Roommate Arrangement

SAXON JAMES

Created with Vellum

About the Book

Payne:

In search of: room to rent.

Must ignore the patheticness of a forty-year-old roommate.

Preferably dirt cheap as funds are tight (nonexistent).

There's nothing sadder than moving back to my hometown newly divorced, homeless, and lost for what my next move is.

When my little brother's best friend offers me a place to stay in exchange for menial duties, I swallow my pride and jump at the offer.

I need this.

I also need Beau to wear a shirt. And ditch the gray sweatpants. And not leave his door ajar when he's in compromising positions ...

Beau:

In search of: roommate.

Must be non smoker and non douchebag.

Room payment to be made in meal planning, repairs, and dumb jokes.

Since my career took off, I barely have time to breathe, let alone keep my life in order. I'm naturally chaotic, make terrible decisions, and scare off potential dates with my "weirdness".

So when Payne gets back into town and needs somewhere to stay, I offer him my spare room with one condition: while he's staying with me, I need him to help me become date-able.

And while he does that, I can focus on my other plan: ignoring that Payne is the only man I've ever wanted to date.

Prologue

PAYNE

The internet is an amazing place for cooking recipes, watching cat videos, and finding out your husband is a filthy, lying cheater.

My mouth is dry as I punch in fake details and my credit card number to access the OnlyFans account that was sent to me. The thumbnail is so clearly him, but I need to know for sure, because there's that tiny part of me that can't accept it.

My heartbeat picks up as his page loads and ...

Fuck.

A quick scroll shows, well, way too many videos. This isn't a one-off.

The most recent is date-stamped yesterday.

Yesterday.

I don't know if he fucked this guy yesterday or just uploaded the video, but either way, this was obviously on his mind while we spent the morning together. Right before he went to the gym.

Is this guy "Jim"?

And because I must be dead in the brain, I tap on the video.

That fucking. Mother. Fucker.

I'm an understanding, open-minded guy. If Kyle had come to me and told me he wanted to do porn, we could have talked about it. I might have watched. I might have done it with him. If he'd wanted an open relationship, it's something we could have discussed …

But when Kyle shoves the other man onto the bed and roughly pushes inside him, I see red.

Not totally because of the cheating, though that's making me pretty fucking ragey.

Or seeing him with another man.

But because I've suggested a few times over the years that he top me and he's always said no.

He hates it.

It doesn't feel right.

We rarely have penetrative sex at all anymore.

And yet …

I scroll through his page and find videos dating back *two years*.

My stomach rolls.

Two years of that asshole cheating. Two years of him doing with other men what he'd never do with me.

We are *done*.

I force myself to watch another three scenes, to watch his

orgasm face and the way he smacks the other men around, and I let my rage build.

And build.

And wonder if he's out there, right now, with his dick in some guy.

The thought crosses my mind to go and film myself fucking someone else and send it to him, but I'm not so convinced he'd care. And the thought of retaliating that way makes me sick.

But I have to do something.

Revenge is burning through my blood.

Pumping so hot and thick through me that it sets off a ringing in my ears and makes it difficult to think.

I stalk into the bathroom, grab his toothbrush, and drop it into the toilet, where I take a photo of it before popping it back in the cupboard.

But it's not enough.

My gaze lands on his laptop, charging on the side table, and fuck, was he lying in bed beside me last night, reading the comments on his OnlyFans?

My hands shake, and I stalk over to it, tug it off the charger, and open the top. The password screen blinks at me, and it only takes a few attempts to get the right one. That's how well I know him. A man I've spent *twelve years* with.

Well ...

I *thought* I knew him.

When I get to the OnlyFans site, his username and password are pre-saved, and a second later, I'm in.

All his filthy secrets are at my fingertips.

He has a ton of unread messages, and I know I shouldn't do it, but I click over to them anyway. Hundreds of different men, dick pics exchanged, dirty talk and cybersex, and ... my heart squeezes. Messages arranging hookups.

... wait until my husband is at work ...

I shove the laptop off me and suck down a breath, trying to stop the rising vomit. It's a struggle to hold on to my anger when betrayal and embarrassment are attempting to take over instead.

My nostrils flare, but I refuse to cry over this asshole.

He's not fucking worth it.

My head knows that, but my heart is struggling to catch up.

I grab his laptop again, find the *Go Live* option, and turn it on.

My face is reflected back at me, and I look *wrecked*. Fuck it.

"To everyone subscribed, this is the page for my husband, Kyle Rousle, and despite being married for five years now, I've only just found out it exists. So thank you for subscribing to two years' worth of evidence of my husband cheating on me." I rattle off his phone number. "Feel free to give him a piece of your mind or to arrange hookups, but now that he's single, it might not be as hot for him. Also, he chews with his mouth open, talks like an obnoxious monkey, and apparently has issues with commitment." I wink. "Real catch."

Then I end the video, walk out onto the balcony of our fourth-floor apartment, and drop the laptop over the edge. It hits the ground with a satisfying *crack*, but the silence that follows is stifling.

I stare down at the broken computer like I'm staring at our shattered relationship, and I'm hit with an overwhelming sense of grief.

There's no staying with him, and facing the end of a twelve-year relationship is a complete mindfuck.

How do we split our things?

Work out joint finances?

Finances? Screw him. He must have a secret bank account with the number of subscribers he's got, so I'm clearing our accounts out.

I pack everything I can into my car, knowing I have a couple of hours until he's finished work.

Shit ... I'm going to need to get tested.

The thought hits me out of nowhere and sends me spiraling.

If that son of a bitch has given me something ...

A sob builds, and no matter how much I try and swallow against it, my vision blurs.

I block his number in my phone, then flee the house before he's home. There's no way I can face him.

I leave, brokenhearted and at a loss.

What the fuck do I do now?

The drive from Boston to Kilborough, the town I grew up in, takes a bit under two hours. We're located in Hampden County, in the foothills of the Provin Mountain. It's been a while since I visited, the last time being for my niece's birthday, and *that fucker* was with me.

I push the anger back.

I promised myself by the time I got to my brother's, I will have put it behind me, which seems laughable as I make my way through town. Two hours isn't enough to erase over a decade of memories.

The thing is, I *should* hate him. And I do. But I also miss him already, and I'm glad I blocked his number when I did, because I'm not so sure that if he called and begged me to come back that I'd be strong enough to say no.

Kilborough is a tourist town. Right now, it's the off-season, but in a month, the place will pick up again. Winter is our only downtime, with summer being crazy and Halloween having sold out accommodation all week long.

It never used to be that way apparently, but forty-five years ago, they closed the massive prison here, and all the people who worked there moved away. Now, the prison and surrounding "ghost" town are a hot location for people who crave being terrified to come to.

The rest of Kilborough has been built around the historic site, and the whole town has embraced the theme of being a *Halloween Town* of sorts. With the Provin Mountain behind the prison, a walkway around the lake on one side, and farmland on the other, we're snug in our corner of the world.

Instead of driving to Marty's place, I change my mind at the last moment and head straight to the Kilborough Brewery. It's a huge warehouse just off the boardwalk that serves as an axe bar, brewery, market, and café. The words "The Killer Brew" are stamped over the faded brick building.

Being midweek, the market on the other side and the café out front are both busy, but inside the brewery is quiet, missing the steady *thunk* that usually comes from the back room as people throw axes at a target.

There are still plenty of stools left at the long bar, and the second my butt hits the seat, I wave down the bartender and order two shots, followed by a beer to wash them down.

And as I'm sitting there, staring at the mirror over the bar, I hear my name being called.

"Payne Walker, what are you doing round these parts?"

I glance up to see the permanently cocky expression of one of my high school friends. Art de Almeida slides onto the barstool beside me, propping one elbow on the bar top, head tilted like he's trying to figure me out.

Despite the shit day, I muster up a smile. "Hey, man. What are you doing here?"

"I run the place now. Mom and Dad took a step back and handed over the brewery."

"Holy shit, congratulations."

"Thanks." His dark-lashed eyes narrow. "Why are you drinking on a weeknight?"

"It's a long story."

"I'm in no hurry."

It's strange. Even though Art and I haven't stayed in

touch and we haven't spoken in years, I'm immediately comfortable in his presence. Plus, I'm going to have to tell people eventually, so I might as well try it out now.

"I found out my husband has been cheating on me."

"Ouch. So, we're drinking to forget, are we?" Art asks.

"Yup."

"Wanna talk about it?"

I grunt. Because that's a solid *no*, even though I'll have to eventually.

"Okay ..."

"I just ... I don't understand. How could he *do* this?"

Art squeezes my arms. "Sometimes people aren't who we think they are. Even when we've known them for a really long time."

"Twelve years." I drain my beer.

"How did you find out?"

I swallow, the sting I felt when I saw the message hitting me afresh. "Someone we work with gave me details." Details I won't be uttering out loud. Ever. "It was going on for a while."

Art only stares at me, then turns to the bartender and orders two more shots. "That fucker."

I snort with amusement, even though I feel sick, and down the shots as soon as they hit the bar top. Art orders another one for himself. The atmosphere between us relaxes, and suddenly it's like twenty years ago, when we were thick as thieves and could talk about anything. "I think ... I think I want a divorce." And even saying the word feels like the biggest failure of my life.

"I'm so sorry. Divorce is never easy."

I frown and suddenly remember the excitement just after I finished college when Art was one half of the first gay couple to be married in Massachusetts ... and also the first to divorce. "How did you handle it?"

His lips twitch. "I went back to sleeping around and didn't look back."

"Not sure that's me."

"Well, unless you've changed dramatically since high school, I agree. These things take time. You'll grow from it, but it takes a while to clear the storm clouds and see it for the blessing it is."

Blessing? I snort again. "What the hell do I do now?"

"Do you need to figure it out this second?"

I smile glumly. "I have the rest of this week on leave from work. If I don't go back, I'm going to have to quit. I'll have no job, no home, and the only money I have to my name is the ten K I cleared from our account." I rub my forehead. "I'm forty years old, and I have nothing."

"Nope, we're not following that path." Art reaches over the bar to pour me another shot and presses the glass into my hand. "You're a qualified ... gym teacher, right? And didn't you buy an apartment down there? Either kick him out or sell it. You don't have to quit your job if you don't want to."

"But do I want to stay in Boston now?"

"Do you?"

"I don't know." My whole body feels tired. "I miss so much of my nieces growing up while I'm down there, and there's no way I can stay in our place, knowing what he did, and I'll never afford a place close to the city on my own."

"You have a lot to figure out," Art says. "If you break up or choose to stay with him. No judgment. Only you can make that call."

"It's already over." I scrunch up my face. "Think I can organize the divorce without having to see that fucker's face?"

"Of course you can. But for some totally unsolicited advice, go back, take a minute to organize your life, and see where you end up."

What he's saying is completely reasonable. But I don't want reason. Only alcohol and self-pity.

"And if you do end up back in Kilborough, let me know. I started a group for guys like us."

"Like us?"

"Divorced men. It's a support group, and there are a fair few of us now."

"No offense, but that sounds sad. A group of guys hanging out and trying to act like they love their lives when they're one breakdown away from a midlife crisis."

Art laughs loudly and slaps my back. "You would think that. Hell, most people do. And that's the point. Society has made divorce into this twisted, negative experience when all it is, is a fresh start. The DMC is a safe space. If a guy needs to vent, he can vent. If he needs pointers for dating again, we've got him. A lot of splits result in friends taking sides, and it's usually always the man who's the bad guy—or for queer couples, there's always one on the outer. We're friends, we're a listening ear, and we're motherfucking cheerleaders when our boys find love again. Maybe you won't need that at all. But the offer's there if you want it."

I might not know what my next steps are, but I do know I'm touched. "Thanks, man." I'm not going to take him up on the offer, but I appreciate it. "I'll let you know if I'm interested."

Chapter One

PAYNE

It's been a long month, but when I drive back into Kilborough, knowing I never have to go back to Boston and my old apartment again, I finally feel like I can breathe.

Kyle's betrayal still stings when I let myself think about it, but I've reached a point where I'm able to thank my lucky fucking stars that I found out what he was getting up to and got out of there.

And he can thank *his* lucky fucking stars that my tests came back all clear.

He's tried reaching out through email a few times, and the only time I responded was to demand his test results, which he sent—after assuring me that he always used a condom, like that makes any goddamn difference.

I've never been so happy for our dry spell.

It's surprising how easy it is for me to cut him out after

twelve years together, and maybe it's because the fucker cheated on me the way he did, or the relationship was already over and I hadn't realized, but walking away was easier than it should've been.

Staying away will be the hard part, because even though I think I'm over it ... our relationship was like a warm blanket. It was familiar. That doesn't exactly scream madly in love. I thought the moment I fell out of love with him was the moment I saw him with someone else, but maybe it was sooner than that.

Sex is just sex.

The betrayal of trust is what stung. The failure of not being able to keep my husband satisfied stung. But as more and more people find out about the divorce, and more and more people expect me to be devastated about the split, it's made me think that I don't know *what* my marriage was.

I'm angry and embarrassed, but I don't think I'm heartbroken.

Since I took everything I wanted from our apartment on that first day, it means I've been able to mostly avoid seeing him for the month I spent in Boston, crashing with a work friend as I tied up loose ends.

I resigned from my job at the high school we both work at, where thankfully he kept his distance after I threatened to send the link to his OnlyFans to the school board. It's not something I ever would have done, and the fact he believed me shows he didn't know me the way I thought he did.

All of the people I thought were my friends disappeared, and it became obvious very quickly that I had no life left in

Boston. So as soon as my notice period at work was up and our apartment hit the market, I left.

Once the divorce is organized, I'll never have to think of Kyle again.

Which is a relief, because I'm going to need to use that brainpower to figure out what the hell I do now.

Normally that line of thinking would send me spiraling into a panic, but since talking to Art, I have a better outlook on life.

This isn't a failure.

This is an opportunity.

Or whatever bullshit he's been feeding me.

I park down from Killer Brew, where I'm meeting Art and two other guys. They're part of the DMC—the Divorced Men's Club—which at first I thought was a group of depressed dudes sitting around feeling sorry for themselves, but is actually more of a title in theory than practice. We're just guys who are in varying stages of divorce—or in Orson's case, who have lost their significant other—who understand the shit stereotypes that go along with what we've been through.

We're a safe space for each other.

When Art first told me that, I hadn't wanted to listen, but I'm glad now that I reached out.

I immediately spot Art, Orson, and Griffin as I approach the outdoor café and make my way over to them. Art and I were friends in high school, and Griffin was a few years older than us. Orson only moved here shortly after I left, so I don't know him well outside of the group texts and the one and only time before now that I met up with them.

What I do know is that these guys are so different, there's no way we'd have become friends outside of this group, but without them, I might not have made it through the last month without going back to my fucker of an ex. I'm not clear on how many other guys are in the group, but from what Art says, it's a lot. There's no way I'm ready to face all that.

"Payne!" Art calls loudly across the cafe. Since the Kilborough Brewery has been in Art's family for years, everyone knows him, and everyone knows how loud he is.

I grin and join them at their table. "It's official, I'm a kil-boy again."

Art and Orson pretend to applaud while Griffin smiles softly.

"Well done," he says. "You feeling good about the move?"

"Nope. But my apartment is on the market, and with any luck, I'll have the down payment on my own place soon." I don't mention that we made a lucky investment with that one. On two teachers' salaries, we hadn't been able to pay the mortgage down as much as I would have liked, but the place is worth a lot more now than what we paid for it. Thank you to a decade's worth of inflation.

I place my order with the server when she comes around, then turn back to the guys.

"Any more luck with finding a job?" Orson asks.

There are no open positions for a high school gym

teacher in Kilborough, and since it's all I've ever done, I don't have experience with anything else. "I still want to do something with kids. Something sporty. I haven't figured out what yet."

"And you're staying at your brother's place?"

"Yep. It's not ideal, but it'll do for now."

All three of them have offered to help, but Orson only has a one-bedroom place, Griffin still lives with his wife, who will become his ex-wife once their son goes off to college, and Art and I tried living together for a month after high school, so I already know he's a pain in the ass and total control freak to share a space with.

So for the time being, I'm going to be sleeping in a tiny single bed, while my nieces share the other.

Fun times.

I glance toward the counter and see my brother's best friend, Beau, waiting. After he orders, he scans the room, and I hold up my hand in a wave to get his attention. His eyes widen when they land on me, and he hesitates for a second before making his way over.

"Hey," he says when he reaches us. "You're ... I, umm, didn't know you were visiting."

"I'm not."

His forehead creases in confusion. "Then ..."

"I'm back for good."

"You're what?"

I laugh because the poor guy looks legitimately in shock. "Moving back. I'll be staying with Marty for a bit, so I'm sure I'll see you around."

"And Kyle?"

Yikes. As positive as I am about moving forward, having to explain the breakup over and over isn't going to be a good time. "We split."

"Oh." Something crosses his face that I can't work out, and then it disappears when his order is called. "That's ... I'm sorry to hear that."

"Don't be," Art cuts in. "It's good news, not bad. Sometimes we have to cut the shit out of our lives in order to level up to our best selves."

I grin at him because he's always saying stuff about spreading our wings and exiting our cocoons or whatever. Beau clearly doesn't know how to take him.

"It's cool." I wave his concern away. "Thanks, but Art's right. This is a good move for me."

Beau hurries to agree. "Of course, yeah. Well, I'm glad, then. I'm actually on my way to meet Marty now, but I'll see you soon?"

"For sure."

His face breaks into a wide smile that's impossible not to smile back at. It defines his jaw and lights up his blue eyes behind the clear-rimmed glasses he always wears. "Right, okay." He backs up. "See you then."

As soon as he's gone, Orson laughs. "Wow."

"What?"

He rubs at his stubble. "The man was *very* nervous around you."

"He's always been like that."

Art nods. "It's true. Though it was worse when we were younger."

Oh yeah, I'd almost forgotten about that. The stuttering and blurting out random comments. I'd forgotten because the past few years, it had all but disappeared. What's brought it back now?

Griffin hums. "Weird or not, he's hot."

"Agreed," Art says. "I'd bone him."

"Is he single?" Griffin asks.

I shrug. "I'm not sure actually. He was the last time I saw him, and Marty hasn't mentioned anything."

"Maybe when Poppy and I officially split, he'll be interested in a date."

I eye Griffin. He's the more serious out of us all, with the least relationship experience, but he's gorgeous, with dark brown hair, neat stubble, and insane piercing blue eyes.

Art's distinguished, with Portuguese good looks, the kind of presence that demands attention and an attitude to match.

Orson's the oldest of us, with a short beard that has more silver than black, but his hair is still dark. His face is lined in a friendly way, and he looks rough around the edges, but is the biggest sweetheart I've ever met.

I'm ... well, the laid-back one out of us all. Well, usually. The whole cheating thing was hard to be laid-back about.

And trying to picture any of them with Beau ... I can't see it.

"How much longer until the split now?" I ask Griffin.

19

"End of summer. Once Felix leaves for college, we'll separate and then tell him when he's back for his first break."

"No second thoughts?"

Griffin shakes his head. "None. Poppy was a great wife, but we're both ready to get on with our lives now."

"And you don't think you should do it before Felix leaves so you can work through it together?"

"I'd rather wait until he's off at college and has plenty of friends there to distract him."

"You really think he'll be that upset?" Art asks.

"Yep." Griffin stares at his tea. "He doesn't like change and can be a bit ... dramatic."

I've gotten enough of a read on the situation through our texts, so I remind him, "You and Poppy are going to support each other through this, and you'll both be there for Felix like you always were. You guys will adjust." *And at least Poppy never cheated on you.*

That part I keep to myself.

"True." He sighs. "But fuck I'm ready to get laid again. It's been years."

They've stayed exclusive even with the plan to split because they haven't wanted anything to get back to their son, and while Griffin is ... let's go with *quiet*, it makes me respect him to be putting his kid first like that.

It's been a month since I left Kyle, and I haven't had sex since. Truthfully, it's the last thing on my mind after what he did, but I know it won't take long for that urge to come back.

The urge will need to wait a little longer though because

while I'm staying with Marty, I'm putting all my energy into family time. My brother, my sister-in-law, and my nieces are going to be spoiled filthy rotten. Well, with love. My money only extends so far right now, which is why I can't find my own place. Yet.

We finish up, and I tell the guys I'll see them next week before I head for my car. It's late enough that Lizzy should be home with the girls, and the thought of seeing my nieces immediately boosts my mood. They're adorable. And full-on.

I reach their place and pull up by the curb before grabbing the things I've brought with me on this trip. Most of our furniture I left with my fuckhead ex, so the things I do have are minimal. And there's no way I wanted to take that bed.

I let myself inside with the key they gave me.

Lizzy's on the couch flipping through the TV, while the girls are playing at the LEGO table behind her.

"Uncle Payne!" Bridget cries and jumps to her feet. She throws herself across the room and into my arms. I melt, and holding that much pure sunshine reminds me my life is still awesome.

"What are you guys building?" I ask.

"A military base. The aliens are coming."

"We better get to work, then." I spare Lizzy a quick smile as she watches on with amusement, then slump down next to Soph, who's eyeing me strangely. It always takes a minute for her to warm up. "Remember me?"

She drops her head and watches me from under her eyebrows, and it's so adorable I do my best not to laugh.

"Is this a new one?" Bridget asks, angling my forearm to see my most recent tattoo.

"It is. I made sure it had lots of detail, just for you."

Her face lights up. "I'm going to grab my markers."

"You okay?" Lizzy asks the moment Bridget is out of the room.

"As well as I can be. It still hurts sometimes, but I'm ready to move on from it all."

"Well, you're welcome to stay as long as you like."

"Careful. I'm getting a *whole* single bed—you might never be rid of me."

"You're ridiculous."

"I really do appreciate this."

"I know you do. I still can't believe—" She cuts off, face tense, and I know the only reason she's holding back her thoughts is because of the girls. Lizzy has subjected Marty and me both to long rants about *that fucker*.

Listening to her swear like a sailor has been enjoyable, at least.

Bridget returns with a pencil case full of markers, so I yank my shirt over my head and lie facedown on the floor. I guess the aliens have been forgotten about already.

Soph eventually joins her coloring in, and I'm so peaceful while they work that I start to drift off. That is until Soph speaks. "Where's Uncle Ky?"

Urg, straight to the heart.

Lizzy jumps in to explain that Uncle Ky won't be around anymore while I bury my face in my folded arms.

I'm one hundred percent over him.

Mostly.

But in moments like this, all I can think of is *why*?

He destroyed our lives.

And I'm the one left to deal with the fallout.

Chapter Two

BEAU

Wow, am I a bumbling idiot or a bumbling idiot?

Thirty-six. I'm thirty-freaking-six, and I still trip over my words when Payne is around, like I'm going through puberty again. It definitely doesn't help that the years have been kind to him.

Instead of looking *older*, he looks *manlier*. Broader and scruffier. From the short beard to the messy hair, to the way his shoulders strained that T-shirt.

I was caught totally off guard.

Normally, when he visits, it's for a family thing. One of the girls' birthdays or Christmas or something so I'm able to prepare and psych myself up. Plus, being married put a damper on things, to the point I'd thought my crush was on the way out. But nope. Still here. Still strong. Still want to lick his neck.

I clench both coffees tighter as I reach the place where I'm meeting Marty. Every Friday, we catch up for his lunch break and take a walk around the lake. It gets me out of the house and socializing because if I'm left to my own devices, weeks could pass before I realize I haven't spoken to anyone in that time.

I'm ... well, lonely isn't the right word. I like my space and solitude, but some days I wish I had someone to live alongside me. Someone who won't interrupt while I work, someone who accepts my quirks and won't make me feel weird about them.

But apparently that someone doesn't exist.

Or, if they do, I've probably been set up on a date with them and forgotten about it.

I've been called *scatterbrain* too many times to count, but this morning, I'm not the one who's conveniently forgotten something.

I pin Marty with a look as I approach. He has the same light brown hair as Payne, but unlike his brother, it's short, he doesn't have tattoos, and he's clean-shaven. Plus, Marty has lines around his mouth and eyes where Payne's skin is still mostly smooth. And gorgeous. They might look similar to most people, but I don't see it.

For me, Marty is like an annoying brother.

Payne is like ... a wet dream.

Marty goes to smile when he spots me, but it dies before it can properly take hold. "Uh-oh. What's wrong?"

"Oh no, no, nothing. Nothing at all."

"Something's telling me not to believe you."

I hand his coffee over. "Apparently Payne is moving back?"

"Oh, that." He gives me a weird look. "Yeah, he and Kyle split. What does that have to do with anything?"

"Just surprised to see him, that's all."

Marty looks confused, and I don't blame him.

I want to push and ask more, but it's hard to do that when Marty is blissfully ignorant of my crush on his brother. If Lizzy was here, she'd give me all the information I want without me having to say a thing. It's baffling how it's so obvious to her when Marty is completely unaware, but I'm grateful she's never said anything.

"What happened with the breakup?"

Marty's expression darkens as we fall into step with each other. "I still can't believe it."

"Believe what?"

"Look, I'm not sure how much Payne wants people to know, considering he hasn't even told us the full story, but ... Kyle cheated. Maybe a lot, but it's definitely over."

My mouth drops. Kyle *cheated*? On *Payne*? My heart thumps as angry indignation creeps up my throat.

Ever since I hit puberty and discovered how good jerking off felt, Payne's been a constant in my fantasies. Not only is he so hot he makes me drool, he's got a relaxed confidence about himself. Where some of our other friends' older brothers were dickheads, Payne always included Marty and me.

Then he went off to college and moved to Boston, where he met Kyle. His wedding day was the one time I wished

Payne wasn't a decent enough human to invite me. Sitting through him promising some other guy forever was painful.

Kyle got to have that. Payne's loyal—he would have been married to that guy until they died—and that stupid *fuck* threw it all away. I don't even have it in me to be excited by the prospect of Payne being single when I'm too pissed that someone would do that to him.

If Payne was my husband, I'd make sure he knew how amazing he is.

"Wow." The one word is too inadequate to encompass my feelings, but I don't want to give myself away.

"Yeah. All I can think of are the times he stayed with us and played the part of happy families. Was he sleeping around on my brother then?" Marty almost growls. "I want to kill him."

"Happy to take a drive to Boston with you if you want backup."

"If I knew where he lived now, I'd probably take you up on the offer."

"Probably a good thing since neither of us knows how to swing a punch." Marty is a lover, not a fighter, and so am I. Where the other guys in high school were looking to get *into* fights, we both ran the other way. "At least Payne's home now."

"Exactly."

"So where is he planning to stay?" I ask.

"Our place." Marty pulls a face. "We offered to move both the girls' beds into one room so he could have the other to set up in, but he tried to insist on the couch. So, we're compromising. He's taking one of the girls' beds, and they're sharing."

My lips twitch. "Payne? In a single bed?"

"I know. I give him two days before he caves and buys something bigger."

"Payne's not the kind of guy to complain. I bet he makes do."

Marty suddenly stops walking. "Hang on. You have a spare room, don't you?"

"Umm ..." *Yes, Beau, the answer is yes.* "I do ..." And the thought of Payne living in that room? It both fills me with anxiousness and so much want that I might pass out.

"How do you feel about a roommate?" Marty laughs like he's joking, but he's really, really not. "It'd only be for a couple of weeks. Or so. Probably."

Crap.

A couple of weeks is exactly enough time for me to become embarrassingly addicted to having him around.

Or ... maybe it would cure me of my crush once and for all.

I hate people in my space. I've had roommates before, and those arrangements did *not* end amicably. They always found me too fussy, and I found them too loud. And intrusive. And ... inconvenient.

One part of me doesn't want to let this crush go, but the thing is, I *do* want to find my person, and it's going to be doubly hard to do that with Payne back in Kilborough all ... gorgeous and irresistible and *available* with me comparing every man I meet to him. It was easier to date when he was gone and married.

Easier, but still not successful. I'm worried I have no clue how to date. How to relate to people and loosen the reins so that I'm boyfriend material. "Fussy" isn't something I want to be, but I don't even know what I'm doing to project that trait.

I'm not easygoing like Payne, as much as I'd like to be.

And then, like a light bulb going off, I'm hit with the most fantastic, terrific plan of all plans.

If Payne moves in, we can *both* focus on the other's flaws. I'll cure my crush, and he can point out the things I'm doing wrong. He can make me *dating material*.

Oooh yes, I'm liking this.

It's more or less foolproof.

The thing is, Payne will probably say no. He doesn't like to put people out, but maybe if I can get the girls on board ...

"You know what, I think I could do it for a couple of weeks," I say.

Marty lets out a long breath. "As much as I'd love for him to stay with us, I think everyone would be happier if he wasn't squished into Digit's room."

"Including Bridget." She's a bossy little six-year-old—in only the best way, of course—so I can't imagine she's too happy with the arrangement. "And I can't let my oldest niece be inconvenienced in any way, can I?"

"Heaven forbid she *doesn't* turn into a spoiled brat."

I chuckle into my coffee. "Don't worry. I'm still thinking about getting her a pony. I'll turn her into a diva yet."

Marty swipes at my head, and we finish our walk without mentioning Payne again. It takes nearly all of my self-control to keep my thoughts to myself, but I play nice and talk to him about work, and the kids, and the book I'm working on.

We make our way back over to the office building where Marty works. "Why don't you come around tomorrow for lunch? Then you can suggest for him to move in? Please? I can't do it because I don't want him to think that we don't want him there."

I promise I will, then set about a hundred reminders in my phone so I don't forget. Though with how nervous I am about seeing Payne again, I don't think I'll be able to focus on anything else.

What am I *doing*? This is going to be the most self-indulgent, torturous thing I've ever done. Payne in small doses keeps my feelings controllable, but him around all the time? Maybe getting to know each other better one-on-one?

I fan out the collar of my shirt, suddenly feeling borderline hysterical.

The silver lining to this is that since I know he's here now, I won't make a fool of myself like I did earlier. When I'm prepared to see him, I can behave like a normal human; it's only when I'm caught off guard that my words become a mess.

Shit.

This is going to be interesting.

Chapter Three

PAYNE

A **rt:** *Rise and shine you sexy mofo. Time to take today by the balls.*

When people warned me against sleeping in a single bed, I'd thought the concern was overboard. Sure, I knew it wouldn't be comfortable, but you can deal with anything for only a few weeks.

This morning, I'm thoroughly regretting sticking to my guns.

When I try to stand, every part of me hurts.

Normally, I take pride in the way I don't look and feel forty.

This morning, I'm feeling every one of those years and more.

"Morning, family," I murmur on my way into the kitchen. Soph immediately launches herself off the counter to latch onto my back, and while I'm glad she's gotten over the shyness toward me, I'd prefer she save it for after coffee.

"Morning, Uncle Payne," Bridget says.

"Morning, cutie." I hold back my yawn as I switch on the coffee maker and try to remove Soph from where she's attached herself like a barnacle to my sore back.

"Let's talk about something," Bridget announces.

"Like?"

"You come up with the topic."

"Ah ..." I try to think. "Tea parties?"

She ponders that for a moment. "Sure, that's okay. Have you been to a tea party?"

Kyle and I used to do brunch with friends—is that the same thing? Not mentioning it anyway. "Once or twice."

"Tell me about it. Like, what was your favorite part? Who did you go with? Were there cakes?"

One thing I've learned since spending time here is that six-year-olds never shut up. "My favorite part was the tea, I went with my friends, and there was lots of cake. Now, new topic—I say we have a few minutes of quiet time."

Bridget pins me with a stare. "That's *not* a topic."

"Okay, you two," Lizzy says, walking in and saving me. "Uncle Payne needs grown-up time. Go watch cartoons."

Soph immediately drops from my back and runs toward the front room. Bridget hesitates for a moment before following.

"Thank you," I say, pouring coffees for us both.

She eyes me with amusement. "How do you feel?"

"Sore."

"Not too late to buy your own bed. It's not like you won't need one when you find a place."

She's right. It's not a terrible idea, but to do that, we'd need to take down Bridget's bed, and she's already been disrupted enough as it is.

With any luck, it's only a few weeks. I've stayed on their couch now and then over the past month, which I managed fine. Surely I'll get used to the tiny bed?

I take my coffee out onto their back deck and pull up the job listings. As a high school gym teacher, I'm not expecting much since there are only two high schools in Kilborough. I broaden my search to include anything to do with sports and kids ... still nothing.

Goddamn it.

We're a small town, but we're not *that* small.

I set my phone down and pick up my coffee as Marty walks out to join me. "You could try not looking so depressed about living here."

"I can't help it when I have to see your face every day."

"Ooh, ouch." He chuckles and takes the chair next to me. "What are you doing?"

"Looking for jobs and failing."

"Might I suggest that you remove the failing part?"

"Ha ha," I say dryly.

"Seriously though, why not find a job that won't be high stress? Once you sell your place, you'll have money from that, plus some savings that you cleared out of your accounts, plus you're living here for now, so what's the rush? Pick up anything until you find something you'll love."

He has a point, but that reasoning goes against everything our parents taught us. You go to college, get your degree, and then use it. I checked off those steps. I also did the dating and marriage thing too though, and look at how that turned out for me.

Maybe I can take a time-out from being a regular adult and think through my choices. Not that I have many to consider. When it comes to sports and kids, there aren't a huge number of options out there.

"I'll think about it."

It's a nice day, so after a quick call to update our parents on the move, I spend most of the morning outside with the girls to give Marty and Lizzy some quiet time. I love my nieces like no one in the world, but they're high-energy, and I couldn't imagine doing this full time. Wrestling on the trampoline and piggyback rides are constant requests before we start working on building a fort. Aren't little girls supposed to, I dunno, sit down quietly and play with dolls?

I laugh at the thought before grabbing the wrench that Soph is waving around as she runs past. I might not know much about small kids, but I *do* know that can't be safe.

"This looks fun." I glance up at the voice and find Beau stepping into the backyard. Soph's attention is immediately diverted.

"Uncle Bo-Bo!" She flies across the yard and throws herself into his arms. I watch as Beau pretends to struggle to lift her and throws her over his shoulder.

"Oh, no, Soph disappeared! I hope the gremlins haven't taken her!"

She cackles and squirms as Bridget jumps up and runs over to them.

"She's right there."

"Where?" Beau turns dramatically. "Here?"

I flop back in the grass, not able to stop watching the way he plays around with them. He has ... an imagination, that's for sure, and he doesn't seem self-conscious about looking like an idiot. Not that he does, but the way he's singing about Fair Knight Bridget could definitely come across as dorky. It doesn't take long for him to have them giggling so hard they can't speak.

"Fly!" he cries, throwing them both onto the trampoline. Then he zips up the side and walks over to drop down beside me.

"Thank fuck you're here," I say. "I never realized how old I was getting until I tried to keep up with a four- and six-year-old. I'm beat."

His smile is almost shy. "They're a lot, but I love visiting."

"Me too."

"At least when I visit, I get to leave again though." His words are calm, but his hands are twisting constantly in his lap. "I hope you know that being out here is setting a precedent you'll have to meet for the whole of your stay."

I groan. "Tell me they're not this full-on every day."

He mimes locking his lips.

"Shit." I let my eyes fall closed. "If I lie here and fall asleep, will they pretend I'm a dead monster from one of their games?"

"That won't work."

My eyes snap open because I didn't realize I said that aloud, and the first thing I see is Beau's eyes. So freaking blue even through his glasses and trained right on my face. "Well, dammit, then. Looks like you'll need to tag team with me more often, Bo-Bo."

"Tag ..." He stares for a second, then gives a short laugh. "Only the, uh, girls get away with calling me that."

"Aw, come on. I'm going through a divorce. I'm depressed and shit. Take pity on me."

"If I thought you were actually, you know, *depressed*, I might. But you seem okay. To me at least." He cringes. "I'm just hearing how that sounds, and it was insensitive, so I'm sorry if you actually are still sad about it all."

"Eh, I am mostly over it. I mean, it still hurts, but I'm more mad than upset."

"What did your friend say? Leveling up? Evolving?"

"Evolving?" I tease. "I'm not a Pokémon."

"What? Ah, no, I—"

"Only teasing, Bo-Bo."

"Moving on." His face flushes, which is cute as hell. "Yeah, so I brought lunch. Only some sandwiches, but the girls will be okay out here for a bit."

"Sandwiches sound incredible." I jump to my feet and reach a hand out for Beau.

Then he does something odd.

He sucks in a sharp breath and pretends not to see it.

It's not like I was implying he *needed* help. It was an automatic thing.

My stare doesn't leave the back of his head as I follow him into the house, wondering what that was about.

Lizzy and Marty have already set the tray of sandwiches out on the table, and I collapse dramatically into one of the chairs. "Your kids are life stealers. I feel ten years older after this morning."

Marty points to his forehead. "Where do you think I got these wrinkles?"

I laugh and reach forward to grab some food, not waiting on the others. The meat-and-cheese combo is exactly what I need, but until I find a gym, I have to be careful about what I eat. My job keeps me fit most of the time, and while I have a six-pack, I work damn hard for it.

"How did you sleep last night?" Marty asks, and I glance up to find the three of them looking at me.

I level him with a stare. "Not interested in an I-told-you-so, thanks."

"Lizzy mentioned you felt like shit."

"Thanks, Liz," I say dryly.

She smiles back innocently. "Totally welcome."

I wave off their concern. "It's fine. Hopefully the apartment won't take long to sell, and then I'll be out of your hair."

"*I-have-a-spare-room.*" Beau's words come out so fast I'm not sure I've caught them at first.

"You do?"

Lizzy answers before he can. "Payne's fine where he is."

"Is Bridget though?" Beau replies.

The look Lizzy's giving him is hard to read, but Marty jumps in before she can.

"That's actually a great idea," he says. "Beau only lives ten minutes away, and he's got a nice place."

"Well, nice when it's not a total bomb site," Beau jokes.

Bomb site or not, the temptation of my own room with a proper bed is strong, but there's a reason I'm staying here instead of leasing somewhere. "That's nice of you, but I don't have a job or anything, so I couldn't contribute rent. The money I do have, I'll need to ration until I work out what's next."

That makes Beau laugh. "Who said anything about rent? I own the place outright."

"I'm not going to take advantage, Bo-Bo."

"It's not taking advantage when I'm the one who offered," he points out. "You need somewhere to stay, and I have somewhere. It's not like I'll lease it out to anyone else, so you either use it, or it stays empty. Sounds like a waste to me."

For the first time since he mentioned it, I let myself consider it.

Marty nudges me. "Beau's right. There's more than enough space, and he doesn't need the money since the film rights to his books got him a big, fat check."

Beau shifts. "Yeah, no money."

"Trying to get rid of me, brother?" The joke doesn't have much conviction, because I'm wavering. If he was planning to rent the room, that would be one thing, but it's literally sitting there unused. I'd be ridiculous to turn it down, but

I'm also not going to rely on Beau's kindness, whatever he might say. "At least let me contribute something."

An idea lights up his face. "Actually, there is something."

"Yeah?"

"See, I'm a bit, umm, messy ...?"

"Total slob." Marty nods. "Continue."

Beau gives Marty a flat look and turns back to me. "I'm not a slob, I'm low on time. When I'm not working, I'm stressing about working, and before I know it, the whole day has passed, and sometimes I haven't done a single thing. If you really wanted to help out, keeping the place tidy and stocked with food would actually be a lifesaver."

"Like a live-in maid." I weigh up that option, and it actually sounds perfect. "All right. You're on."

"Yeah. Cool." Beau shrugs, then shrugs again, some of that weirdness from outside hitting him. He's a hard one to read. On one hand, he was almost pushing for me to accept, but now he's being awkward about it.

Jesus fucking Christ.

This is going to be interesting.

Chapter Four

BEAU

I told myself I'd be ready today. I promised. And yet I'd gotten up early and then become distracted by, well, everything. As I look around the apartment, I can't put my finger on exactly what I've been doing all day.

My dirty clothes are sorted, but none of it made it into the washing machine, my dishwasher is full of dirty dishes, but the clean ones are piled on the countertops so I could wipe out the cupboards, and the toilet cleaner and bleach are sitting on the floor by the bathroom door, where I left them before I got an idea I needed to jot down.

When did my life become such a mess?

For all of my hard work, the place is disgusting. I'm behind on my deadline. And when I open the fridge to grab something to settle my stomach over the thought of Payne's impending arrival and note the suspicious lack of food in there, I remember too late I was supposed to go shopping yesterday.

I go to slump onto my couch when I catch myself in time.

He'll be here any minute, and I'd hoped to have the place in some kind of order.

For a thirty-six-year-old man, I'm embarrassingly disorganized.

I redirect my attention to the clean dishes, and just as I'm about to put them away, there's a knock at the door. *Shit.*

I grab the stack of plates and shove them in the cupboard above my head. Out of sight, out of mind. Though there really is no more procrastinating. I need to let him in. I do. I can do this. But before I reach for the handle, I take a second to prepare myself. This is ... fine. It's totally fine.

Payne is any other guy.

Who's incredibly good-looking and out of my league and makes my gut all twisted but ... *a guy.*

Who I also somehow have to convince to look out for my flaws.

I know it's the best decision long term, but it isn't my favorite plan to ask the man I have a thing for to focus on my bad qualities. I'd rather wow him with my exceptional blow job skills.

There's another soft knock, then the door pushes open, and I spring back out of the way.

"Hello?" Payne peeks inside, and his face breaks into a

smile when he sees me. "Sorry, I didn't think you heard me."

"No, no, that's fine, come in." It takes effort not to gawk as he steps into my space, bag slung over his shoulder, and closes the door behind him. Then he looks around.

I try to take in my home the way Payne must be seeing it and barely hold back my cringe. It's modern, but you wouldn't know it with the clutter and mess on most surfaces. "So, it's possible I'm only now realizing that Marty is right. I'm a slob."

Payne's deep laugh is friendly. "That's why I'm here, right?"

Riiight ... "Umm, about that."

He shoots me a confused look as he drops his bag next to the island. "You don't want me to look after the place?"

"Oh, no, definitely. Look around, the place needs it. I wasn't lying about that. But the thing is, I maybe had another idea of something you could help me with." I want to swallow down the words, so the best thing I can do is get them out as fast as possible.

"Oh yeah?" He casually folds his heavily tattooed arms and leans into the counter, totally at ease in my home. For some reason, that makes me even less comfortable.

Which won't work for this conversation. I pull out a stool at the island and sit, trying to gather my thoughts. All it takes is a glance at Payne's concerned expression to get me talking. "I'm lonely," I admit. "Mostly. Like, I like my own space and doing things my way, but I'm reaching an age where I need someone."

"Ah, Beau ..."

"Not you," I hurry to clarify, though, yeah, I'd love him to throw me a bone. Euphemism included. "I've tried to date, and it's never gone well. Apparently, I'm *fussy* or whatever and cause secondhand embarrassment." I'm still mad the last guy I dated said that.

"What do you want from me, then?"

"Teach me how to live with someone."

His lips quirk. "Teach you?"

"Yes. I'm not good at it."

"Living with people?"

"It's more people *in general*."

He barks out a laugh, and a trickle of pride hits me at causing it. "So, what does this entail, exactly?"

"Well, you'd point out whenever I do something weird or annoying or frustrating. When it happens—and it *will*—you tell me, I'll make a note of it, and then I can avoid it in the future."

He's silent for a moment. "You're going to change yourself for someone?"

"Improve," I correct, because change just sounds sad. "I'm going to *improve* myself with your help."

"I don't think you need to change or improve anything though."

It's my turn to laugh. "You're also not trying to date me, and in the last year, I can probably count on one hand how many times we've seen each other."

"True ..."

"You don't have to." I want to make that clear. "It's not a condition. Neither is the cleaning, honestly, and you also don't need to rush to try and find a place either. Whether you're here for a week or months, that room is yours, and I want you to feel comfortable."

"Thank you. I appreciate that." He eyes me. "Okay, you're on. If—and that's heavy on the if—I notice anything strange, I'll give you the heads-up."

"Perfect."

"Right." Payne hefts his bag back onto his shoulder. "You going to give me the tour now?"

"Oh, shit, yeah." I slide from my stool and lead Payne through the apartment. He's mostly quiet, occasionally commenting on something he likes.

He points to my work desk set up in what should be the dining room. "Why didn't you use the spare room as your office?"

"That was the original plan, but it felt too claustrophobic. Like I was in a cell. Or a coffin. Sometimes I'll go a week of writing nonstop, and when I finally come out of that weird place I go when I focus, I realize it's been that long since I had any other human contact. At least here, I have a view of the street outside. I like seeing the sky."

"Well, I can't wait to see my coffin." He grins at the morbid humor, and it relaxes me.

Which does nothing to help with the not-liking-him thing.

"The bedrooms are down here."

Payne follows me into the hall, and we pause outside his bedroom.

"Mine's there," I say, pointing to the door across from

his. "And I actually remembered to put fresh sheets on your bed this morning, so high fives for me."

"Very impressed."

He's definitely humoring me.

I go to turn away when I remember something. "I also keep unusual work hours. When inspiration hits, I'll zone out to the point I won't even notice you." I sigh and lean against the wall. "It's been a while though. My brain is fighting me. So sometimes I'm up late, others I'm up early. And I'm very, very easily distracted at the moment."

"Don't distract you. Got it."

It's unnerving how easygoing he is. There's no fighting me or pushing for more information. I don't get it. I like it though.

I can't quite commit to my words, but I try anyway. "I'm glad you're here."

"Thanks." His dark eyes watch me steadily.

A nervous sound bubbles up my throat, and I almost trip over my feet as I back up. "Welcome to Casa De Shitraw —" I blanch. "I mean dickraw—ahh, *Rickshaw*. It's Rickshaw."

His laugh fills the space between us as he pushes the door to his room open. "Shitraw or dickraw ... I'm glad to be here too."

I smile until Payne disappears into his room, then flee into the living area. Stupid, stupid, stupid. I walk over to my keyboard and keysmash to let out some of the nerves. It wakes up my computer screen, but I ignore it and grab my phone to order Chinese instead. Maybe some takeout and a drink or two will help ease us into this roommates thing. The sooner we can get comfortable, the easier this will be.

I order a bit of everything and wait until it arrives before I knock on Payne's door.

"Dinner's here."

The door opens suddenly. Payne's changed into a soft-looking T-shirt and sweats. Black, unfortunately, but tight enough to hug his thighs. I swallow.

"You ordered something for me?" he asks.

"Yeah, I assumed you wouldn't want to cook."

"You assumed right." He follows me out. "What did you get?"

"Chinese."

"My favorite."

I know. That part I keep to myself though. Payne helps me clear off the kitchen island before we open the containers and spread them out between us. There's way too much food for us to get through, but the leftovers will do us for a day or two. Then I go for the bottles of beer. I crack the lid on mine before offering one to him.

"Is this to make things less awkward?" he asks, taking it.

"That's the plan."

Payne drops onto one of the stools, and I take the one beside him, pulling it out a little so we're not touching. Even this feels too close though. Too ... intimate.

I can see every hair on his forearm as he reaches for the chopsticks, and I let myself stare for a moment. Curing this crush won't be an automatic thing, so in the meantime, there's no point beating myself up over indulging in some eye candy, is there?

Hey, maybe he'll be terrible at using chopsticks and end up covered in food?

Almost as soon as I have that thought, Payne loads his plate up with practiced confidence. There goes that theory.

He doesn't talk with his mouth full.

He doesn't get food stuck in his teeth.

He *does* talk to me in his low, smooth voice about how much he likes the room and how concerned he is over finding a job here.

This isn't helping issues.

Not when his voice has one-way access to my cock.

I shift so I'm positioned farther under the counter.

"Can I ask how you are? Like, really?"

I regret the words instantly because his eyes immediately meet mine. "I told you I was doing okay."

"It's okay if you're not though. And if you are. Like, there's no right answer here, and if you wanted someone to talk it out with, I'm your guy. No judgment."

"Thanks." He turns back to his plate. "You didn't like him, did you?"

"Umm, well, it wasn't so much that as ..."

"As?"

I deflate. "Okay, no, I didn't."

"Sorry. I always noticed when that fucker was around, you'd go quiet. I guess you were smarter than the rest of us."

I drum my fingers, unsure whether to tell the truth or not. The problem is everyone liked Kyle. He didn't seem like a bad guy overall, but he got to be with Payne, and I didn't. I was bitter. "He ... made me uncomfortable." Not a total lie. I'm pretty sure Kyle could tell how I felt about Payne.

He straightens. "Why?"

"It's nothing. Really."

"Beau ..."

"Just, you know ... Some people you get along with, others you don't. That's all."

The skeptical noise that comes from him makes it clear he doesn't believe me. "Either way, I'm sorry he made you feel that way."

"Thank you."

He hums, turning toward me, one elbow propped on the counter. I greedily drink in his powerful, spread thighs and wish I could drop down and kneel between them. Everything about Payne that's ever attracted me to him has amplified in recent years.

His broad back, his rough-looking style. His light brown hair has grown out from the short cut he used to keep it in, and now he has tattoos down both arms.

Being closed in those arms would probably make me pass out.

But more than his looks is the calmness that radiates from him. He's the stillest person I've ever met. Where my hands are always busy and my knees bounce unless I tuck my legs underneath myself, it's like his entire body owns the space it occupies.

He lifts the beer to his full lips and holds my stare as he drinks. "Kyle cheated on me."

"I heard."

He grimaces. "And then I did something I shouldn't have."

"Which was?"

"I threw his toothbrush in the toilet and unblocked his number long enough to send him a photo of it the next day."

"His ... toothbrush?"

Payne waves a hand at me. "I don't want to get into it. But I shouldn't have done that."

The bitter, vindictive part of me rears its ugly head. "There was a lot he shouldn't have done to you. Does it make me a bad person to like that you retaliated?"

"Do you?" His eyes are twinkling, and it makes my gut feel unsteady. "Maybe it does. But if so, then it makes me a bad person too, because smashing his laptop felt so fucking good."

I can't help it, I start to laugh. The thought of Kyle arriving home to a smashed laptop and Payne gone makes me so happy. Holy shit, I *am* a horrible person. A horrible, horrible person. A horrible person who almost wants to suggest that Payne use me as a rebound fuck. Maybe even tell Kyle about it.

When I glance back over, his smile is the one I remember from before all this heartache. Shit, he makes me weak.

I need to try harder to put my plan into action.

But then there's that tiny voice that doesn't want to.

I shake the conflicting thoughts away. "How did you find out?"

He chuckles. "You're nosy, has anyone ever told you that before?"

"A lot. How else would I get ideas for my characters?"

"What?" His eyebrows shoot up. "I don't want you writing about this."

I hold up my hands. "Joke. I'm sorry, just a joke. I don't write about real things anyway, but even if I did, I wouldn't use people I know."

"Yeah. Of course." He shakes his head. "Sorry."

I sigh. "I guess my jokes are an area I need to work on. Got it."

He makes a noise I can't decipher.

"What?" I ask.

"Nothing."

I cringe. "And now that I've epically screwed up a nice conversation, I'm going to spend the rest of the night going over and over it in my head, trying to work out what I should have said."

"Really?" His gaze slides over me. "Why?"

"I can't help it."

"But it won't make a difference."

"I don't do it because I think it will make a difference, I do it because I like to torture myself with all the ways I could have been better, funnier, sounded smarter or more interesting. I work out everything I would change if I could."

Those unnerving eyes meet mine again. "Funny. Because I don't think I'd change a thing."

My mouth drops, and I want to point out why he's

wrong, and where I could have been smoother, and maybe moments I could have made him more relaxed.

But then Payne's large hand is patting my arm in a completely casual way, and I damn near swallow my tongue.

"I think I'm going to hit the sack," he says.

All I can do is nod.

DMC Group Chat

Art: *Hey, how's things? Settled in okay?*

  Payne: *Depends on how you define okay.*

  Orson: *Oh no, I sense a story.*

  Payne: *Haha no story. Just ... different.*

  Griffin: *Dude, you're living with Beau, even if everything is ducked, at least you have the eye candy, right?*

  Griffin: *Fucked, dammit.*

  Payne: *He's cute all right, but also ... I dunno. He has a routine at home, I guess, and I'm trying not to disrupt him too much.*

  Art: *If you walk on eggshells around him, all you'll end up with is messy feet.*

  Orson: *What Art and Griffin are TRYING to say is that sounds tough and we're here if you need to talk.*

  Griffin: *^WHS.*

  Art: *Sure. That. But also, this is your time. You don't need* to explain yourself to anyone or make excuses. It's your place. Live the way that makes you happy.

Payne: *Thanks for the ... I want to say support, but that doesn't sound right.*

Art: *Any time, brother.*

Orson: *Maybe next time message me direct.*

Griffin: *Hey, do you think you could snap some sneaky shirtless pics? Asking for a friend, of course.*

Payne: *JFC.*

Chapter Five

PAYNE

I tuck my hands behind my head, staring up at the bright white ceiling. It's new, like everything else in the apartment, but unlike everything else, it's still perfectly clean. I know, because in the week since I've moved in, I've spent a bit of time studying it.

All thanks to my ... let's go with *interesting* roommate.

There's noise from out in the living room, and it makes my lips twitch. Beau is different than I thought. It's weird that I've known him for over twenty years, but apparently I didn't actually *know* him. When we were younger, he was my kid brother's friend. Always around, cool to chat to and shoot the shit with, but during our college years I barely saw him, and since then ... he said that fucker made him feel uncomfortable, and the more I think back to how Beau behaved with him around, I realize how different it was to when it was only me visiting home.

In the last week, I'm seeing a different side to Beau.

And it's a side of him I'm not sure how to take.

He's ... high-energy but in a controlled way. Every time I duck out there, he shoots to his feet and hovers around me, trying to force conversation, eyes constantly darting back to his desk. It's clear he doesn't know how to react to someone being in his space, and if this is what he was like when he had people cleaning the place, I'm not surprised he stopped having them come. There's a difference between needing to fill silences and needing to make yourself available for every possible second. Beau is firmly in the latter category.

And during the few times I've snuck out there without him noticing, I've watched him. He's constantly doing *something*. Swinging his chair, or tapping his pen, or punching random keys on his keyboard. Being around all that energy makes even *me* feel awkward, and that's not a feeling I'm used to.

So, I've been spending time in my room. Too much time. I get what Beau meant about it feeling claustrophobic. The window here looks into the next yard, so I like to have breakfast out on the balcony, looking up at Provin Mountain and the old Kilborough Penitentiary—or Kill Pen for short.

I get up and stretch, then head out into the living area, which is ... well, *not* the same room as it was yesterday.

My feet halt in their tracks. Every item of furniture has been dragged into the room and piled together. Chairs and stools, the dining room table. One couch has been pushed up onto its side, and the other is blocking the entrance to the kitchen. Dark sheets cover the windows, and a mattress—I'm assuming Beau's—is propped against the door to the balcony, preventing any light from getting in.

Did someone break in? And, what? Caused polite and mildly annoying chaos?

"Ah ... Beau?" I call out.

His head pops up like a meerkat in the middle of the mess. He blinks at me for a moment and then, "*Shit*. Sorry. Umm ..." He glances around, like he's seeing the mess for the first time.

"What is all this?" Somehow I manage to get the question out without sounding *too* amused.

"A fort ..."

"A fort?" Okay, I stumble over my amusement on that one.

"Sorry, just—just give me a second and I'll take it down. I was, umm—" He cuts off and shakes his head. "Never mind. It will be gone. Momentarily." He disappears inside, and I choke back my chuckle before approaching. Peering over the side, I find Beau scrambling to pick up a mess of papers and notebooks that surround his laptop. "Whatcha got there, Bo-Bo?"

His head jerks up, face flushed and glasses slipping down his nose. "Nothing. It's nothing."

Instead of pushing him to explain, I duck down, find the entrance, and crawl inside.

It's obvious he knows I'm here by the tension in his shoulders, but he doesn't look at me.

"So, it's possible I forgot you were home," he says in a rush.

"And you regularly build forts for yourself when you're alone?"

"Of course not." He gives me a look like the question is ridiculous.

"Then ..."

He sighs and drops back to sit on the floor. "I'm stuck."

"Stuck?" I pretend to glance behind me. "The entrance is *right there*."

"Funny, but I mean on my book."

That makes more sense. Good to know Beau isn't losing it. "What are you stuck on?"

A scowl crosses his features. "I have this impenetrable fortress. Like, the whole series has been well established that it's impenetrable. No one in or out unless it's approved."

"Okay ..."

"And now the stupid hero's stupid love interest has been stupid, captured, and taken there."

I don't mean to laugh, I really don't, but it slips out anyway. "Sounds stupid."

He makes an affirmative noise.

"Well, your world, your rules, right?"

"Sort of. But it doesn't work that way. Once it's established, I have to work with it, otherwise the whole series crumbles if the world building can't be trusted."

"I know nothing about this stuff, but surely one tweak

isn't something people will notice. They're there for a good time, not to pick the thing apart."

He cocks a pale eyebrow, and it makes me grin. "One time I spelled a minor side character's name as J-U-N-A-E-A instead of J-U-A-N-E-A and had thirty-seven emails about it."

"Yikes."

He nods. "They notice. Which I love. But it's also taught me to be meticulous about everything. I stress over things most people wouldn't even know to stress over."

I can see that. He *is* stressed. It's in the way he holds himself and how his mouth turns down and his eyes have dark smudges under them. Beau's a good-looking guy; even with all that going on, I can only imagine what a good night's sleep would do for him.

"That's really interesting."

"Code for boring as fuck?"

I bark out a laugh. "No, I'm being serious. I wouldn't know the first thing about writing. Whereas you can create a world out of nothing, using only your brain ..."

"I'd appreciate the compliment more if my brain hadn't written me into a corner."

I think for a moment. "Could you have the love interest not be taken there?"

"No, it's how I ended the last book. Which just published."

"Well, I'm not creative, so I don't have a lot of ideas for you, but I'm here if you need to, I don't know, throw ideas out there?"

"Thanks."

Before an awkward silence can fall, I change the subject.

"I applied for ten jobs last night." Basically all entry-level, which I'm trying not to think about.

His whole face lights up. "No way."

"I've already been turned down for three of them." I wave off his surprise. "You're going to have to put up with me for a little longer."

"I've already said there's no rush. That wasn't pity. I'm serious."

I'm sure he thinks that, but if this fort is anything to go by, he's used to being on his own. "Don't you want your own space back?"

"No." He looks at me like I've grown an extra head.

"You don't feel weird having a roommate at our age?"

"Our age?" He snorts. "I'm four years younger than you, thanks. It counts."

"Sure, it does."

"I'm not in my forties yet."

"Unlucky." I lift my hands. "Being forty is awesome. Unemployment, infidelity, homelessness, and divorce. Who wouldn't want to be hit with all that at once?"

"You're right. Sounds like a dream." Beau leans back on his arms. "But you're not homeless. You live here. This is your place too."

I know he's trying to make me feel better, but while he might not have an issue with having a roommate, it makes me feel ... like I've gone backward. "Well, I'm in no hurry to leave, not when you've been so kind to me. But once I have a job, I will be on the hunt for my own place."

"All right, but my offer stands. It's not as lonely with you here."

He doesn't say it like he wants sympathy, but I can't help feeling bad for him again. "You have friends."

"It's not the same. Like, even when you're in your room, knowing you're here is nice. I don't always want to talk to people, but having them around without expectations ..." He cuts off. "Sorry, that sounds dumb."

"Not really. You want the companionship, without the pressure to be social."

He looks surprised that I get it. I mean, I don't under-stand it, but the way he describes it makes sense.

"Exactly. And until I find a boyfriend, your company will have to do." He blinks innocently at me.

"Glad to know I'm an acceptable consolation prize."

He opens his mouth like he's going to say something but snaps it closed again.

I glance around at the furniture towering over me. "So, this is what an *impenetrable fortress* looks like, huh?"

He cringes. "I'm sorry. I thought it might give me some stroke of inspiration." He frowns. "Wait, is this one of those things you're supposed to be pointing out to me?"

"Pointing out to you?"

"Our deal, remember? Anything weird, you're supposed to tell me."

Oh. *That* deal. The one I'm doing my best to forget he even asked about. He can call it improvement all he likes, but what he actually wants is to change himself so people will like him better. That doesn't sit right with me, not that it's my decision to make, but I've always liked Beau. Sure he's ... different in ways, but that's not a bad thing.

"I'll admit this isn't what I'd expect to walk out to—"

His face falls.

"—but it doesn't matter what I think."

Beau looks like he wants to roll his eyes.

And fair enough. If this is something he wants to do, I'm not going to stop him, but I'm also not going to encourage it. Convincing him he's fine the way he is isn't my place.

"I'm going to cook lunch. You hungry?"

"Yeah, thanks." He goes back to gathering up the paper. "I'll put everything back and—"

I cover one of his hands to make him stop. "Leave it."

"What?"

"You're working, and if this helps, then it stays for as long as you need it. I'll slide lunch in through the, ah, door when it's ready."

Beau's forehead creases as I climb out, but I pretend not to notice.

Sure, the fort thing seems like a leap in logic to me, but it's a minor thing. This is his place, he can do what he wants, and if building a pseudo-replica impenetrable fortress is what he needs to get past the writer's block, then why shouldn't he? Beau doesn't take himself too seriously, and it's refreshing.

My fuckhead ex took everything too seriously. From our

furniture to his clothes to where we hung out and with who. I'd liked it at the time, but thinking back on it makes me sad.

How much different would things have been if we'd taken a step back and built a blanket fort in the living room to watch movies from?

I know exactly what that fucker would say to those kinds of suggestions though. That we're too old. Like I just told Beau we're too old to have a roommate.

The whole time I'm cooking the rice for lunch, I keep glancing over at where I can hear Beau shifting papers and tapping at his keyboard as he mutters to himself. He's like his own center of energy, filling the apartment with his presence.

I'm still not sure how to take him.

But I'm curious anyway.

Chapter Six

BEAU

My brain is wired today. Hopped up on overthinking and hyperfocus with no outlet to unleash it on. I woke up at midnight, and the second I opened my eyes, I knew there was no getting back to sleep. Sneaking down the hall so I didn't wake Payne, I closed off the door into the living room, made a coffee, and then switched on the computer. Words tumbled from my fingers with the steady tapping of keys, and an hour later, I had a scene written about a seashell pining for the ocean.

It's too on the nose for anyone to ever see it, so I save the scene to the depths of my hard drive and open the novel I'm working on.

The next chapter stares back at me blankly—white screen, pulsing cursor, brain urging me to type *something*—but my hands are unwilling to listen.

Instead, I keep thinking back to the other day when I thought it would be a good idea to build a fucking fort. *Am I a child*? I shake my head. I have no idea what Payne must have thought of me. My brain keeps projecting images of him and his friends having a good laugh about the weirdo he lives with.

My subconscious itches to write more irrelevant scenes, and I end up giving in. It feels good to get back into the flow of things, even if this allegory is so obviously about my crush on the Payne tree who parted its branches so my little bushy self could be bathed in sunshine. I mentally gag at how heavy-handed and dramatic the whole thing is once I'm done, then save that to the darkest depths too.

The rapid typing still wasn't enough to shake this buzzing under my skin.

Sunlight peeks through the curtains to the balcony and tells me I've been here for hours.

Shit.

I rummage through my drawers for one of my coloring books and come up empty, so I grab the yoga mat rolled up beside the cabinet and put a workout on to try and clear my head. The sooner the noise stops, the sooner I can sleep.

It takes me a while to zone out, and just as I think it's not going to happen today, my brain starts to relax, even as my muscles ache with the poses I'm putting them through.

The door to the hallway clicks open when I'm mid-downward dog, and I tilt my head toward the noise to see Payne's upside-down form.

His lips twitch. "Morning."

"Morning." Of course I'm sweaty and the armpits of my shirt feel damp. All I can hope is I'm not stinking up the space.

"Care if I join you?"

"Ah ..." I quickly nod. "I mean, *no*, I don't mind. You can, of course."

He leaves and is back a moment later in gym shorts and no shirt. I should have said no. Told him I was done.

Because I basically am now, since it's near impossible to do these poses with a fucking hard-on.

I've been at it for longer than I normally would be, but there's no stopping me now. Payne's body, stretching and moving beside mine, is better than porn, and when he begins to sweat as well, it *definitely* isn't stinking up the place. It's manly and sexy, and I want to bury my face in his neck and inhale.

A shiver passes through me as my dick starts to thicken.

Shit.

I drop my pose, and my ass hits the mat with a thud. "*Ouch.*"

"You okay?" He's got the fingertips of one hand brushing the carpet and the others stretched into the air, providing a view of that wide, tattooed chest for my fantasy memory bank.

"Totally. Just bruised my coccyx," I joke.

"Better than your cock, I guess."

My blood pressure skyrockets. He cannot say *cock* around me. I scramble to my feet. "Right, so, umm, breakfast."

"I'll make it." Payne drops the pose he was in and straightens, stretching those long arms over his head.

I realize I'm staring at his muscles like they're crack and yank my gaze away. "I feel like I should fight you on it, but I can't actually cook, so my options are a bowl of cereal or yogurt."

His hands land on my shoulders as he steers me toward the hall, and if he wasn't totally oblivious to my feelings, I'd say he was deliberately trying to tease me. "Go take the first shower. I'll jump in after breakfast."

An image of him completely naked and covered in water flashes through my mind, and I lurch out of his grip. "First shower sounds great. I'll be right back." After I take care of my dick.

The second I'm behind the closed bathroom door, I turn on the shower to drown out all sound and drop trou.

I'd feel embarrassed or guilty, but this is far from my first jerk-off session since Payne moved in.

I wrap my hand around my lengthening cock and give it a long, hard stroke. It's more frustrating than anything, so I pump hand soap into my palm, and this time the glide of my hand makes my eyes flutter closed.

It makes it easier to picture Payne in here with me. His dominating presence, the muscles, his steady gaze. How the hell could Kyle give that up? I'd sacrifice my left nut to spend the night with him. To feel his lips on my skin, to run my fingers through his hair, to finally find out if his scruffy beard is soft or spiky. I'm almost sobbing as I start to jack off properly.

When he was away, it was easy to forget my crush, to put it behind me and only torture myself with it whenever I was reminded of him. But now he's here, in my space, sharing proper one-on-one time with me for the first time maybe ever ... having his full attention, being the one who gets to be here for him, it's driving me crazy.

My hand speeds up to the slick squelches of the hand soap, and I have to bite my lip to hold back a groan. My cock is pulsing with pleasure, zaps of need filling my balls, my muscles tense as I stroke faster.

I picture his chest, his forearms, that smile that makes me weak. Seeing those gym shorts slide to the ground as his dick comes into view.

"*Fuck ...*"

My cock pulses, and then I'm coming. Waves of relief sweep over me as I unleash the pent-up need into my fist, stroking myself to completion.

When I trust my legs to move again, I climb into the shower and clean off.

Readying myself to go back out there and face him.

The breeze from the water blows through the café at the Killer Brew, sending a chill down my back. I tuck my hands under my arms and place an order for Marty's and my usual coffees, then move to the side.

Ford Thomas is already there waiting. "Hey, Beau, how's things?"

"Yeah, not bad. Just meeting Marty."

He makes an affirmative noise. We're usually here at the same time, so of course he already knows that. His garage is down the street, and he stops by here for lunch a lot.

"What about you?"

He tilts his head from side to side. "Mostly good. Just had to let another pain-in-the-ass kid go, so I'm looking for an assistant. Again."

"Ouch. What's that? Three in the last month or so?"

His chuckle is as loud and large as he is. "Easy now. It's not my fault they don't want to show up for work."

"Well, you keep hiring teenagers."

"I've had some good teenage apprentices before. The problem is with the low pay rate and minimal job responsibilities, no one older is applying."

"Could you combine the work?"

He grunts as his coffee order is called. "Maybe. I'll think on it and figure something out."

I say goodbye, and then when my order is up, I grab both coffees and head out to meet Marty.

He smiles wide as I approach. It's funny that he and Payne are totally different, yet both feel like home. Marty is a bookkeeper for small businesses and always looks well-groomed and put together. Button-up shirts, clean-shaven, short and tidy hair. He has more lines in his face than Payne, even though Payne is four years older, but the lines make him look happy, instead of old.

My erratic sleeping patterns and tendency to work until I drop when the muse hits means I look way older than either of them.

Not in a hot way.

In an exhausted way.

I hand over his coffee, and we start on our usual path along the boardwalk.

"I have an odd question."

"Uh-oh."

"Do I ever annoy you?" I ask.

"What?"

"With, you know, how ..." I struggle to think of a word that describes me properly. "*Absentminded* I am."

He stares at me. "What's brought this on?"

"Been thinking. Obviously, I'm worse at the moment because of the writer's block, but outside of you, who do I have? Everyone else has decided I'm too much work, so why not you?"

"Beau ..." He squeezes my shoulder, and with a jolt, I'm reminded of Payne. "It's one of your ... *quirks*. You're not doing it maliciously."

"Never."

"Then how could I be annoyed? Seriously, what's this about?"

"Nothing. I'm being melancholy. Ignore me."

"You're okay though, right?"

"Yes, actually." I hesitate over how much to say. "It's been good having Payne live with me."

"How does he seem to you? Whenever I ask, he says he's

fine, but you know my big brother. He wouldn't admit if he wasn't."

If he's told Marty he's fine, it's not up to me to say otherwise. And it's not like it's a *lie*—he is fine. Mostly. Until I catch glimpses of a man who's had a shitty thing happen to him and is trying to pretend he hasn't. "I think his main problem at the moment is finding a job."

"That makes sense. He's never been great at having nothing to do." Marty takes a long drink. "I think he'd take anything about now."

"Exactly." I frown. "Wait, anything?"

"From what he was saying."

I hum, wondering whether the job Ford has would class as "anything." Being an errand boy for the garage wouldn't be Payne's first calling.

"What's that noise?" Marty asks.

"Ford mentioned he was looking for someone again, but I can't see Payne picking up spare parts and cleaning out car interiors."

"You could suggest it and let him decide."

"True ..."

Payne's reliable. And if Ford has been messed around, he'll be far more likely to hire someone like Payne than some fresh-faced high school graduate.

Who knows? Maybe Payne'll be so thrilled to have any job, he'll want to reward the one who gives him the lead.

I indulge the fantasy for all of a second, because I notice Marty watching me again.

"What is it?" I ask.

"You're different today."

I shift. "Did some yoga this morning."

"Hmm ... maybe that's it."

Silence creeps in, and I know he wants to say something. "All right, out with it."

He chuckles. "You always know."

"Because I know you. What do you want to say that I'm going to hate?"

"I have this friend ..."

He pauses so I can let out the required groan. Every couple of months, he tries to set me up with someone, and it never ends well. "Why are we doing this again?"

"Because the last date you went on was six months ago. If you didn't want to find someone, it would be one thing, but you do, and, Beau, my pool of available friends is getting very small."

I never should have told him I was lonely. "It's fine. I have Payne now, so there's always someone around. I don't need to date."

"Yeah, but that's short term. He's a roommate, not a boyfriend."

And this is the perfect opening. The moment to tell Marty how I've always felt about his brother.

I force a nonchalant tone. "Maybe Payne could be my boyfriend."

Marty spins suddenly, cutting off my path. "You're joking, right?"

"O-of course."

"Thank fuck." He lets out a long breath and starts

walking again. "Imagine if I'd pushed this roommates thing on you while you were hoping for more. He's not in that place, and I'd feel guilty to see you get hurt. Besides, *you two*?" Marty laughs. Properly. Out loud. "What a disaster."

Ouch. "Total disaster." I think the words hurt more because they're true.

"The sooner he's out of there, the better," Marty says. "I think he needs to be on his own for a bit."

I disagree. Even though things are shaky and he clearly doesn't know how to take me, when we do hold down a conversation, he seems to enjoy it. He's a social person. At least I can give him that.

But he's already echoed what Marty's said. He does want to get out on his own again. Selfishly, it's the last thing I want, and telling him about this job opening could be his foot out the door. Am I going to sabotage myself like that?

Yes. Yes, I am. Because if it makes Payne happy, there's no way I can stop myself.

PAYNE

The second Beau tells me there's a job going at Ford's Garage, I'm straight on the phone.

Is it what I want? Far from it. The problem is though, I need *something* to keep me going, or I'll blow through my money and have no cushion to fall back on. How embarrassing to be living with Beau *and* having to ask if I can borrow money.

The thing is, I know he wouldn't care. If the seventy-five times he assured me that I don't need to leave as soon as I have a job is any indication, I'd say he likes me and wants me around.

Either that or he's more awkward than I thought.

From what Marty says, Beau is loaded after selling a bunch of rights to his books. I don't understand how any of it works, but I *do* know publishing isn't an easy business to make it in, so if he's doing all right, he must be good.

I focus on the rock music playing in the large garage instead of what I'm going to find as I reach under the front passenger seat of this car I'm detailing. My hands close around *something* and pull out ... I cringe. I don't want to know. This is not what I had in mind when I finished college, that's for sure.

Or on my wedding day.

Or when that fucker and I bought our apartment.

I grit my teeth and push that thought away because it's done now. This is temporary, and I'm not going to let him affect my life moving forward.

I tilt my head to see if there's anything else left under there before moving on.

As far as bosses go, Ford is cool. If the rumors are true, he's done time, and while he's rough around the edges, I like him. He's no bullshit.

It makes up for the pay being shithouse.

Since starting this job, I've seen a lot less of Beau, so I guess it doesn't matter what the pay is like when I can stay there indefinitely anyway. He's either out of the house or napping in the afternoons, and some mornings when I'm up beginning my day, he's only just going to bed. Without crossing paths, it's like having the apartment to myself.

And it's a nice apartment. Especially now that it's clean.

But I know what Beau means about being lonely. I've lived with someone almost all my life, from home to the college dorms to the shared house. I spent a couple of years solo, and then that fucker came along, and we've lived together ever since. So now whenever I see Beau, I basically jump on him for company.

I've never been needy before, but I like having a friend, and his lack of attention makes me want it more.

I've got friends still around, and I'm catching up with Art again soon, but having someone in my own space to shoot the shit with is maybe my favorite thing.

I still think having a roommate at my age is pathetic, but maybe I want one anyway.

Besides, I like Beau's nosiness. When some people ask about the separation, I can tell they're after gossip, but Beau actually gives a shit.

Keeping the house clean isn't enough for what he's done for me. That part's easy. Despite the epic mess I walked into, Beau isn't actually a slob. Sure, I've had to remind him about garbage left on the counter a few times, but otherwise it's not a big issue. He'd left the cleaning for too long until it had backed up to unreasonable levels.

I don't understand him. But I don't need to, I guess.

When I get off work, I swing by a Thai place on the way home to pick us up dinner. If he's sleeping, he can reheat it, but I keep my fingers crossed he's awake.

And when I get home, I'm in luck. Beau's at his desk, frantically typing, and I like the sight of him working rather than staring off into space.

I try to keep quiet and not disturb him, but even when I pop the food in the fridge he doesn't notice, so I assume that he's deep into whatever it is he's working on. I leave to shower and change, but he's still going when I come back out again.

I have no idea what the etiquette is here. Do I let him know I'm home with food? Eat my half and leave his? Wait to eat together?

My empty gut groans its disapproval at that.

Yeah, I'm not waiting.

Before I can open the fridge, the steady, rhythmic typing stops, and Beau spins in his chair. "You're home."

He looks like he's coming out of a daze as he blinks rapidly, glasses halfway down his nose and usually neat curls a frizzy mess. There's food down the front of his shirt, but I hold off from pointing it out.

"Have been for a while, but you were clearly busy."

His face flushes, which is interesting, before he hurries to switch off his screen. "It was nothing, just messing around."

"Not on your book?"

"Nope."

"Well then, I don't feel so bad about interrupting you." I grab the food from the fridge. "I picked up dinner and thought we could chill and watch a movie or something if you don't have plans?"

"I don't."

I smile at how fast the words come out. His brand of awkward is fun. "Good. Well, I'll plate up if you want to get us drinks?"

"The hard stuff? Because I have to say, I need it after this week."

"You and me both."

We grab everything and head through to the living area to eat in front of the TV.

Only, he doesn't make a move to switch the TV on.

"You okay?" I ask.

Beau pulls a face. "Marty wants to set me up with someone again."

"Well, that's good."

He doesn't look any happier though.

"Right?"

"I don't know. Maybe. I don't like the dating scene. Of the last three guys he's set me up with, the first one I forgot about the date and stood him up, the second was scared off by the end of the first date, and the third hung around for a few weeks of banging and then totally ghosted me."

"Ouch."

"Yes. See why I need your help?"

Annnnd we're back on that. "How do you know my brother doesn't have terrible taste in blind dates?"

"Just things they said. I really hate the getting-to-know-you part."

"Well, that part is a necessity. You can't build a good foundation with anyone unless you know them first." And even as the words leave my mouth, I realize how ridiculous they are. "Actually, don't listen to me. I spent seven years getting to know my husband before we took that step, and fat lot of good that did me."

"That wasn't your fault." Beau's tone is harsher than I'm used to hearing, and his cheekbones are going red the way they do when he gets angry. I shouldn't enjoy him being pissed off on my behalf anywhere near as much as I do.

I manage a tight smile, because there are days where I wonder if it was. "I guess once I get in gear and have the paperwork organized, I won't need to worry about it again." I'm about to start eating when Beau responds.

"You deserved better."

It makes me laugh. "Doesn't anyone? I trusted him more than anyone I knew, and then he went and did that to me." I swallow back my words. "My point is, maybe you've got the right idea. Relationships are too much work. Once I have a proper job, I'll get my own place, then hook up all I like, but fuck dating."

"You're going to give up on relationships?"

"I'm forty." I shrug. "I might not feel it or act it some days, but the older I get, the less time I have for bullshit. And after what I've been through, I'd like to do everything I can to make sure it doesn't happen again."

Beau's voice drops low. "Do you still love him?"

"Is this for another one of your characters?" I ask dryly. He ducks his head, and I take pity on him. "In some moments I do. In some weak moments where I wish he'd show up and apologize and we could go back to everything being the way it used to be."

"And in others?"

There's something in the way he asks, like he knows he shouldn't but can't stop himself, that amuses me. "You really can't help it, can you?"

"Sorry."

"Why don't I believe you?"

His lips twitch, and it draws my attention to how full they are. "I might struggle with a brain-to-mouth filter when I'm curious."

"Well, we can't have you being curious, can we? Most of the time, when I'm not being a whiny moron, I know this is better, and I hate him for the choices he made. I'd be happy if I never saw him again."

"Well, no one is going to tell him you're here."

"Another reason why moving from Marty's was a good idea. You're a total lifesaver, you know that?"

He rubs the back of his neck. "It's just a spare room."

"It's so much more than that, and you know it."

"Okay." He bites his lip like he's trying to hold back another question. It doesn't work. "Since I'm a lifesaver, can I ask another personal question?"

"The last few weren't enough for you?"

"I'm very, *very* curious." His innocent expression has a mischievous tinge to it that has me folding like a clipped hurdle.

"Fine. One question."

"Oooh, we could make a game of it. One question per day."

"I'm not sure I'm interesting enough to get more than a week out of that game, but go for it."

His excitement dims slightly as he drums his fingers on the coffee table we're eating at. Then his blue eyes collide with mine. "How *did* you find out?"

I cringe, automatically reaching up to rub my chest.

There's a sting there, but it feels more like betrayal than loss now. "You want me to reopen that wound, huh?"

"Okay, maybe let's skip that question. Sorry. I wasn't thinking."

The odd thing is, though, I don't mind. I tap Beau's forearm to cut off his apologies and then smile. "Well, you already know the condensed version. I caught him red-handed, smashed his laptop, and took off out of Boston before he was done teaching for the day."

"And now the real version?"

The real version is something I've been trying to forget, but Beau asking doesn't feel weird. It doesn't make me angry or embarrassed, only resigned.

"The real reason is I was sent a link to his OnlyFans page and found two years' worth of video evidence of him cheating on me."

Beau's eyes shoot wide and make me feel vindicated. "Two … years?"

"Yup. Who knows how much longer it was happening though." And for some reason, I'm hit with this stupid, reckless urge. The same urge that slams me in the face late at night when I pull up his page and force myself through one of the damn videos. "Can I show you?"

Beau's clearly surprised, probably because of how closed off I've been about it all, and now I suddenly want to drag him into it.

"Porn?" he asks.

"Yes."

"Starring your ex-husband?"

I screw up my face. "You're right, that's weird."

"No. It's ... yes. Show me. As long as you're, you know, okay with it."

"Truthfully, the day I found out isn't the only time I've seen it."

He tilts his head. "What, you watch it?"

"Whenever I'm scared I might go back."

"Don't." The word is soft and hesitant, but I catch it in the quiet.

"It's not like I want to. I'm ... weak."

"Excuse me?"

I rub my jaw, not used to talking about feelings like this. "Sometimes. It's been a big change, you know?"

"Okay, I hated him before, and then I hated him again for doing this to you, and now I hate him a bit more for making you doubt that you're a strong, badass mother-fucker. Where's this porn?"

I blink at Beau, hardly prepared for that little outburst. Instead of commenting on how much I appreciate it, I pull out my phone. Then I navigate to the account I'm still subscribed to and try to ignore how the number of subscribers has only increased since I posted my video.

I like to pretend that doesn't hurt.

Beau takes my phone, and before he clicks on the first video, he glances at me. "You sure about this?"

"It's fine. I've watched that one enough times I've desensitized myself to it."

His thumb hovers over it a couple of seconds more. "Fine." He hits Play.

I try not to hurl.

It's one thing to watch this privately and feel humiliated, it's another to watch Beau's face as he watches it and see the horrified expressions play out. He looks disgusted. Shocked. Angry. When the sound of skin slapping together as they fuck plays out through the speakers, Beau closes the video and sets my phone on the table in front of us.

To my surprise, his eyes are glassy. He swallows, frown deep, eye contact unwavering.

"That is so completely fucking unacceptable. I—" He growls, and then he grabs me and yanks me into a hug. His arms close tight around my shoulders, and something inside me snaps.

Lizzy and Marty have both hugged me since, and so have the girls, but none of them felt like this. Like Beau's trying to force my shattered pieces back together.

I don't cry, but I want to.

Instead, I grip him to me, not wanting to let go.

All the anger and embarrassment I've been living with loses hold on me, and for the first time since, I have ... hope. Like things can actually get better.

"You deserve so much more than that loser could ever give you," he says.

I drop my forehead to his shoulder. "Thanks."

He clears his throat, and when he pulls back, I force myself to release him.

"I think you should unsubscribe," he says.

A few minutes ago, I would have argued, even though I know he's right. Instead, I pick up my phone.

"I think I should too."

"Go on, then."

I unlock my phone, then stop, surprised at how hard this is. I could give it to Beau and make him do it, but I want to be the one to take that step. I peek over at him. "I know you just said a bunch of awesome things about me, but I need some help here."

"What can I do?"

I wriggle closer to him until I'm leaning against his body. "Another one, please."

He laughs as he wraps an arm around my shoulders, and then we both watch as I follow through.

"There, feel better?" he asks.

"I do." And it's probably not for the reason he thinks.

Chapter Eight

BEAU

Since our dinner last night, Payne seems better. I'm trying to pretend it has nothing to do with me, but I can't stamp down that twinge of pride at being the one who got to support him like that.

Seeing Kyle with another man though ... I saw red.

I'm not a violent guy, but if he'd been right in front of me, I would have punched him. The guy he was with had nothing on Payne.

Stupid, horrible, dumb loser.

Words have been coming easily, practically pouring out of me, but still not on what I'm supposed to be writing about. They're nonsensical snippets of pining and loss and betrayal, and while none of it is anything I'd ever publish, it feels good to follow the muse.

I'm keenly aware of Payne behind me, watching TV,

volume down so low it's a hum of noise. And even with him doing his best not to distract me, I can't stop the weird feeling of *needing* to say something. To make it clear I'm not ignoring him.

I open my mouth to suggest we get lunch when he cuts me off.

"Don't."

I slump. "I wasn't going to say anything." It's not my fault his presence is so *big*.

He angles his head so he can smile at me over his shoulder. "Yeah, you were. I swear you have the loudest inhale in history. Not to mention I can practically hear you thinking about it from here. You need to get used to working with people around since you want me here and I'm not hiding out in my room every day."

"You're going to stay?" My voice hitches with excitement.

"You're doing it again ..." he sings.

"It was a legitimate question!"

"Legitimate procrastination, maybe."

I turn back to my computer with the biggest grin on my face. Maybe he only means short term, who knows?

I'll take it though.

And if I'm really, really lucky, I'll get the chance to hold him again.

My fingers fly across the keyboard.

And as I write, I zone out. The room around me disappears as I'm transported into the world beneath my fingertips.

When I blink back into reality, my hands are cramped, and it's darker than it was earlier. I glance over my shoulder and find the TV off and Payne gone.

Beside me, though, is a bright yellow paper crane, with a note along the wing.

Babysitting the girls tonight. Be home later.

Nerves that have no right to show up hit me out of nowhere. I know it's dangerous, and I'm leaning into the fantasy too far to be safe, but all I can picture is Payne in the role of my boyfriend, letting me know when he'll be home.

I drop my head onto the desk.

Bad, Beau!

Determined to behave somewhat normally and not totally smitten with my roommate, I go shower, then forage for leftovers in the fridge. It's well stocked, and I *could* cook something—if I wasn't so worried that I'd put it on and forget about it. Luckily, the leftover Thai smells mouthwatering as it reheats.

I sit at the kitchen counter as I eat, letting the silence settle over me. Normally this is the moment where I'm most lonely. Where the end of the day hits me and I realize I've been holed up here with no human contact, and my thoughts usually head in a dark direction, but this time, when I ask myself if anyone would even notice if I was here or not, I come up with a different answer.

Payne would notice.

Butterflies hit me again, and I wish they'd stop. I wish I could be immune to him, but even more than that, I wish he was in a position where I could tell him how I feel. Going through a breakup isn't stellar timing for unloading that onto him, but for the first time in our whole lives, I actually have the opportunity.

We're not teenaged punks. Neither of us is leaving for college. We're in the same town, the same fucking apartment. I could … I could actually do it.

I stare blankly at my food as I realize, with total certainty, that I'm going to tell him. Not now. Not even soon, since I want to make sure he's in a good place first, but in the coming future, I *will tell him how I feel*.

He'll probably let me down easy.

But my brain can't stop conjuring pretty images of him saying he feels the same.

I'm an idiot.

A hopeful idiot, but just as stupid all the same.

Since Payne is with the girls, I assume that means Marty and Lizzy have gone out together, so instead of messaging my best friend like I normally would, I take a photo of the crane and send it to Payne.

Me: *Man of many talents.*

To my surprise, he texts right back.

Payne: *I'm good with my hands.*

I bite my lip and try not to read too much into that, but … it sort of sounds flirty. Maybe? Sort of?

Me: *So am I, but clearly we use that superpower for two very different things ;)*
Payne: *Oh yeah? What do you use your magic hands for?*
Me: *Typing, of course. Whatever else could you possibly be referring to?*
Payne: *LOL*

I give him a minute, but nothing else comes through.
Fuck it.

Me: *They're also good for jerking off.*
Payne: *We have that in common.*

Nrgh. Payne. Jerking off. Standing in the shower, water running over his hair and down his tattooed body, forearm flexing with every stroke. Goddamn I want to see that. My fingers are itching to write more, to flirt, to push boundaries I have no business pushing. Instead, I close my phone and will myself to forget about the maybe almost kinda flirting that's probably all in my head and look for distractions instead.

It's too late to go for a walk, and I can't be assed pulling the yoga mat out. I still haven't grabbed another coloring book, and the one time I'm actually considering cleaning the place, it's already clean.

I could go to bed, since I was up at four, but even that isn't calling to me.

Instead, I flop back onto the couch, about to turn the TV on, when I'm hit with the faintest whiff of Payne's cologne. My eyes fall closed as I breathe more of it in. His scent floods my senses, and my cock thickens with interest.

Guess I've figured out how to spend my time.

I duck into my bedroom for the lube, then head back for the couch. As I'm passing Payne's room, the idea to go in there flickers through my mind. While it would be hot as fuck to jerk off in his bed, even my feelings know what the word "limits" means. Apparently jerking off over him is fine; doing it in his space is not.

Good to know I'm not yet beyond rational thought.

Back on the couch, I turn my face and press it to the cushion. His scent is still there but frustratingly faint. I squirt some lube in my hand and hook my sweats beneath my balls. Then I take a deep breath and relax.

I stroke myself slowly, almost teasingly, as I wait to reach full hardness. All I can concentrate on is how amazing my couch smells and how good Payne felt in my arms last night. Only a foot from where I'm sitting now. His large, warm body, pressed against me, making me hard.

Mmm. Sighing, I drop my head back. My hand circles the tip of my cock before I give myself another long, hard stroke. Desire is pooling in my balls, driven by the image of Payne on his knees between my spread thighs, leaning in, his hot breath on my swollen, needy cock.

I've never jerked off so much as I have since he moved in.

He's everywhere in my place. Filling every room with my filthy thoughts of him. I walk into the kitchen and can see him bending me over the island. I sit at my desk and can picture him spinning me in my chair before shoving his cock into my mouth. He's in the shower with me while I clean myself, and in bed with me at night. My need for him is growing stronger, more tangible every day. And sure, maybe I should focus on my plan to pay attention to his flaws, but those flaws only make me want him more.

My balls tighten with the need to come, so I draw back and loosen my grip. I want this to last. To enjoy my fantasies. It's so fucking difficult though when all I can think about is him.

Payne Walker Payne Walker Payne Walker ...

I groan deep in my chest, and I jerk off with purpose, getting myself so close before backing off again. I do it over and over, until my thighs are trembling with the pressure of holding off, and I know I'm not going to last much longer.

I'm so lost in the delicious arousal flooding my system that I don't register the small click.

The light footsteps.

Then movement catches my attention as Payne walks into the room.

My heart stops.

He freezes.

My hand keeps fucking going.

"P-Payne ..."

His dark stare drops to my cock and sends a full-body shiver through me.

"I ... I'm sorry—" He goes to turn, and I speak without thinking.

"*Stay.*"

Payne whirls back around, confusion on his face, but

even that isn't enough to embarrass me. I know any normal person would have stopped touching themselves by now, maybe tucked their junk away, but when Payne's gaze falls to my cock again, my hand only moves faster.

My eyes are locked on him as he crosses his arms and rests casually against the wall.

"Okay."

Fuck yes.

My balls throb as I jerk off, greedily drinking in Payne's long, muscular body. I want to ask him to take his shirt off, but somehow I manage to cut off that thought. I'm panting, body alive and thrumming with my impending orgasm. Then I notice something that catapults me over the edge ...

The long, hard outline of Payne's cock.

I bite off a cry as I come, head tossed back and thighs tensing through the pleasure. My cock throbs and throbs, and the weight of Payne's stare sends tingles through every limb. The high lasts a blissfully long time, and when I finally crack open an eye, I'm hoping Payne will have done the decent thing and left me to my embarrassment.

Instead, he's still there. And as soon as we make eye contact, he lifts his eyebrows.

"You really do have magic hands." Then he reaches down and adjusts himself before disappearing into the hall.

All I can do is stare at the place he disappeared and try not to picture him going to relieve himself.

Over me.

Chapter Nine

PAYNE

Well, that was the last thing I expected to see when I walked through the door.

And I can't say I hated it.

The sight of Beau sprawled out across his couch hit me with a sack of lust so hard I feel like I have a concussion. It has to be the only damn reason I stood there ogling him like a creep. All I know is it took herculean effort to turn away, and then he'd said that one word, husky and deep and so fucking turned on it made it impossible to argue with. When he asked me to stay, my self-control snapped. There was no walking away.

There was no closing my eyes.

I stood there and took in every expression that crossed his face as he gave himself what looked like the greatest hand job in history.

Damn I wanted in on it.

There's no doubt if Beau wasn't the person standing between me and being back on the couch at Marty's, if he wasn't my little brother's best friend, if he wasn't someone I legitimately like and want to be friends with, I would have closed the distance between us and had my way with him.

God fucking damn that was one sexy show.

In my defense, it's been a long time since I've had anything resembling decent sex, and after what that fucker did, I thought it would take me a while to ease back into that side of my life.

But apparently, nope.

All it took was Beau with his cock in his hand, and I'm already ready to get back out there.

Specifically, out *there*. In the living room. With my cock in Beau's mouth.

I go to bed, determined to ignore my dick's need to jerk off to what I saw. No need for things to get even more mixed up in my head than they already are, and I know if I touch myself, it'll be Beau's dick I'm thinking about.

That long, pale, mouthwatering dick ...

No! Nope.

I roll onto my side and deny myself anything even close to friction. All I need is to sleep it off, then tomorrow, everything will be back to normal.

Except next morning, there's nothing normal about the way Beau's entire face flushes when he sees me.

And if I needed anything to break the tension, it's the mortified expression he's wearing.

I crack up laughing.

"Guess we're not pretending it didn't happen, then," he says.

"Bit *hard* to forget."

He scowls.

I poke his shoulder on my way to the toaster. "You're bright red. Feeling *hot*?"

"Here I was thinking I'd have to apologize."

"Apologize?" I snort. "For what? Giving me an eyeful of the goods?"

"Making things ... weird."

"Oh, come on. I'd be a *jerk* to get weird over that."

"Payne ..."

I slide my bread into the toaster. "It's fine. Really." If he's ignoring the way I got hard over watching him, I can ignore the way he ... *fuck*. It's going to take some time to get his O face out of my mind.

"You don't ... you're not feeling awkward?"

I shrug. "Who hasn't been caught by their roommate while jerking off?" I know that isn't the awkward part he was referring to, but I'm set on forgetting about it. Apparently, Beau is too, and who could blame him? He might have asked me to stay in the heat of the moment, but no one wants their friend's brother eye-fucking them. Talk about creepy.

"I can't say I make a habit of it," he says.

"Different *strokes*."

"You can stop now." He pins me with a dry look.

I laugh. "Maybe I shouldn't say this, but if you weren't, you know, *you*, and I wasn't me, that would have been hot as hell to come home to. I'm surprised no guy has locked all that up already."

"The thing about finding someone is you have to actually leave the house."

"Good point." My toast pops up, and I cover it in peanut butter. "Why don't you come out with me today?"

His stare immediately flicks to his desk, and I hold back a chuckle. He has to be the biggest workaholic I know. "Where are you going?"

"Not sure yet. Out. The place has changed a lot since I lived here last, so I thought I'd get reacquainted with it."

He cringes as his eyes stray back to his desk.

"Let me rephrase. Are you planning on working on your book today or something else?"

"Ah ..."

"That's my answer. Go get dressed."

"You don't understand. I have to follow my muse."

"Oh yeah?" I give him a blank look. "Was it also your muse that told you to get your cock out last night?"

His eyes widen. "You couldn't pretend to let me forget, could you?"

"Nope." I spin him around, then slap him on the ass for good measure. "Get dressed. You're *coming* with me."

Our eyes lock for a moment, and I realize that I took it one pun too far. The way that sounded ... the sight of his dick flashes through my mind along with filthy ideas on how he actually can come with me, and I force a laugh to ease whatever this tension is between us.

"Coming for a drive," I clarify like I could possibly mean anything else.

Way to make things awkward.

Luckily, Beau is as intent as I am to pretend the whole thing never happened.

He grumbles the whole way down the hall to his bedroom but doesn't try to fight me on it. When we're both dressed, we head out, still with no clue on where we're going.

"Okay, where would you say has changed the most in the last twenty years?" I ask on the way to the car.

"Take your pick. Pretty much everywhere."

Hmm, well, we don't have time to see everywhere. "In that case, where will be the best place to go to kick that muse of yours into gear?"

"My muse?"

"Yeah, you said you're struggling to write. Maybe you just need to, what's it called? Where you find inspiration again?"

"You think I'm lacking inspiration?"

I unlock the car and wait for him to climb in beside me before I answer. "You're not stuck for words—those are happening. It's your book that you're holding back on."

"True."

"So, what do you write?"

He shifts in his seat. "Fantasy, mostly, with some heavy romance throughout."

"Romance?"

"Don't '*romance*' me." He pins me with a look. "Men can like love too."

My laugh fills the car as I turn it on and get moving. "Of course they do. Why do you think I got married? It's the fantasy stuff that has you stuck at the moment though, right? With the fortress?"

"Right."

"Okay, I know where we can start."

Thankfully, he doesn't try to get it out of me, clearly content to come along for the ride. I make a mental note to attempt to get him out of the house more often while I'm living with him, because the farther we get from the apartment, the more *tense* he gets.

"You can't stand to be away from your work, can you?"

"Am I that obvious?"

"Would you prefer I lie and tell you I'm really good at reading people?"

He nods. "That would work."

"Why are you such a workaholic?"

"I'm not." After I cut him a look, he continues. "*Usually*. The deadline is what's stressing me out. I'm used to planning my time in a way that I can do small amounts each day, but the closer the deadline gets, the more work I need to do, and it stresses me to the point where I can't do a single thing."

It's no surprise he's so on edge all the time. Working under that kind of pressure would be enough to make me freeze up too. "I know it will be hard, but can you try—just for the day—to forget it and pretend to enjoy spending time with me?"

He scoffs, and I grin his way. "Can't make any promises."

"It'll be a real struggle, I'm sure."

"I'll do my best not to *cock* it up."

I bark out a laugh, and whatever lingering tension there was between us completely disappears. This Beau is one I can get on board with. Now if only I can forget what he looks like as he comes, we might be able to nail the position of world's greatest roommates.

It takes twenty minutes for us to get to the ghost town on the outskirts of Kilborough. The whole place is a tourist trap. Ticket prices, tours, and souvenirs, plus the expensive themed motels. Locals rarely come out here because during tourist season it's busier here than in town, and the only time I've ever been to Kill Pen was on a high school field trip. I'd be willing to bet Beau's the same.

My suspicions are confirmed when I pull into the parking lot and he whistles. "The prison? Really?"

"It was supposed to be inescapable. That's your fortress."

He gives me this weird puzzling look, but I jump out of the car instead of sticking around to try and decipher it. Because the second I start thinking about the looks he's giving me and what they mean is the second I start thinking about *other* looks I've seen on his face and then *other* body parts that caused those looks. And I really, really don't want to be the creep who keeps picturing what Beau must look like naked.

He's Marty's friend and my roommate—those lines are clear, and the best thing I can do is not blur them.

Even if he does have a pretty fucking cock.

"I'll pay," Beau says before we reach the ticket booth. Since it's still early in the season, it's busy but not ridiculously so.

"Why? This was my idea, and I have money."

"I didn't say you didn't. But I have more money than I know what to do with, so let me spend some of it."

I wave him ahead of me. "You won't hear me arguing."

We pay for entry and a tour, then make our way through the ghost town toward the prison at the base of the hill. There are people running tours through the tunnels underground, shops selling souvenirs, tourists exploring the abandoned buildings, and brightly colored signs everywhere with reenactment schedules on them.

Everything is themed too. The costumes, the food and drinks being sold, the site maps, and the signage to stop people from getting lost.

It's old and intimidating. The front of the prison is surrounded by a stone wall, housing a courtyard and front entrance, then when we pass through there, we reach the main compound. It looks exactly like I remember it but less menacing than when I was a teenager. Barbed wire tops the heavy, metal fences, and the gates to enter are thick steel and at least fifteen feet tall.

Our tour guide is a grumpy, balding man with missing

teeth who was a resident of Kill Pen back in the day. He goes over the history of the place, why it was built, and the reason they closed and shows us through the high-security wings.

Beau and I walk side by side, arms bumping against each other. I'm listening to the guy up front, but we've clearly lost Beau. He's studying everything with interest, and when we pass through cells and into common areas, I can tell he's cataloguing every detail. He hasn't picked up that I'm watching him, and the more I watch him, the less interested in the prison I am. His expressions are constantly shifting, light eyebrows drawing together, eyes glazed behind his glasses, lips silently repeating certain facts, and it's almost as though I'm getting a glimpse at the conversations taking place inside his head. It's ... different. I can't look away.

"And this is the main guard booth for the high-security floor. The CCTV systems were replaced shortly before the closure, and as you can see on each of those screens, they had every cell covered. No such thing as privacy in them days."

We wait for the rest of the tour group to pass us and then take our turn inside. Beau immediately drops into the chair and starts inspecting ... everything. The screens, the desk setup ... I watch him and his constant energy.

The voice of our guide begins again outside the booth, and I watch through the glass as our group moves on.

"Ready to—"

I turn back to Beau and ...

He's on the floor, chest flat to the ground as he peers under a bank of drawers.

"What are you doing?" I ask.

"Looking."

"Uh-huh." I lean against the desk. "See what you're after?"

He searches for a bit, wriggles under the desk and out again a moment later, then straightens and sits back on his heels. "It's all wired in. No good." Beau looks so serious, I have to remind myself not to laugh. If I was a dick, I'd point out to him that this is the kind of thing that might weird some guys out. But I'm not "some guys," and it's kind of fun to see someone with a complete lack of awareness on how they're perceived.

Instead, I play along.

"The ... CCTV?"

"Yep. I need something else."

"Your fantasy world has electricity, then?"

"Of course." He tilts his head. "It's a semi-contemporary setting on earth, but instead of the world having a huge focus on technology, it's on magic."

"That sounds fun."

"It's the world I wish we lived in."

There's a longing in his voice that makes me curious. I hold out my hand to help him to his feet. Unlike the last time I tried it at Marty's, he takes it. "What's so great about this world of yours?"

"Are you saying you've never read one of my books? Should I be offended?" There's a mischievous spark in his eyes that I like.

My mouth drops. "Are you teasing me, Bo-Bo?"

"Wouldn't dream of it."

I pretend to narrow my eyes. "I'm onto you. And I'm also well aware you're deflecting." But if he doesn't want to tell me what's so great about his world, I won't push.

"I have no idea what you mean." He smiles angelically as we leave to catch up with the rest of the group.

And fine. Maybe he doesn't want to tell me right now. But hopefully he will, because I want him to feel comfortable confiding in me, exactly the way I've been doing with him.

Chapter Ten

BEAU

Payne is a genius.

I'd never made the link between prisons and my fortress before, but since he connected the dots in my head, I researched other prisons, ones that were supposed to be impossible to escape, and I finally found my answer.

My hero doesn't actually *have* to do anything.

Alcatraz was supposed to be impossible to break out of ... until it started to deteriorate.

I might not have salt water, but my world has magic, so why not use that?

With my fortress slowly crumbling, my block *should* be gone. This was the issue I was having, so technically I know the direction I'm taking things, but ... something still isn't right.

It makes me even more irritable than usual.

My work hours become so erratic to the point I barely see Payne. He's at work during the day and sleeping while I'm up and down all night.

The one small mercy about my scattered concentration is it means I haven't had to face him again since he saw way too much of me to be comfortable.

I'm not embarrassed over it, not *really*, because it was an accident and we're grown men and Payne was so cool about it, blah blah blah. But when I think about that night, I think about the way his pants hugged that thick, hard outline of his cock, and saliva pools in my mouth.

I've taken to jerking off strictly behind locked doors, stroking my cock into total submission so it doesn't have the opportunity to get excited when I catch a whiff of Payne's shampoo in the shower or hear him moving around in the apartment when I'm trying to force sleep.

Maybe asking him to move in wasn't the smartest idea, because this crush I'm supposed to be getting rid of has other ideas. It feels like it's growing and taking on a mind of its own. I'd planned to eventually tell him how I feel, but it's gotten to a point where I'm scared of these feelings, and I think it would be better off for all of us if I can pretend they don't exist.

Marty is having a few people over for drinks this weekend, so I know I'll have to face Payne again by then, and for some reason, the nerves combined with my frustrations over this book are sending me spiraling.

Yoga is my new best friend, and I've taken to unfolding and refolding the paper crane Payne left for me that night.

I've ordered a bunch of coloring books, which still haven't arrived, and pound out the sit-ups before bed until I'm at the point of passing out.

It's past midnight, and I'm typing furiously at one of these nothing flash fictions that are coming so easily to me when the air behind me shifts. My fingers pause and hover over the keys, while awareness slivers down my spine.

It's either Payne or someone who's broken in to kill me, and considering I'm not interesting enough to kill, that leaves me with only one option.

I'm not sure which choice is better.

Payne.

Axe murderer.

Payne.

Axe murderer.

Nope. Too close to call.

"Please tell me those words are on your book?" His deep voice, tinged with a hint of amusement, warms my insides.

I turn in my chair to face him. "Unfortunately not."

All of the lights are off, and what I can see of Payne is illuminated by my computer screen. He's in sleep shorts and ... nothing else. Damn. His sexy chest and all those tats are ... I physically shake my head and try to meet his eyes again, only to find them trailing over me.

Normally I'd assume it's because I have food down my front, but this is a fresh T-shirt, and when Payne's gaze flicks back to mine, even in the darkness I can tell there's something different about them.

"Wha—" I clear my throat. "What are you doing up?"

"Couldn't sleep, and I knew you'd be out here. I haven't seen much of you."

I shift self-consciously. "I told you I keep weird hours."

"I think it's less weird and more unconventional." His smile makes me shiver to my toes. "Like you."

"Is that your way of pointing out maybe this is one of those things I should work on?"

His amusement dies. "Did I say that?"

"To be fair, you haven't actually pointed out anything though."

"And why is that?"

I consider the question. "I guess I haven't been around you enough for you to do it."

"Yeah ... *that's* it."

"Well, you'll be at Marty's this weekend, won't you?"

"Yes."

"Then let's go together, and if we hang out there, you'll be able to keep an eye on me, and every time I do or say something weird, you can tell me. Oooh, maybe we could come up with a code?" I drag my hand back through my hair as I think. "Maybe a cough? No, maybe you can tap your nose? Wait, no, what if I'm not looking? Umm ... you could pinch me, or—"

"I'm sure we'll think of something." The amusement is back in his tone.

"Deal."

"Are you sure you'll even be there? I swear you haven't seen sunlight in a week."

"Most of the time when I'm up during the day, you're at work."

His eyes hold mine. "You're not avoiding me, are you, Bo-Bo?"

"What? No. Why would I?"

He narrows his eyes.

I try to look innocent.

We're locked in a standoff for what must be minutes of intense eye contact and me fighting the need to tremble. Goddamn I want him so bad.

Eventually, he grins. "No reason."

"Good. No reason."

"Are you feeling okay?"

"Fine. Why?"

"You seem ... more, I dunno, high-energy than usual."

"Oh. Yes. *That*. My concentration has gone completely out of the window, and I'm not able to focus on anything."

"Because of the book?"

"Yeah, I get unsettled when I don't feel like I'm making progress."

"What helps?" he asks, sounding like he's genuinely interested.

"Well, yoga, usually. And recently I've taken to refolding the crane you left for me, but the paper is wearing thin." I laugh softly. "Coloring is usually the best thing because I don't need to concentrate on it—I can fully zone out. But I didn't realize I'd finished the books here, and doing it on a tablet isn't the same."

"Coloring?"

My face heats. "I *know* people think it's for kids, but you can get some really detailed adult—"

"No, no." He holds up his hands. Big hands. Instead of placating me, all it does is make me focus on those thick fingers and how desperate I am to suck on them. "I know coloring is a thing. I was going to say, when I visit Bridget and Soph, they usually color in my tattoos. If you think it would help, you can use me. Best part is that I can wash it off, and you can do it again."

Use ... *him*. I will my voice to come back to me, but it's stuck somewhere in my throat behind a tongue that feels too big for my mouth.

"You ... tattoos ..." is the best I can get out, but somehow, Payne doesn't notice the weirdness.

He moves closer, then opens my top desk drawer. "You have markers in here?"

"N-next one down."

The top drawer closes with a click, and then Payne opens the second and pulls out my black marker case. He throws it up and catches it with the other hand. "Coming?"

Coming? I might. Is he trying to kill me?

"Now?"

He shrugs. "Sure, why not? I'm already awake, and you're clearly not getting to sleep until you've shut that brain of yours off."

"Wait. Stop. You want me to color in your tattoos?" Why is my brain struggling with this so much? "The ones on your skin? You want me to touch the tattoos on your skin?"

Payne laughs. "If you don't want—"

"I want."

"Okay, then. Where do you want me?"

And I must have serious issues because my brain takes that one line and turns it so dirty, my cock takes interest. "I … umm …"

"Normally it relaxes me enough to fall asleep, so come on. If we do it on my bed, I'll probably crash right after."

He needs to stop talking. Immediately. Because there's no way he can say "do it on my bed" and have me not immediately think about sex. I force a nod because I don't trust myself to speak, then stand numbly and follow him.

I've always noticed Payne's tattoos, but as a method of self-preservation, I've never let myself focus on the specifics. They're all line work, which makes them perfect for coloring. He's got flames over his abs and characters woven together up both arms, then across the back of his shoulders. The simple lines make it hard to tell what they are from a distance, but when he crawls onto his bed and lies facedown on top of the covers, I have time to drink in my fill.

Payne tosses the case to me, and I realize this is it. I'm about to touch Payne Walker … for as long as I want to.

Fuck, is there no oxygen in this room? Why am I light-headed?

And even though I'm ninety percent certain I'm about to blow my plan to resist him to pieces, I can't stop from moving toward the bed.

His back rises and falls with each breath, and he tilts his head from where it's rested on his crossed arms so he can see me.

"Will this work?" he asks.

"Yep. This should be ... this is fine. Good."

"Awesome. I'll drift off, so take as long as you need."

Payne's eyes fall closed, and I stand there for a moment, unable to believe this is happening. If anything, his plan has already worked, because I'm not having an issue with concentrating now. All I can focus on is Payne, half naked and asking me to touch him.

I don't want him to pick up on me hesitating, so I crawl up beside him and open the case. The tattoos across his back are underwater themed, and the more I look, the more I see. There are mermen, a sea castle, starfish and dolphins. It doesn't make any sense, but as I uncap the first marker and try to figure out where to start, my mind is already putting together a story from it all.

When I begin, I try to work out a way to do it without touching him, but that plan is derailed when I keep going out of the lines.

So I give in and place my hand on his back to steady myself. The warmth under my palm is hotter than I expected. His skin, smoother. I swallow thickly and try to focus on the images instead of burying my nose into his hair. I'm so close. It would take no effort to lean forward and press my lips to the soft skin where his neck meets his shoulder. To nuzzle into his jaw. To press my hard cock against his ridiculously round ass.

I lick my lips as my gaze pulls again and again to the two round globes covered by his sleep shorts.

Fuck, I need a cool shower.

I need to jerk off.

But both of those things would require me to stop touching Payne, and there's no way in hell that's happening.

I'm going to sit here and endure this sweet torture for as long as I'm able.

I don't manage to completely zone out, but the longer I work, the more relaxed I get, even as my cock stays persistently hard. Payne's deep, rhythmic breathing falls into sync with my own, and having him close, being surrounded by his scent, and allowing myself to fall into those things as the coloring clears my mind ... it's perfect.

He overrides my senses, and for the first time all week, I'm calm.

Chapter Eleven

PAYNE

I've had the best week's sleep of my life.

It was a stroke of genius, suggesting Beau use my tats, because now when I'm struggling to sleep like I have been since the divorce and I hear Beau up and pacing, all I have to do is poke my head out of my bedroom door, and he joins me in minutes.

It's not awkward anymore either. At first, I could tell he was doing everything he could to keep his distance, but last night there was maybe a minute or two of him trying to get comfortable before he gave in and draped himself across my back. We don't talk much when he's there, and I don't know if he feels the same way I do, but there's something about the dim light, his breaths fanning over my skin, and the warmth seeping through his T-shirt that feels … intimate? Is that the right word? Like it's something just for us.

I always fall asleep before he's done, and by the time I wake, the only evidence I have that it happened is the bright colors staining my skin.

It's also the only time I get to see him all week, so when I get home from another pointless day at the garage with arms full of groceries, I'm surprised to see him up and pacing.

"Question," he says before I get out so much as a *hey*. "If I was a twenty-five-hundred-pound dragon and I jumped from the top of this building, would I have enough time to unfurl my wings and take flight, or am I likely to create a massive crater? And if it's the crater, how large are we talking? Equivalent to dragon-size, or would the impact be larger?"

"Hold on, I've been playing errand boy all day and need to switch my brain back on." I place the bags on the kitchen counter and turn to him. "Purely from a guesstimation perspective, my vote would be on the crater. And when you look at those huge ones left by meteors, they're usually bigger than the rock. So even though they're falling a lot faster than a dragon would, I'd still imagine a dragon crater would be bigger than the animal itself ... right?"

He blinks, mouth open, then abruptly heads for his desk. "Good enough for me." He scribbles out something on the paper in front of him, his forehead is bunched up with concentration.

I stand there for a moment, watching, content to just take him. "You working tonight?"

"I was going to try, but I already wrote a bunch."

"On your book?"

"Yeah, but it doesn't feel right."

"Why not?"

He laughs, and I recognize the sort of glazed look he gets about him when he's in another world. "I don't know, that's the problem. Our visit to the prison fixed the fortress issue I was having, but it's like Jaciel doesn't even want to save Klein."

"And you can't ... make him?"

"People judge me when I say this, but when you get to know a character really well, they take on their own life in your head, so when you try to force them to do something they don't want to, it doesn't work out great."

"Well, I don't understand it, but I'm not going to judge." I pull out a packet of microwave popcorn. "Want to watch a movie instead?"

He shifts his weight, and I think he's about to say no when his expression shifts. "Yeah, sure."

"You grab the drinks, and I'll change and cook this."

I duck in for a quick shower, then pull on some casual clothes and head back out. Beau is on a stool in his kitchen, grabbing a bottle of scotch from the top shelf, and when I round the corner, I come face to, ah, crotch with his *gray sweatpants*.

And I'm pretty fucking sure he's freeballing.

I clear my throat and step away, scooping the popcorn from the counter before throwing it in the microwave. Given the thin sleep shorts I'm wearing, the last thing I want is to start chubbing up, so I will myself to focus on nothing but the smell of melting butter.

"This okay?" Beau asks, holding up the bottle as he climbs down. "We're out of beer."

"Yeah, sure. I think I need to kill a few more brain cells after the boring week at work."

"That bad, huh?"

"Eh. Ford is a great boss, and he's offered to put me through some courses if I'm interested, but cars aren't for me. I want to get back to sports and working with kids."

"I'm sorry."

"Oh well, it'll happen. I'm trying to be patient."

The microwave beeps obnoxiously, so I check it's ready, dump the popcorn in a bowl, and head for the living area, Beau just behind me. We settle for an action movie where the girl is kidnapped early on and the hero spends the movie trying to find her.

The movie doesn't hold much of my interest though.

Not when every time Beau shifts, my attention is drawn back to his spread thighs. I hold in a groan at the inappropriate direction my thoughts are taking. It's been too long since I got laid, which explains why, ever since I copped an eyeful of Beau's cock, it's been all I can think about.

Well done, Payne. You're creeping on your little brother's friend.

Only Beau isn't the same guy he was when we were growing up. Sometime over the years, he got ... hot. His features are finer than mine, and his hands are soft, but the light hair on his arms and chest has thickened, his shoulders have widened, and his body is perfectly solid. He's completely different from Kyle, who hit the gym every day, and I think that's what I like about him.

I'm not clueless though.

I know I can't go there.

Not only would Marty be weirded out by me screwing his friend, but I don't want to mess up our current arrangement.

And then Beau shifts again, crossing his legs at the ankles and jittering his legs up and down like he can't help himself.

The problem with that is it makes the bulge under his pants move too, and I'm watching, shamelessly, as it comes to a rest with his soft sweats molding around it.

Jesus fucking Christ, do I see head?

Motherfucker, I need this movie to be over, like, now.

It's my turn to shift nervously as I lift my leg to try and hide the situation that's evolving down south.

"See? He has motivation," Beau says. "I'm not feeling that in this book. My guy should be hell-bent on getting his man back—"

"Your romance is two dudes?"

"Of course."

I arch my head back to where his books are lined up neatly on a shelf above his desk. "I want to read one."

"Go right ahead."

I make a mental note to grab one of them before I head to bed later. "Are there sex scenes?"

"Yes." His cheeks redden. "And the rules are if you read one of my books, we both pretend like you aren't. Don't tell me if you like it or hate it—we just act like it's not happening."

"Deal." But the sex scenes have me interested. "Are they filthy scenes?"

He gets redder.

"They *are*!"

"Well, no, they're—"

"How filthy are we talking?" I cross my arms and lean back into the couch.

"Not ... filthy. It's part of their relationship. A way for them to show they care."

"HJs? BJs? Anal?" I need to shut up, but thinking of *Beau* writing those things, of him *doing* them? I can't stop my gaze from dipping down to his crotch again.

And when I glance back up, I've totally been busted.

Our eyes lock, and the air between us seems to crackle. Awareness of his body, inches away, prickles my skin. I want to move closer. I want to inspect that bulge myself. My own cock is thickening with the need to touch him.

There's this little line between Beau's eyebrows as he watches me, completely silent. His mouth opens, and a long, shaky inhale rattles the still air.

I'm about to make a joke of the whole situation, anything to ease the tension—

When Beau surges forward. His mouth on mine before I can react.

Through parted lips and the swipe of his tongue, I taste scotch and popcorn, mixed with raw need. I have barely enough brain cells still firing to grab his shoulders and push him back. "What are you doing?" I gasp. My stare doesn't leave his mouth.

When I lick my lips, I can still taste him. Even his shoulders feel good in my grip, and when Beau inhales loudly again, I can't hold back. He moves, and I meet him halfway.

He pushes me against the backrest and straddles my thighs. His mouth is warm and insistent, and when he licks my bottom lip, I open my mouth to let him inside. His tongue slides against mine, and I let out the groan I've been holding in all night, because *damn* I swear kissing never felt this good.

Hot breath, needy moans, strong body pressed against mine.

I don't have time to stop and consider what I'm doing, or maybe it's just that I don't want to think about it. Beau is here, and willing, and so sexy, I'm not going to say no. Whatever the fallout of our decision, we'll deal with it tomorrow, hopefully the way we always do. With him being awkward and me cracking jokes.

The real problem will be facing Marty at his thing and not spilling to him that Beau and I crossed all sorts of lines.

My mouth breaks from his to taste his jaw. "You sure this is okay?"

"Please. Oh fuck, don't stop."

That's what I want to hear. I lick his jawline and nip at the place where it meets his neck. "Shit, I need this," I murmur.

"Me too."

"Can I touch you?"

Beau whimpers before pushing his sweatpants down, and suddenly his hard, swollen cock is between us.

Fuck. I spit into my palm and wrap my hand around him.

Beau shudders, one hand tangling in my hair as he brings his forehead to mine. Even through his glasses, his eyes are so blue close up. "Make me come."

Gladly. I ignore my aching cock as I close my free hand over his nape and hold him to me while I jerk him off. I love the feel of him in my hand. His skin is hot, as overheated as I am, and silky smooth. Every pass over the tip brings out more precum for me to smear over him, filling the air between us with the smell of sex. It goes to my head, makes me dizzy. It's been so long since I've felt this desperate sort of urgency for another person that I want to draw it out and make it last as long as possible, but at the same time, there's no pacing this need inside me.

"You're right," he says. "You are good with your hands."

I squeeze tighter, stroke faster, and Beau's breathing loses rhythm. I need him to touch me—my body is begging for it—but I ignore the urges as I focus on bringing him as close to the edge as I can.

I want to see that usual frenetic energy burst from him, leaving him boneless and still.

"Kiss me," he begs.

I tilt my face up and catch his mouth with mine. Soft lips and needy gasps are all that's between us. I still can't get it out of my head that it's Beau I'm doing this with. Beau, who I've known forever. Beau, who I caught jerking off and haven't been able to think of anything else since.

Marty will fucking kill me.

But for tonight, I don't care.

We're both single. We both need this. And we're both taking advantage of every second.

Beau thrusts into my fist, faster and faster, breathing ragged. He breaks from my mouth on a string of curses, and as his hips fall out of rhythm, he stiffens beneath my hold.

"*Payne* ..."

His cock throbs as he comes, and I keep stroking him, working him through every drop. I end up with his cum all over me, but Beau doesn't stop for a breather. He yanks my filthy shirt up over my head and tosses it to the floor, then leans down to nip my shoulder. He sucks a mark against my skin, then presses his lips to my ear.

"I want to taste you. Please."

I growl and lift my hips to shove my sleep shorts down my thighs. Beau scrambles off my lap to kneel in front of me and tugs at my shorts until they're around my calves. Then he leans forward and presses his face to my abs. "These are fucking divine. Damn, I wish I came on them instead."

Yesss. That would have been hot. Maybe if we play our cards right, we might get to make another attempt at that.

But right now, it's my cock that needs attention. "Beau." His name comes out needier than I mean it to. "Suck on me."

The second his hot, wet mouth wraps around my cock, it's heaven. I moan, long and loud and completely unrestrained. There's nothing hotter than seeing that glazed look take over his face when he works his mouth lower and tighter over my shaft. He doesn't dive in and try to get it over with; he takes his time. Licking and tasting, he pulls back to suck on the tip, and his eyes flutter closed before he takes a deep breath, then slowly sucks me down, all the way into his throat.

I have to hold back from thrusting, he's so tight. My cock is weeping, reveling in the attention, and there are zaps of pleasure racing from the base of my spine to my balls. I let Beau set the pace, let him take total control, and the way he's humming and working me over is hot as fuck.

"Shit, you look like you love that."

"You have no idea." His voice comes out raspy, attention still locked on my dick. His lips are swollen, cheeks flushed, being a complete fucking cocktease every time that pink tongue darts out and licks along my slit.

"I'm close," I breathe.

Beau dives on me. He bobs up and down with purpose, sucking hard, saliva running down to my balls. I can't stop myself from reaching out and resting my hand on his head, coaxing him to a faster rhythm as I forcibly hold back from thrusting. Holy shit can Beau give good head.

My balls are drawing up tight even as I try to hold off, but I'm spiraling out of control. It feels amazing, tight, hot, slick ... He cups my balls, tightens his hold, and *fuuuck* ...

"I'm ... I'm gonna ..."

I finally give in and start to thrust, and the sound Beau makes when he gags on my cock is so fucking obscene, it's all over. My orgasm smacks me in the face so hard my head drops back against the couch as I hold Beau in place, making sure he stays put until he's caught every drop.

I wait until my cock stops throbbing, then loosen my hold to stroke my thumb along his cheek. "That was incredible."

He reaches up to wipe his chin, then rests his head on my thigh. "Ah, so, there's something I should probably tell you ..."

I frown but stroke his cheek again and wait for him to go on.

"I have a teeny, tiny crush on you."

Chapter Twelve

BEAU

The moment I take in the horrified look on Payne's face, I know I've fucked up.

So much for saving my confession for the right time, when he was over his divorce and I had the smallest chance of him returning my feelings. Lust drunk and full of his cum was not on my list of options, but when I'd looked up at him from my knees, he'd taken my breath away.

This is ... definitely not the reaction I was hoping for.

"You ... you ..." He shakes his head. "You're not a virgin, are you?"

And even though he usually jokes to lighten the mood, I know this isn't one of those times. I laugh anyway. "No."

"Then ... what"—he yanks his shorts back up—"what do you mean?"

Great, now he's going to make me spell it out for him.

That sounds like a really fun time for me. I tuck myself back away and drop onto the couch beside him. My insides are in knots, but I'm going to pretend like this is no big deal, because I don't want to scare Payne back out of my life.

"A crush. It's nothing, seriously. Please don't worry about it. I've had it for years, and it's never caused any issues.
"

"Years?" If possible, his eyes get wider. "How many?"

"Umm ..." I play with the bottom of my T-shirt. "Since high school ..."

"Ah, fuck." Payne leans forward and props his elbows on his knees before burying his face in his hands.

"Look, I swear you don't need to worry. I know it's not returned, and I'm okay with that, but I was hoping we could do something like that again, and I figured you should know that first." Even if I totally undersold how much I feel for him.

"Beau ..." He turns to me with pity in his eyes, and I hold up my hand.

"No. Nope. No sympathy here. I'm okay with you not feeling the same way, and I mean, can you blame me? You were part of my whole sexual awakening. You're hot and kind, you always make time for people and make sure they're comfortable when they're really, really not ..."

I'm trying to reassure him, but the more I talk, the more wary his eyes become.

"I'm so sorry," he says. "I didn't know. If I did, I never would have—"

I snort. "I don't need your pity. I knew about my feelings, and I was more than happy for that to happen, knowing it might be the one and only time. I like being attracted to you. It's better than me crushing on someone who's an asshole to me."

"I feel like an asshole."

"You didn't know. I didn't tell you."

"You should have."

"Why? So you could make my choices for me?"

He lets out a heavy breath. "You've been good to me. I don't want to hurt you, Beau, but I'm going through a divorce. This was—"

"If you say a mistake, you *will* hurt me."

He gives me a sad smile. "No mistake—I knew what I was doing. I'm attracted to you, and I was interested in it happening again, but not now. Emotionally, I have nothing to offer you."

"Did I say I wanted anything emotional from you? All I said was we should hook up again."

"Can you honestly tell me if we keep hooking up that it won't make things weird for you?"

Okay, honestly, I can't tell him that. Things are already weird now that I know how perfect his cock is and have heard the sexy noises he makes during sex. "Yeah, it probably will."

He exhales loudly. "Do you need me to move out?"

"What? No." I turn to face him straight on so he knows I'm serious. "We'll chalk tonight up to some hot fun that we both needed and move on. We were friends before, yeah? So there's no reason getting each other off should have to change anything." I'm praying he agrees with me. My feelings for him aren't incapacitating. They're just ... a lot. So much that I don't want him to move out. Even if it's hard, even if it means jerking off nonstop, I want him to stay.

"It doesn't?"

"Nope."

He eyes me. "Can I say something that might be shitty of me?"

"Always."

He catches his bottom lip before releasing it. "It feels good. To know someone thinks of me that way after everything my fucker ex did, which is shitty because I really like you, and I don't want you to get hurt."

"I promise I won't get hurt."

"You can't promise that."

"It's fine." I wave my hand, faking a confidence I so don't feel. "Let me stroke your ego after how good you stroked me."

He laughs. "Shit, don't say that."

"Why? You weren't lying when you said you were good with your hands. That was maybe the best hand job I've ever had."

He shoves me. "*Beau.*"

"And I sucked your dick good, didn't I?"

"Fucking hell ..." He grins as I nudge him. "You're playful after you've blown your load."

"You think this is different? You should see me after I've taken a pounding."

We lock eyes, and Payne doesn't try to hide the interest

in his. He sighs and looks away, so I take that as my sign to get out of here. Now. Before my orgasm wears off and I begin overthinking everything.

Before I leave, I lean in, lips to his ear, and drop my voice. "It'll only be weird if you let it." Then I kiss his cheek and flee to my room.

To my surprise, Payne acts like last night is totally forgotten, and without the orgasm high to make everything fine, I'm grateful.

Because I'm low-key freaking out.

I didn't mean to blurt feelings all over him, and I'm grateful I didn't go so far as to tell him that I'm actually totally smitten with him and I'm scared it will never go away.

Because *that* would have been a fast way to lose myself a roommate.

We head over to Marty's Saturday drinks together, and Payne seems like his usual happy self. Almost like last night didn't happen.

And if I hadn't felt the mortification bone-deep this morning, I might have thought it was a dream.

But nope.

Payne's cum-covered T-shirt was still on the living room floor when I got up.

We're half an hour late to arrive, so most people are there

before us. It's a combination of Marty and Lizzy's work friends and a handful of people from school. They're people I've met a few times before, but other than one or two guys from our graduating class, I'm not friendly with most of them.

"About time," Marty says, walking over and holding out a beer to me. "I almost thought you weren't going to show."

"Late night," I say without thinking, and the second the words are out, Payne's eyes fly to mine. Well, I guess if I was unsure about it happening, that's my confirmation. "Had lots of work to do."

The tension leaves Payne's body, and thankfully, the moment goes right over Marty's head.

"Come on, I have someone I want you to meet." He winks, and *ooh no*.

I suddenly understood why he was so intense about me being here. "I'm not in a mood to meet people," I say, the sudden onset of panic hitting me the way it always does when I'm put on the spot.

"Don't play. Lee's a great guy and mentioned he thought you were cute last time you were here."

"Marty, I ..."

"You keep saying you want to meet someone, don't you? No pressure, but he's a good guy. At least come and say hi."

In Marty's defense, the guys he sets me up with usually are nice. It's me that's the problem. He also couldn't have timed this any worse. Trying to set me up on a date in front of the guy I confessed feelings for last night.

Wow. I should have stayed in bed this morning.

I expect Payne to break away from us as we cross the backyard, but he sticks close to my side. If it wasn't Payne, I'd assume he was uncomfortable around people he doesn't know, but Payne isn't uncomfortable anywhere.

Marty comes to a stop by a group of guys sitting around the paved fire pit area. I recognize most of them as Marty's work friends, and they say hi as Marty introduces Payne.

"And Lee, Beau. Beau, Lee."

"Hi." A guy a little younger than me stands and holds out his hand. He's ... gorgeous. Brown curls and a big smile. Confidence rolls off him, but where Payne's is a lazy, relaxed confidence, this guy makes it look intentional.

I shake his hand. "Nice to meet you."

He holds on for a second after I relax my grip before releasing me. "Marty's, uh, told me a lot about you. Friends from high school, right?"

"Middle school."

"And what about me?" Payne cuts in. He offers his hand to Lee. "Surely Marty's told you about his cool older brother."

They shake hands, and Lee gives him a friendly once-over. "From Boston, right? Go Bruins!"

Payne hums. "I'm more of a New York man myself."

"Damn. I've caught a few live games, and that Ezra Palaszczuk is as hot in real life as he is on TV."

"Eh. He reminds me of my ex-husband."

I choke back a laugh. I guess Palaszczuk *is* known for sleeping around.

Lee's attention drifts back to me. "Do you follow hockey?"

"How much trouble will I be in if I say not really?"

The look Lee gives me is straight-up flirtation, and even if Marty hadn't given me the heads-up, I would have picked that he was interested from a mile away. "Somehow I think I can forgive you."

"So what do you think Boston's chances are for the Stanley Cup next year?" Payne asks loudly, and Lee reluctantly returns his attention to him.

"As good as any other."

"My money's on Vegas. That Tripp Mitchell, am I right?" He pumps his eyebrows suggestively, and all I can do is stare. What is he doing? Is Payne seriously oblivious to what's happening here? I would have thought he'd be ready to marry me off to the first guy who showed interest after last night.

"Hey, Payne," Marty says, taking his brother's elbow. "I think Lizzy needs us inside."

Payne shrugs him off. "I didn't hear anything."

"Nope. She definitely called us. Come on, we can't leave her waiting." Marty physically yanks Payne, and only then does he move.

Lee rubs his arm. "Is he an ex-boyfriend?"

"Nope."

"Does he see you like a brother, then?"

After last night, that would be creepy. "Definitely not. I'm clueless what that was." Other than totally out of character.

"I'd hoped to catch you tonight, actually. I mentioned to Marty that you're my type, and he said you're not seeing anyone, so if you were free, did you want to go on a date?"

Ah. We're jumping straight to it.

Do I want to go on a date with him?

No.

Should I want that?

Definitely.

Lee's attractive. Not in the rough way that Payne is, but he's conventionally attractive. He also seems to be nice, just like Marty said he was.

Then why do I have absolutely no desire whatsoever to go on a date with him?

The problem is, I'm not good at letting people down.

And faced with Lee's kind eyes and hopeful expression, I say the only thing I can. "Sure. Let me give you my number."

DMC Group Chat

Payne: *How do you let someone down easy?*

   Art: *Not my area of expertise.*

   Griffin: *Or mine.*

   Orson: *I've never done it either, but I'd assume just being honest about why it won't work. Who do you need to let down?*

   Payne: *Nobody.*

   Art: *Okay, we'll pretend to believe you.*

   Griffin: *Why do you need to let this "nobody" down?*

   Payne: *Because he's ... I'm not in a relationship place right now.*

   Orson: *So tell him that.*

   Payne: *Hmm ... maybe.*

Chapter Thirteen

PAYNE

Drinks with Marty used to be fun.

Visiting Kilborough during my time off, catching up with familiar faces, seeing the girls, having a few beers until I'm happy and buzzing, ready for Kyle to drive us back to a hotel room ... where I'd end up passing out.

I scowl as I think of what he probably got up to on those nights while I was blissfully sleeping off my alcohol coma.

All of our memories together are tainted.

It's probably a good thing. It makes it a lot easier to ignore that niggling in the back of my mind that I should go back so I don't spend the rest of my life alone.

Forty isn't old. But it does feel way past the premium dating age, and going through that again only to find someone who I don't think I could ever trust properly seems exhausting.

I agree with Beau. Dating sucks.

And yet ... I narrow my eyes and watch him with Lee. They're sitting around the fire pit where we left them and flirting up a storm. Lee looks ready to eat Beau alive.

Should I be offended that Beau can go from having a crush on me one day to being completely consumed by this other dude a day later?

Though it does confirm my suspicions that hooking up made him loose-lipped and he said something that felt right in the moment but was grossly exaggerated by the mind-blowing orgasm.

It should be a relief.

It shouldn't annoy me as much as it does.

Beau's back to his usual awkward self, and it was easy to slip into what we were and not acknowledge what happened last night. I wasn't sure if it was the right move, but he doesn't exactly look cut up about it.

I take another long drink of my beer, still watching them.

Am I offended? I think so. He claimed I gave him the best hand job of his life, and here he is ready to wrap those lips around another guy's dick, and I ... don't like it.

I'm also well aware I have no ground to stand on here since I wasn't lying when I said I had nothing to offer Beau.

I'm not so sure Lee does either.

What I want to do is go over there and interrupt them again.

What I *should* be doing is asking Marty if I can move back in here.

I don't want to though. I like living with Beau. I like my room. I like his eccentricities. I like when I'm falling asleep and can feel his breath on my back, the steady lines of the marker running across my skin.

That's something that's going to have to stop though. I think. I can't argue it isn't good for the both of us, but if he does have this crush that he claims he does, that's the sort of thing that can blur lines.

Although ...

I hate to admit this, but if Beau was dating someone, it wouldn't be an issue.

We could go back to exactly how we were.

It means no possibility of a repeat of last night, but I think that's off the table anyway. Unfortunately.

Because fuck me, he has one talented mouth. And that glimpse of his playful, happy self right after is something I'd like to see again.

But that Beau isn't for me.

"You're quiet today."

I turn to find Lizzy assessing me. "Geez. 'Payne you're a loudmouth,' 'Payne you're too quiet.' Between you and your husband, I'm getting mixed signals."

"When did he call you a loudmouth? Normally I'd agree, which is why seeing you here by yourself is weird."

"Apparently I was interrupting his matchmaking." I wave my hand toward where Beau and Lee are.

Lizzy follows my gaze, looking confused for a moment before it clicks. "Ah, he introduced them, did he?"

"Looks like it."

"About time. I swear the last two dinners Lee has been over for, it's all they've talked about. I almost banned Beau's name from the dinner table."

"You guys have Lee over?"

"Sure." She shrugs. "We're an old married couple, but we do have friends, you know."

I pretend to look around the party. "Shit, is that who these people are?"

"You're funny."

"Seriously though, why Lee? He's ... showy."

She tilts her head. "You think? I've always thought he was nice."

"Nice. Wow. Ringing endorsement."

"Better than what I tell people about you."

"Oh, yeah?" I play along. "I would have thought world's greatest brother-in-law ever was a good thing."

"Sure. That. But also, total pain in the ass."

That makes me laugh because I couldn't picture Lizzy saying that about anyone. "That decides it, no more chocolate deliveries for you."

"Oh no, I take it back."

"Where are my wild nieces today?" I ask.

"With Mom. They get a sleepover, and Marty and I get to pretend we're still fun adults."

"At least you know you're preten—*oomph*!"

She backhands my gut. "That's enough from you."

I know Lizzy and Marty need the night away from the girls, but I wish they were here. They're always good at being a distraction.

"So, are you going to tell me what your problem with Lee is?"

"He's not our people."

"Uh-huh. And what *is* our people?"

Fucked if I can describe it. "Laid-back. Cool. He's trying too hard."

"Of course he is. He's talking to the guy he has the hots for. Trust me, normally he's way more relaxed."

And would you look at that? Her words do the opposite of what she'd hoped they would. I dislike him even more now. I don't want to hear that he's nice and cool, even though the smarter part of me knows it's a good thing.

She sighs happily. "It might work out this time, but I'm trying not to get my hopes up. Selfishly I want more couple friends, but also, Beau deserves to be happy. Every time Marty sets him up with someone, he never puts in the effort."

"Maybe he's uncomfortable with dating."

"Or maybe he's not giving any guy a chance."

From what he said, they're the idiots who haven't given *him* a chance. "Why do you think that? If he actually wants to find someone, wouldn't he be trying?"

"Yes, but I think the problem is he's hung up on someone unavailable."

I swear under my breath. "Tell me you don't mean me."

Her surprised stare meets mine. "You *know*?"

And I guess that confirms that, then. "He told me."

"That's surprising. What did you say?"

"What was I supposed to say?" I ask defensively. "I'm

140

going through a divorce. I'm not gold-standard relationship material."

"You do know those things don't go hand in hand, right? You can be divorced—because an asshole cheated on you—but still be an awesome person to date. Just because one guy didn't see your worth, doesn't mean another won't."

"Well, after-school special aside, I'm not anywhere close to dating, worth it or not." Which is why I'm going to have to encourage Beau where Lee is concerned. If he is as interested as Lizzy and Marty are saying, then it's a good match. Even if I don't think he's good *enough*.

"You're not freaking out about it?"

"The feelings thing?"

"Yeah."

"I did at first." Not that I'm going to tell her why. "My main concern is I don't want to lead him on or have things get out of hand. He said it's a crush, so I guess dating someone else will fix it." Even if he did say something about a sexual awakening, which was flattering as hell.

She grasps my arm. "You can play matchmaker with us. You can help Beau get ready for his date and tell him all the things he can talk about."

That suggestion sits too uncomfortably close to his one about *improving* that it's hard to hold back my annoyance. "He doesn't need anyone to tell him what to say. He'll be fine on his own."

"Yes, but the Beau we know and the one who ends up on

those dates are two totally different guys, apparently. He has an issue with nerves."

"And? If the guys he's dating can't deal with that, they shouldn't be dating him at all."

"It's not like that. But, well, you know how conversations go when it's one-sided. It makes it hard to get to know him. I've never seen that side of him, so it's weird to consider, but when I see him with other men"—she gestures to where Beau and Lee are sitting—"it's like he clams up."

Now she's pointed that out, I realize she's onto something. Beau smiles and nods a lot and offers the occasional sentence, but it's definitely less of a conversation and more Lee monologuing. Beau's hands never stop moving, all that excess energy coming out through his fidgeting.

It shouldn't make me happy.

It does though.

As the day moves on and the beers go down smoother, it becomes easier to relax. Lee takes up a lot of Beau's time. At one point, I see Beau get up to take a piss, so I give it a minute before I follow him inside. I've barely said hello, though, when Lee pops up again.

It's not until late, when my brain is swimming in alcohol and I order a car to pick us up, that I give in and make my way over to them.

I throw an arm around Beau's shoulders, ignoring the look Lee gives me. "Car will be here in five to pick us up."

"Perfect." His cheeks are red, probably from drinking all day.

"It's okay," Lee says. "I can ride home with him."

"That's pointless when we live together."

It's like I can hear the thoughts racing through Lee's mind. The intent. The need for more Beau. And maybe it's stupid or petty of me, but I don't want Beau so much as kissing this guy twenty-four hours after we've hooked up.

"The night is still young. You don't want to go yet, do you, Beau?" Lee asks.

"Uh, well, I'm a bit tired ..."

"We were up late last night," I point out, loving the sound of those words. When Beau stiffens though, I reluctantly add, "Watching a movie. Besides, Beau isn't the type to hook up on a first date, so you're out of luck there, friend."

I love the way Lee frowns. He doesn't look so pretty now.

"That's not what I meant."

"Ready to go, Beau?" I ask.

"Yes. Please."

"I'll text you," Lee adds.

Of course he fucking will.

We leave without so much as a goodbye, and it's not until we climb into the back of an Uber that Beau looks at me.

"What was that?"

"What do you mean?" The question is stupid though, because we both know what he means. "Fine. I know you said you hate the small-talk part of dating, so I was trying to save you. You're welcome."

He hums. "I *was* trying to think of how to get away."

"It's easy. You say, 'I'm leaving now, bye,' and then you leave."

Beau laughs. "It's not that easy *for me*. This is what I mean. I struggle with things like that. I don't like letting people down."

"You're not going to go on a date with him just because you can't say no, are you?" Because while I might have been a dick by stepping in when I shouldn't have, the last thing I want is Beau feeling uncomfortable.

"I *should* go on a date with him."

"Right."

"Because he seems nice."

I snort. "That fucking word again. *Nice*. What an endorsement."

"He's hot too."

Okay, that one I don't like, and I shouldn't say the thought that pops into my head, but I do. "Hotter than me?"

Thankfully, Beau laughs. "Different than you. But since you're mentioning it, that's exactly why I should give him a chance. Do I want to go? No. But if I don't give anyone a chance, I'm going to end up pining after you alone, and I don't think either of us would like that."

That's the reality though, isn't it? And that's exactly why I need to keep my nose out. It's not up to me to decide who is good enough for Beau. "You're right. I shouldn't have stepped in."

"I'm glad you did."

"I know you are. But I shouldn't have done it anyway."

His phone lights up, and he tilts the screen to show me Lee's name.

"Guy works fast." I grunt.

"Yeah. He wants to catch up next weekend. I should do it, right?"

"It's up to you, Bo-Bo."

He chews on his bottom lip for a moment before nodding. "Yeah, I should."

He's right. I don't like it.

"But you know what this means, don't you?" he asks.

"Oh, yeah? What's that?"

"You *really* need to get onto pointing out the dumb things I do. Fast. Because if this works out, crush gone."

Crush gone. "And as flattering as it is, I think that's for the best."

BEAU

It's for the best.

I keep repeating Payne's words to myself the whole day while he's at work.

He didn't say it to be a dick, and thankfully he isn't treating me any differently than usual, but he also hasn't walked in and told me he wants to bone me, so I think it's time to acknowledge that is solidly off the table.

Now I need to convince *all* of me of that.

Because my dick disagrees in a big way and is determined to harden the fuck up every time Payne walks into a room. Because lucky me, suddenly my body is on normal people time, which means seeing him in the morning wearing those tight shorts and the polo for Ford's Garage, and then again all afternoon while we eat dinner together and settle in front of the TV for the night.

I thought for sure Payne would come up with every excuse under the sun to avoid me, but so far, he's doing the opposite. Like he *enjoys* my company, but that can't be right.

He's also taken my book like he said he would. That bare space on my shelf is haunting me, and I want to ask him what he thinks, but I also really, really don't.

It's one thing to have a bad review by some random person on the internet; it's another to have the guy you're pining for think your life's work is trash.

I'm still making progress on the next book, but it's frustratingly slow. I know I can be done by the deadline if my muse hits, but struggling with a few hundred words a day is painful.

So instead of working on what I should be working on, I open another file and smash out a few thousand words on betrayal and heartbreak without a second thought. It's a waste of a few hours though, so I reluctantly close the window I'm working in and turn back to my book.

Maybe if I skip this part and write a scene I'm excited to write, that might help?

A sword fight, maybe?

My hero, Jaciel, is one of the best, and I include at least one sword fight with Tombra in each book. They're usually my favorite scenes to write because the antagonism brings it alive. They might be fighting with the intent to kill the other person, but the way Tombra plays with Jaciel is a fun dynamic.

They're also scenes that take forever to write because logistically it's a balance between making sure it works and writing it in a way where it's not bogged down with details but shows just enough.

I plan it out, research the steps, then jot out on paper the beats I want to hit. Now, to make sure they'll work.

I'm nothing if not thorough. When I have a scene where there are a lot of steps, I like to walk through them. I grab the umbrella I have next to my desk specifically for this purpose—buying an actual sword seemed excessive—and walk through it.

Two steps forward, one back. Block. Swing. Lunge to the left. I'm caught up, seeing it play out in my head, when the front door opens and Payne walks in to find me kneeling on one knee, umbrella held above my head like goddamn Simba.

Oh, fuck my life.

Payne's lips twitch as I shoot to my feet. "Am I interrupting?"

"*No.*"

He doesn't look convinced and my heart sinks as I realize that first, I'm going to have to explain this to him, and second, I *really* need to pay better attention to the time. "Fine. I have a sword fight coming up, and I was working through it. There's just this one part ..." I glance back at the paper and raise my umbrella, trying to visualize how Jaciel will block *and* slice consecutively.

Then I realize the umbrella is in the air again, and Payne is still watching.

I drop my arms. "Nothing to see here."

"I dunno. Seems fun to me."

I sag. "*Funny*, you mean. Shit. This is one of those things, isn't it? That normal people don't do?"

Payne gets this crease between his eyebrows as his stare runs over me. I can tell he's thinking. Maybe trying to come up with a way to tell me I'll never be dating material.

"I have no idea what you mean." He spares me a grin before heading for the hall.

I assume he's giving me privacy to finish this, but I'm not so sure I want him walking about again and finding me in who knows what position. It's lucky I hesitate too because he's back a moment later.

Carrying a broom handle.

He points it at me. "You're on, Bo-Bo."

"Wait. What?"

"Let's work through your scene."

"You're going to help me?"

"What are roommates for?"

Yep. Just like that, I'm in love.

My face is hot, but I'm smiling wide as I teach him the steps I've choreographed. The more we practice, the better we get, and it highlights the parts that work and the parts that don't.

"What if instead of this"—Payne swings upward—"it's more like—" He spins and slices upward.

It's clear he's an athletic guy because he makes even sword fighting with a broom handle look hot as hell.

"Yep, that works," I say, jotting it down and trying to pretend like I wasn't checking out the way his arms muscles flexed with the movements. "I think we need more terrain though. For some of the jumps."

"I got you." Payne tilts the couch back and moves the coffee table toward where I'm supposed to jump onto a bench. That should work.

"From the top?" he asks.

"This is so much easier with a second person."

"Well, sword fighting usually requires *two* people."

"Both types, in fact."

It takes him a moment to get it, but when he does, his eyes fly to mine. Instead of awkwardness, I detect interest there. "I can't say I've ever tried *that* kind of sword fighting."

"You're missing out."

"You have?" He sounds a second away from laughing.

I point at my face. "Weird, remember? Let's just say I tried it once and never again."

"Why?"

"The guy I was with said it ruined the mood." I shrug because it's no big deal, even if I was embarrassed at the time.

"Well, he was a moron. I bet you're an awesome sword fighter, euphemism or otherwise. You've written enough of them."

And I'm not sure what catches me off guard most—the sex talk or him mentioning my book. "Ah. You've already, umm, read some?"

"No idea what you mean." He winks. "I'm not reading anything. I definitely haven't smashed through the first half of this awesome book when normally I can't make it through a few pages."

I simultaneously love every word out of his mouth and wish he'd stop talking immediately because I struggle with compliments. "Okay. Good. Definitely not reading."

"Nope." He raises his makeshift sword. "Think we can make it through the whole thing this time?"

"Let's try."

We both lift our swords, and then, I lunge. He blocks me, and I spin immediately, trying to get in a hit to the side, but Payne knocks me off-balance before I make contact. He kicks at my leg, I hit his side, and then we bring our swords together. Somehow, we make it through the steps without screwing up, and I'm about to drop my umbrella when Payne goes off book.

He whacks my ribs, my thigh, before I block him.

"What are you—"

"Think you can beat me?"

"You're on."

It's nothing like our practice. Where that was rehearsed and careful, this is a complete mess. Payne gets in a hit to my jaw before I stab the umbrella at his abs, then his back. He grunts in pain, hand flying at my face as I try to wrestle the broom handle off him. Our makeshift weapons are flailing before we drop them, forgotten, and then it becomes a competition of who can get the other to the ground first.

"Damn." He grunts. "You're a lot stronger than you look."

"Yep." I get him into a headlock, shoving him toward the ground, but before he hits, Payne wraps an arm around my waist, heaves me over his shoulder, then staggers us toward the couch. He collapses into it, sends the couch flying back upright, and in my surprise—

"*Fuck*." Payne releases me as he folds in half, clutching at his balls.

"Holy shit, I'm so sorry."

"Yep." His voice is strained. "I think you win."

I can't help it—I laugh, and when the pain settles, he joins in. We're both breathing hard, him sprawled over the couch, me, sitting on the floor, and when we calm down enough and catch eyes, I'm back a few nights ago, on my knees, face buried in his groin.

The humor dies on his face, and I'm pretty sure he's reminded of the same thing.

I can't help licking my lips, desperately wanting to offer it up again.

There's a moment where we both stare at each other, and I'm dying to know what he's thinking. His stare drops to my lips, and then he clears his throat and looks away.

"Heard from Lee?" he asks, and the fun afternoon we've had evaporates.

"Ah, yeah." I look away from him. "He messaged me earlier."

"When's the big date?"

"Friday night." Exactly one week after I hooked up with Payne. It doesn't matter how many times I tell myself it's for the best, I can't get excited over the date. I'd rather stay in. Watch a movie. Eat popcorn with Payne, then maybe swallow his dick again, who knows?

"Want me to stay at Marty's that night? You know, in case ..."

"No. No, no. This is your home. I won't be ... I won't ..." Yikes, I can't finish that.

Realistically, any other time, I'd probably go home with Lee or bring him here; even if the date turned shit, I'm still fine with a hookup.

The problem is Payne was the last guy I was with, and I don't want to let go of that just yet.

So no, I definitely can't explain that.

I clear my throat. "I'm sure we can go back to his place if we ..."

Payne waves his hand to cut me off, thankfully not needing me to finish that sentence either because it makes me feel gross. Fuck, these *feelings*.

I need to make a better effort at trying to move on, despite the tiny voice telling me I don't want to.

It's not healthy.

I'll be so much happier in a relationship with someone who sees me the way I see Payne.

If only I'd kept my mouth closed, maybe we'd still be hooking up.

But that wouldn't be fair on him. The first time wasn't either, but it's not like that was planned. It was spontaneous, and once it started, there was no way I was stopping to be like, "oh, PS, this means a lot to me, just want you to know. Now can I suck your cock, please?" because that would have brought it to a grinding halt.

I needed that one time.

I need more than once, if I'm honest, but I'm not letting that thought get ahead of me. I'll respect Payne's boundaries. Payne's stupid, stupid boundaries because he's disgustingly, stupidly sweet.

Out of nowhere, Payne reaches forward and covers one of my hands. "Hey, what happened? You got real anxious out of nowhere."

"What ... how did you ..."

He laughs. "Your hands started going crazy."

"Oh." I let out a breath. "Yeah, the thought of dating does that." Sure, let's go with that excuse and not the one where I'm desperately trying to downplay my feelings.

His thumb rubs light circles over my wrist, and he surprises me by saying, "Why don't we cook dinner together, and then I'll let you use my tats?"

"You'd let me do that again?"

An adorable, bashful expression crosses his face, and he rubs at the back of his neck. "Maybe we do it here and you can use my arms. That'll be fine, right?"

I'm nodding hard before he's even finished talking. An excuse to touch him again? I should be saying no. Thanking him and protecting myself.

Instead, I wait for him to go and shower off the day's work, then stash the pile of coloring books I ordered into one of my drawers.

Nothing to see here.

Other than an idiot in big, big trouble.

DMC Group Chat

Me: *Date ideas?*

   Griffin: *Getting back on the horse? Good for you.*

   Art: *Want-to-date-you date, or get-in-your-pants date? Important distinction.*

   Orson: *If Payne only wanted to hook up, I'm sure he wouldn't have needed us for that.*

   Art: *Good point. In that case, I'm of no use here.*

   Orson: *Who are you romancing?*

   Me: *Beau. But it's less romancing, and more helping him with a practice date before his one this weekend.*

   Art: *And suddenly I'm interested again.*

   Orson: *This sounds dangerous.*

   Griffin: *And by "dangerous" Orson means Beau is going to be snapped up if you're not careful.*

   Me: *There's no snapping, no danger, I just need a low-key date idea.*

   Art: *Low-key? No. What you need is to give him the most* *mind-blowing date so that whatever this other guy is planning is an utter disappointment by comparison.*

Me: *And again, it's not real. He's nervous, I'm trying to help.*

Griffin: *"Help";)*

Art: *With his dick?*

Me: *You all suck.*

Orson: *What did I do? I think you're being very sweet.*

Me: *I'm not trying to be sweet, I'm trying to be a good friend.*

Griffin: *"Friend";)*

Orson: *Of course we believe you.*

Art: *Nothing friendlier than a suck and fuck.*

Chapter Fifteen

PAYNE

I close out of the chat with a short laugh. I should have known better than to expect those dumbasses to help me. My back is prickling with sweat as I climb out of the car I'm detailing. The fans in the warehouse are rotating above, but they're doing fuck all to reach the ground.

"You look happy," Ford says, holding out a bottle of water.

I accept it with a grateful smile. "Mostly fine, just dealing with annoying friends who like to give me shit."

"Let me guess, Art?"

I grin at him. "No idea how you picked that."

"What's he giving you shit about?"

"The guy I'm staying with—"

"Beau Rickshaw?"

"Yeah, him. He has a date this weekend, and because he's nervous, I thought I might take him on a practice one."

Ford eyes me but doesn't say anything.

I shake my head. "The more I talk about it, the dumber it sounds."

"Not dumb at all. You're helping a friend. It's admirable."

"*Thank* you. That's what I'm going for."

"You got the hots for him?"

Why do people keep asking that? I level Ford with a stare, but he just chuckles.

"It's a fair question. You're a good-looking guy, he's a good-looking guy ... you both live together ..."

"He's my brother's friend."

"Ain't Marty straight?"

"Yes."

"Then what's the issue? If he hasn't slept with him, it's fair game."

"No, it's ... I'm going through a divorce—it's all I can focus on." Though, since hooking up with Beau, I haven't given Kyle a second thought.

He rubs at the sweat on his forehead with an old rag. "Can't imagine how hard that is. I'm here if you need anything."

I eye him. "Do you have any date ideas?"

"Something from the heart is always a good plan. Or something that shows you've put in effort. Just taking someone out for dinner is ... impersonal. Good for people you don't know, but for someone you've known most of your life, a little effort can lead to a big payoff."

What do I know about Beau? Well, other than his work compulsion and keeping weird hours. The way he says things without thinking sometimes. How he needs to wind down when his brain starts going too fast and gets hyperfocused over some things while being completely absentminded over others. He likes seeing the sky ...

"Maybe we could do something outside?"

"Under the stars? Romantic."

"Like a picnic."

Ford claps me on the shoulder. "Sounds good to me. Eating, talking, and fucking under the stars."

"Except for that last thing," I say dryly, even though it's an appealing thought.

"Pity. There're a few guys who'd love to lock that one up, but Beau's never given anyone much of a chance. Maybe this weekend's guy is the one?"

No, Lee better not be.

I try to ignore the way that thought hurts. "Doubt it, but we'll see."

"Either way, Beau's lucky to have a friend like you. I hope it goes well."

"Thanks."

It's not until I leave work that afternoon that I realize that might not be possible though. Heavy, dark clouds are hanging low over Kilborough, and by the time I duck into the store to pick up what I had planned for our picnic, it's already raining.

Well, shit.

What the hell do I do now?

Dinner at home? It'll seem like I haven't tried at all.

For some reason, that thought irritates me. Sure, this is a low-key *non*date, but ... maybe Art was onto something. Maybe I want Beau remembering tonight while he's out this weekend, and I'd like my *very much* nondate to at least measure up.

Surely, a nighttime picnic would have done that.

I stand under the store's awning, watching the rain come down, while I try to think of an idea.

Maybe ...

Maybe we don't need to *be* outside for me to give him the sky.

I jog to my car before pulling out my phone to call my brother.

"Hey," Marty answers. "What are you doing?"

"Organizing dinner. Listen ..." I rattle off what I'm looking for, and even though Marty isn't happy with me not answering his questions on *why*, he lets me borrow everything I need.

Thank fuck for having nieces.

I'm more than prepared to throw Beau out of the apartment for an hour when I get home, except the place is dark and still like it normally is while he's in bed. I get to work, ears strained for any noise so I can intercept him if he's up before I'm finished here. The whole time I'm getting things ready, there's an unsettled feeling low in my gut. Almost like nerves. Almost like excitement.

I also have a very good hunch I know where these nerves are coming from, and acknowledging it the night before he goes on a date with another guy isn't a smart move.

I'm worried my idea is juvenile, or he'll think it's the dumbest thing ever, but it's not like I have a whole lot of options here.

Our date takes me almost an hour to set up, and I think I'm happy by the time I'm done. Beau still isn't up, so I risk a fast shower and then get changed into jeans and a nice T-shirt, and then ... all I can do is wait.

Sometimes Beau isn't up until well past midnight, and I'm praying tonight isn't one of those nights. The longer I wait, the more I doubt, and my brain keeps jumping between Beau being touched by what I've done and him finding it extremely odd.

Half an hour later, I hear a noise and spring off my bed to meet Beau at his door by the time he pops it open.

His sleepy blue eyes blink up at me, clearer up close and without glasses, and his tight curls are a frizzy mess.

"What's up?" he mumbles, still half asleep, even as a small smile pulls at his lips.

"Get dressed."

"Huh?"

"Trust me." I gently turn him to face his room again. "Something you feel comfortable in."

And maybe I should have said something *nice* you feel comfortable in, because he comes back out wearing low-slung gray sweatpants and a long-sleeved T-shirt, his dark blond chest hair visible at the V-neck.

No one has any right to look as sexy in gray sweatpants as he does.

I let my gaze travel over him, and by the time I get back to his face, his cheeks look flushed.

"This okay?"

"Yep." I take his hand "You'll do."

"Do for what?"

Beau doesn't react to his hand in mine at all. Like it's a completely normal thing we do together. I almost wish it was, because when Beau looks up at me ... no one has ever looked at me like that before. As though I'm important. Wanted. Needed, even.

If this was a real date, I'd lean down and brush my lips over his. Maybe back him into the wall and find out how those pink lips taste.

Instead, I give Beau's hand a tug and lead him into the living room.

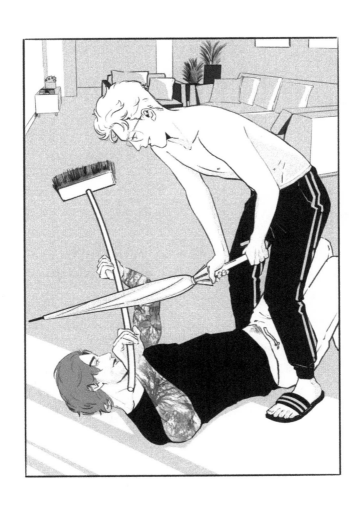

Chapter Sixteen

BEAU

I'm still fighting off tiredness as Payne pulls me through the apartment. The lights are off, and a flash of lightning hits the sky outside, lighting up the space. Including a very large something hunched over in front of the sliding doors.

My first thought is *dragon!* but thankfully I manage to keep that one to myself because duh, Beau, dragons aren't real. But ... what is it?

I squint into the shadows as Payne pulls me closer.

"What am I looking at?"

He turns to face me, large hand still warming mine, and I can make out a hint of his features in the low light. "Well, the original plan was a picnic under the stars, and then this happened." He waves his hand toward where the storm is coming down outside. "So I improvised."

"Okay ..."

"You're worried about your date tomorrow, right?"

My lips part, but nothing comes out, because I'm not sure what to say. *Yes, I'm dreading it, and not only because I hate dating, but also because it's not with you* probably isn't the response he's after. So I hum what I hope is an affirmative sound.

"Well, I thought tonight could be a practice run."

"A practice run?"

"Sure. We'll pretend this is a date. Make small talk, practice flirting, whatever you need."

I give him a cheeky smile. "Do I get a good-night kiss at the end?"

"Now you're pushing your luck."

But as he turns to crawl into a little pink tent, I mourn the shadows hiding that gorgeous ass from my greedy view.

I grab my glasses from my desk, then follow him.

One side of the tent is open onto the glass doors, and the floor is covered in pillows and cushions that look familiar.

"Are those the girls' things?"

"Yup." Payne flicks a switch, and through the flimsy roof of the kiddie tent comes the glow of twinkle lights. He points at them. "As close to a sky as I could get for you."

"If it wasn't pink," I point out.

His laugh is warm and happy. It lights me up inside. "Apparently they don't make kids tents in black. Who knew?"

I watch while he grabs a picnic basket and sets it on the strip of floor in front of the doors. Another flash of lightning lights up the space, but even with it gone, my eyes are adjusting to the low light, and Payne is coming into focus.

"You did this for me?" I ask.

He clears his throat as he sets out the food. "Don't get too excited. I don't have a whole lot of other things happening in my life."

He's trying to brush it off as nothing, so I'll let him, but this is possibly the sweetest thing anyone has ever done for me. I want to close the small space between us and kiss him, but that's not going to convince either of us that I'm getting over my crush.

"Well, cheers to that." I reach over and take the glass of wine that he's poured.

"To having no life?"

"Exactly." We tap our glasses together.

"So, Beau, was it?" Payne says. "How long have you lived in Kilborough?"

My lips twitch. "What are you doing?"

"Just play along."

"Okay … ah, all of my life."

A short silence follows my words until Payne leans in and whispers, "Now you ask me."

"Umm … How long have you lived here?"

"Only a couple of months. You know, I really could use someone to show me around. Someone who knows the area …"

I nod along to his words, showing I'm listening.

"And this is where you offer to show me around," he says.

I hang my head. "I'm *terrible* at this."

"You're not—you're too in your head." He points at the wine. "Have *one* at dinner. Just one. It'll help calm your nerves. Then you need to get out of your head. Some conversation topics that usually go down well are sport, any viral video clips you've seen, work—if you're desperate and need to get him talking—ideal holiday destinations and places you've traveled to ... if you get stuck, ask him about his plans for the future. That should buy you a couple of minutes."

"Huh." I pick at the food he's set out. "So what are your plans for the future?"

"That was good, but you don't need to practice that one."

"No." I shift. "I actually want to know."

"Haven't I already told you everything?"

"Uh, yeah, you've told me about finding a job and moving out. That can't be all though."

Payne considers the question. "I guess those things are the most pressing. I'm still trying to get my head to stop spinning after my life exploded around me, so I haven't thought about it much."

"Yeah, but even before that happened, you have to have had some ideas."

"Honestly, before all that, I thought my life would continue exactly the way it was pretty much forever. I'm a different person now, as douchey as that sounds."

"I don't think it's douchey."

His expression softens. "I think what I really want is independence. Sure I had things, but they were only partially mine, and when you divide your life into halves, it gets very dark when you realize it doesn't leave you with much."

"I never thought about it like that. Whenever I picture finding someone, I dunno, the whole sharing your life seems … nice."

"And it is. Until it isn't."

My teeth clench as the familiar anger at Kyle tries to hit, but I push it back. He doesn't get to interfere with this nice thing Payne has done for me. "Well, now you get to do that. Get your independence. You'll feel better once your place has sold."

"I will." He sighs. "I would have been able to treat you to something more decent than this if it already had."

"In that case I'm glad it hasn't, because this is perfect."

Payne's bashful smile fills my gut with butterflies.

I nudge the food out of the way and lie down on my side. My feet poke out of the end of the tent, but it's … cozy. The storm above my head, Payne sitting across from me. He hesitates a second before he copies me, bending his knees slightly so they almost hit mine.

He's maybe a foot away, the shadows making the fine lines in his face deeper, showing his crow's feet and the lines by his mouth and between his eyebrows. His stubble looks rougher, his eyes more piercing. I lick my lips, wishing I could kiss him again. Always, always wishing for that.

"Favorite ice cream flavor," I ask. It comes out closer to a whisper, like my voice doesn't want to disturb the calm air between us.

"Anything that has caramel in it. You?"

"Vanilla." I try not to think about that in relation to sex. "Anything else is too overwhelming."

"Bor-ring." His voice has dropped to match mine.

"Simple," I counter. "I don't need much to be happy."

"What are things that make you happy, then?"

You. Fuck, don't say that. I swallow the word and think of specifics, then find myself saying. "Paper cranes. And sword fights. Reheating meals that have been made for me, even if I couldn't eat them right away."

"Beau ..."

"Yeah?"

Payne swallows roughly. "Those things make me happy too."

"It's also nice to ... to have someone who ..." I take a deep breath. "Who gets me. It's nice to not feel completely hopeless some of the time."

His eyes bore into mine. The silence is weighted between us, and when he talks, his voice is a low rasp.

"You're not hopeless." His fingers brush the side of my face. "Far from it."

I shiver and shake him off. "You and Marty are probably the only people who think that. And Marty only some of the time."

"Why do *you* think that?"

"Are you kidding? You saw my place before you moved in."

Payne gives me a skeptical look. "You think not being clean makes you hopeless?"

"Well, yes, *that*, but also, I'm not organized. I forget

about things easily. Before you moved in, I'd order takeout or heat ramen for dinner every night. Even basic things like doing the laundry or changing my clothes feel too hard sometimes. That sounds hopeless to me."

"Being clean and on time for things is overrated. Like, who decided that was the marker of a person with their shit together? Because in case you haven't noticed, I tidy up *and* do those things you just mentioned, but I'm a complete mess. Most of the time I'm hanging on by a thread, and that's scary as hell. If you're hopeless, I'm a fucking wreck."

Hanging on by a thread is a frequent feeling for me. Knowing that Payne feels like that too sometimes, well, it sucks of course, because I don't *want* him to feel that way, but it also helps to make me not feel so alone. "Maybe we're all a bit hopeless, then."

"Probably. Which is why when you go on this date tomorrow, you should be yourself."

"A hopeless mess?"

"Sure, let's go with that."

"I doubt that's what most people are looking for in a guy."

He shrugs, then chews on whatever he wants to say for a moment. "I think ... I think you deserve that person. The one who's looking for *you*."

"Does he exist?"

"You won't know unless you try to find him."

"That's true." I chew on my thumbnail. Payne *is* that guy for me though. He's the only one I *want* to be that guy, but Payne said I need to find the one who's looking for me, and that just isn't him. He's a great friend; we're close. He gives me so much of what I need already, but ... I've probably missed out on a lot of good guys because of how hung up on him I am. "Maybe it'll be Lee."

Payne scoffs and then freezes, like it took him by surprise.

"You don't like him?" I ask.

"I don't know him."

"Then what was that noise?"

"There was no noise."

I lift my eyebrows because we both heard it, but instead of pushing, I let it go.

He sighs. "I hope your date goes well tomorrow."

"Well, it has a lot to live up to." I gesture toward the twinkle lights above us. It's quiet and intimate, and maybe not anyone's idea of a perfect date, but I couldn't love this more. Being at home, somewhere I'm comfortable, with good food and a cozy setup and Payne lying across from me ... it's perfect.

"This was nothing."

"To you, maybe."

His smile is hesitant. "You really liked it?"

"I love it. And our date's still going, right?"

"I'm in no hurry."

"Me neither."

We're up most of the night, and while it might be a practice date, I know there's no way any date could ever turn out as good as tonight's has. There are no awkward lulls in conversation, no nervous rambling. Payne encourages my ideas and asks me questions; we talk about the things he missed in Kilborough while he was in Boston, as well as the things he loved while he was there.

It's close to one in the morning when we crawl out of the tent and walk, side by side, back to our bedrooms.

"Thank you for tonight," I say.

"Yeah, it was actually fun."

"You doubted you'd have fun with me?"

"Well, you and everyone else have been telling me you flunk dates, so I thought maybe some kind of pressure was getting to you."

"The pressure does get to me."

"You were fine tonight."

"Yeah, but—" I meet his gaze. "—that was you. That was easy."

Something shifts in Payne's expression, but he doesn't look away. Neither do I. We just stand there staring at each other, and I really hope he's not reading all the feelings on my face because I'm terrible at trying to hide them.

One side of his lips hitches up, and then he leans forward and brushes a kiss over my cheek, pausing when he reaches the corner of my mouth.

My lips tingle. My stomach flips. My fingers are itching to grab him, hold him, tug him closer against me until his mouth is right where I want it.

His breath fans over my skin, which reminds me that I'm not breathing at all.

Payne's slow to pull back, and my brain is full of *stop,*

wait, kiss me again, make it mean something this time, but I force myself to smile.

"I knew I'd get a good-night kiss out of you."

He huffs a laugh. "Sometimes I think you could get anything out of me."

"Anything?"

His teeth rake over his bottom lip. "Night, Bo-Bo."

I'm smiling, heart happier than it probably should be. "Night."

Chapter Seventeen

PAYNE

I message Art halfway through the workday to beg him to meet me at Killer Brew after work. Beau's date is tonight, and I'm uncontrollably aware of the dread sitting heavy in my gut.

This week has been great. Eating dinner one-handed while Beau colors in my arms, talking about absolute shit, and then our date last night, which felt more like a real date than any other I've had.

I'm a moody shit at work all day because I selfishly don't want him to go. We have fun together, and I know if Beau starts dating, the dynamic between us will change. Where everything has been a clusterfuck since that video two months ago, being with Beau is easy. Simple. And it's mine.

I don't want to share him, and I'm starting to feel ...

something. But what the hell do I have for Beau to be interested in? If there's anything my marriage taught me, it's that love is never enough.

Trusting someone again won't be easy, and the thought of a relationship after what I've been through is exhausting. All I can see are the long years ahead of me. The years that were supposed to be spent with one person.

What happens if I jump into something serious and find myself in this exact position at fifty-two? I can't go through it again.

But, on the other hand ... Beau.

Ford lets me off half an hour early. He claims it's because I'm done for the day, but I'm pretty sure he's sick of my attitude, and I really can't blame him. I'd worry about him firing me if he didn't seem to like me so much.

I order a coffee at the café, then head inside Killer Brew and climb the stairs behind the bar to reach the mezzanine level. It's a large, open wood-and-steel space. One side has a hall that leads to Art's office, and the right side of the room has a small bar for functions. Straight ahead under the large mullioned windows is a lounge area, where Art and Griffin are waiting.

Art chuckles when he sees me. "What's going on with you?"

"Am I that obvious?" I ask, sitting opposite them.

"Your message saying 'help, I've done a stupid thing' was a good clue."

Fair point. On both counts.

"What's wrong?" Griffin asks.

"This conversation would work better over beer than coffee."

"That bad, huh?"

I rub my face with both hands, wondering how much to say. These guys won't spread anything around, I know that, and I could use a hand on how to proceed here.

"Everything I'm about to say is between us."

Art nods. "Obviously."

"Beau has a thing for me," I say.

To my surprise, neither of them looks shocked. Instead, Griffin scowls. "Dammit, now I owe Orson twenty bucks."

"What?"

"That day we saw him here, he bet me that Beau was interested in you. Damn guy has a radar for these things."

"Wow. Thanks for the heads-up."

"Dude, you were living with him," Art says. "Saying anything would have messed that up. Besides, Beau used to have the hots for you when we were younger too, so it isn't exactly groundbreaking news. You really didn't know?"

"No clue."

"How did you find out?" Griffin asks.

"He told me."

"Good for him."

"After we hooked up."

And *there's* the shock I was expecting.

"Fuck me," Griffin mutters. "You lucky bastard."

I groan and cover my face again. "I thought so too until he dropped the crush thing on me."

"Crush? What are we, in high school?" Art shakes his head. "The man has feelings for you. At least say it like it is."

"I'm only echoing what he's said."

"And you believe him?" Griffin looks at me like I deserve his pity. "I've been with exactly one person since I was eighteen. I'm naive when it comes to relationships, but even I know crushes don't last twenty years."

Art agrees. "He's downplaying."

"Well, fuck you both very much." This isn't the conversation I was hoping for. "You're supposed to be making me feel better about this whole thing. The crush made it easy to focus on being friends."

"Oh no," Griffin mocks. "A cute guy has the hots for you. How terrible."

I flip him off, and he laughs.

"I take it you don't feel the same way?"

The problem is, it's so confusing to try and work out. I think I do. When I picture Beau, my chest gets warm, and I can't help smile over the thought of him doing something obliviously naive. But what if I'm just latching onto the thought of him because he's interested and my ego has been damaged? "I'm going through a divorce. That's my only relationship focus right now."

"So you need help with what?" Art asks. "How to act with him?"

"No, so far that part has been fine. Not a whole lot has changed, which is good."

"Then what's the problem?"

I cringe and take a long sip of my coffee while I think

about how to word this next part without sounding like a total dick. Because ... the way I feel *makes* me a dick. "He has a date tonight."

"Isn't that a good thing?" Art asks.

"Of course." I tap my knuckles on the table. "Which is why I shouldn't be so annoyed about it."

Griffin leans forward. "Oh, this is good."

"Shut up." Art whacks the back of his head. "I thought you didn't like him."

"I don't. Well, I mean ... If he didn't have a crush or feelings or whatever, I would have wanted to keep hooking up, but beyond that ..." Beyond that, if I wasn't going through a divorce, I'd be all in easily.

"Oh, so this is some kind of toxic masculinity thing?" Art asks. "Beau is *your* toy."

Wow, that doesn't make me sound good. "Is that what this is?"

"You're the only one who knows that."

I scowl because that doesn't help me. "I don't think it's that."

"Then what's the problem?"

"I dunno." It's weird discussing this, but I know I need to. "He's helped me with some stuff to do with my fucker ex, and I've helped him out with some of his book stuff. It's like we both have each other. I don't want that to change."

Art and Griffin are both nodding, so at least I know I'm on the right track with explaining.

"And also, the guy he's dating tonight is a total douche."

Art laughs. "I know what your problem is."

"You do?"

Griffin's studying me. "I think I do too. Maybe."

"Is the brain trust going to share with me?"

"You're jealous." Art says it like it's the easiest thing in the world.

"Yeah, no."

"Oh, yes."

Fuck, I think he's right.

"You might not be there yet, but you *want to* want to date him. With the divorce happening, you don't feel like you have anything to offer, so you're hoping he'll hang around, stroking your ego—"

"And other things," Griffin helpfully cuts in.

"Yes, those too. Stroking your ego and your other things until *you* decide a relationship is on the table."

"Okay, so let's say I *did* have feelings, it doesn't change anything. It would still be too soon, right?"

"Why? And why is it a race? The thing is, you don't have to act on these hypothetical feelings. Maybe they come to nothing, or maybe you want to give them time to grow, or you're still feeling sore from being betrayed. Wherever you're at, just be genuine with him. Spend time with him. Show him you care, even if you're not ready to say it."

"Hypothetically."

Art gives me a look. "Sure, hypothetically."

"And how does that hypothetically help me tonight?"

"It doesn't. You're shit out of luck there."

I stare out at the water. "He could do so much better."

"Beau doesn't think so."

That's true. Beau has been angry over what Kyle did, but he's never looked at me with pity. It's one of the reasons I'm so comfortable around him. Sometimes I catch him watching me with this hopeful puppy expression, and it makes me want to be worth that level of affection. "I'm very confused."

"I wish Orson wasn't working," Art says.

"Why?"

"Because of all of us, he'd understand. My marriage was over in like a second, and I jumped straight back out there."

"And with mine," Griffin says. "It's been a long one, but we're both more than ready to move on."

"Exactly," Art says. "Orson is the only one of us who has felt that kind of raw heartbreak and facing the uphill climb of trying to rebuild a life with someone."

"That." I point at him. "That's what it is. An uphill climb."

"Yeah, but there's a reason people climb Everest." Griffin rubs his jaw. "Sometimes it's worth it. And while I might not know what you're going through, Beau's a catch. If there is something there, my only advice is to stop focusing on everything else because that shit is just noise. If I had a Beau after me, I wouldn't hesitate." He gives me an evil smile. "And if he's still single when my divorce goes through, you better believe I'll be hitting him up."

Art sniggers, and I have no idea why I thought these guys would help. "I hate you both."

Art and Griffin both offer to take me out that night, but I refuse because apparently, I'd prefer to torture myself. So instead of heading out with them to a gay bar and picking up, I go home, shower, then change into sweats and hesitate over a shirt. Beau sees me shirtless a lot, and I sort of want Lee to catch Beau checking me out like I often do, but ... my damn conscience wins. I tug a T-shirt over my head and cross the hall to Beau's room.

He's staring into space, button-up shirt hanging open, and I let my gaze roam down his wide torso, lingering on the light hair that runs from his stomach down into his pants.

When it comes to Beau, there's something there. But feeling a certain way and acting on it are two different things. It's not fair on Beau for me to mention I'm interested when I can't commit to anything.

Would it have been different?

If I'd known Beau had feelings back then, before dickweed, would I be happy now? Or would we have ended anyway? Would I have even looked at Beau like that when he was Marty's friend?

I'm not someone who likes regrets, which is just another reason why the end of my relationship hit so hard. All that wasted time and emotional investment spent on someone who didn't deserve it.

I don't for a second believe Beau wouldn't though.

But Kyle was the same in the beginning, so who knows?

And Lee's the one who gets to be Beau's focus tonight, so I need to suck it up and shut up about it.

I knock on Beau's door, finally catching his attention.

"You're still. I think it's a miracle."

He lets out a self-deprecating laugh. "Lost in thought."

"Everything okay?"

"Yep." His voice does that thing where it gets louder when he's trying to be convincing. "I'm not sure whether I should have the shirt on yet or not. He's picking me up in half an hour. Will I break out in a nervous sweat between now and then? There's a high chance."

"You're nervous?" I'm not expecting that since Beau hasn't appeared all that thrilled by the upcoming date.

"Yes, but I'm always nervous when I'm faced with a night of peopling with near strangers."

"I thought you and Lee have been texting?"

"We have, but—" He shakes his head.

"But?"

Beau forces a smile that is fake as shit. "No buts. Tonight will be fine." He buttons up his shirt, and I farewell the view.

Once he's dressed, I plant my hands on his shoulders and steer him from the room. "You need a shot to relax."

"Yeah, that sounds perfect, actually."

We do a shot of scotch each, and Beau pours out a second, but I take it before he can. The burn is just what I need, and when I open my eyes to find the flat look he's giving me, I taunt him.

"Tastes good."

"You're not the one who needs to calm down though."

"Maybe not," I agree. "But we want you relaxed, not loose. Don't give up the goods too easily."

He hums but doesn't answer, which is annoying. Even though I have no right to know what his plans are or even if they do end up hooking up. I still want to tell him not to though. The thought of Lee touching him makes me want to break something.

There's a knock at the door.

"Shit." Beau checks his phone. "He's early."

"Pushy fucker."

"No, no. It's fine." But Beau's face is a splotchy pink. "I'm not even ready yet."

"You go, I'll let him in."

"Okay, thanks."

Beau darts into the hall, and I frown after him for a moment. The nervousness, him wanting to look good …

I set my jaw and move to open the front door.

And fuck a duck in a pickup truck, Lee looks good. His hair is styled, and he's dressed in a polished way I could never pull off. The friendly expression is what really pisses me off though.

"Hi, Payne. I'm here to pick up Beau." He glances hopefully over my shoulder, and I cross my arms, then lean against the doorframe.

"Leeroy, right?"

"Just Lee."

"Oh, yeah, the dude from Marty's." I take my time to look him over, making sure my expression gets more and more unimpressed the farther I look.

I'd never thought I could be a dick like this, but hey, it's coming surprisingly easily.

Lee shifts. "Can you let Beau know I'm here?"

"He knows. He'll be out soon."

"Ah. Can I wait inside for him?"

"Nope." I don't offer more than that. But, hey, if I can throw Lee off his game, Beau will look like a Disney prince in comparison to my attitude. "So, where are you taking Bo-Bo?"

Lee tries to hide his annoyance with me, which further supports this nice theory everyone keeps throwing around. "Dinner and a movie. Then maybe a walk along the boardwalk."

"Wow. How long did it take you to come up with that?" Because of course the weather is perfect for *their* date.

I see the exact moment he works out that I'm fucking with him, but it's not like he can call me on it. Not without knowing whether Beau values my opinion or not.

He shrugs, going for casual. "Good food, a dark cinema, and starlight." His grin catches me off guard. "It hasn't failed me yet."

Beau's bedroom door closes, and a minute later, I hear him walking up behind me. My glare is locked on Lee, and his stare is challenging me to say something.

"Sorry, I wasn't ready," Beau says when he joins us.

"Of course you weren't." I point out. "That's what happens when people are early."

"I'm early when I'm excited." Damn, he's smooth. Everything from his words to his soft smile.

Beau turns to me. "Why didn't you invite him in?"

"I did. He said he was more comfortable out there." Let's see him get out of that one.

Lee's mask doesn't slip though. "I didn't want to encroach on your space without you being the one to invite me in."

"Oh." Beau looks flustered. I hate it. "That's ... considerate."

"You want to let my *date* past, buddy?" Lee asks.

I reluctantly step to the side so Beau can leave, and Lee immediately leans in to kiss him on the cheek.

"You look incredible."

"Ah, thanks." After a few seconds, Beau's eyes shoot wide. "And you too. You look good as well. Sorry. Sometimes my brain just stops working and ... umm, yeah." He laughs awkwardly, sneaking a glance back at me. "You don't have to ... you know."

Hover. Be here. I rest against the side of the door. "I'm good."

"It's fine anyway," Lee says, and I track his hand as it comes to rest on Beau's lower back. "We were leaving."

Beau nods. "See you later, Payne."

I stand there, watching them walk down the hallway, knowing I shouldn't have interfered but also knowing I couldn't have held back.

Art and Griffin are right.

I *do* want to keep Beau until I'm ready.

Fuck if that doesn't make me a total asshole.

Even that thought can't stop me from leaning out into the hall and calling after them. "I'll wait up!"

Chapter Eighteen

BEAU

I wish I could say Payne's behavior was the worst part of the night, but that was only the tip of the iceberg.

And Lee doesn't even realize it.

When we passed a homeless man on the way into the restaurant, Lee pulled me close and whispered that they should keep the footpath clear because it's a "nice, family area." He didn't stop touching me until we took our seats, despite me moving away, and he keeps pointing out he's paying. Like, a lot.

We'll get the banquet platters. Don't worry, Beau, I'm paying.

Why don't you get a cocktail? It's on me.

Make sure you leave room for popcorn. I'll buy us the biggest one.

I can't help comparing it to how Payne didn't fight me

on paying for the tour. How he doesn't push me to take money, even after he offered me rent now that he's working, and I told him I'd prefer for our agreement to stay the same.

It makes him look comfortable with me.

With Lee, there's no connection, which is probably all on me, but I can't stop picking at the little things he does.

He brought me to a Thai restaurant, which is fine, but then proceeded to order for the both of us, and the dishes he chose were the hottest ones on the menu. I don't like spicy food. At all.

So while I pretend to like his selection so he's not offended, in reality I push it around my plate and eat as much plain rice as I can stomach. He also never. Stops. Talking.

I'd noticed it at Marty's, but I put his control of the conversation down to nerves and the fact I wasn't saying much. But we're on a *date*. Why am I here if he doesn't actually want to get to know me?

I hate small talk and discussing things about myself, but I also know it's an important part of the getting-to-know-you step that needs to be ticked off before we can move forward.

So far all I've worked out is that Lee talks with food in his cheek when he gets excited, cuts me off when I take too long to answer a question or get my words out right, and thinks people who eat blue cheese only do it to look superior.

I mean ... I don't get the appeal, but I'm not going to judge people for it.

"Where are our cocktails?" he grumbles. "You know, I've been noticing lately there are less and less servers in these places. The government keeps taxing the business owners and raising minimum wage, so they can't employ enough people to do the jobs. Whereas if there were enough servers focused on good service, I'd tip more than generously."

"Yeah, but not everyone does that."

"Well, with service like this, what do you expect?"

The server shows up with our cocktails, saving me from a reply.

"Tell me about this book thing," Lee says.

I blink, surprised he's actually asked at all. The problem is "book thing" is a very broad topic, and I have no idea where to start. My feet bounce under the table. "W-what did you want to—"

"You're an author, yeah? How did you get into it?"

That, I can work with. "I read a lot as a kid, then decided to try my own. I won a competition to meet with a literary agent, who gave me some awesome pointers on my book and asked me to resubmit if I made the changes he suggested. At the time I thought it was cool he was interested at all, so I did as he said, resubmitted and ..." My book went to auction, had multiple bids, and sold for a lot more than I would have ever guessed. The translation rights came quickly, and then the movie was optioned, even though last I heard there was no movement there, which is typical.

"Wow, that's really cool." Lee takes a bite of sizzling beef. "So you're a real author, then?"

I pause. "A real author?"

"You know, with a publisher. You're not just out there, throwing whatever up online."

"You mean self-publishing?"

He scoffs. "Can they even call it publishing? I swear, half of those books are barely legible."

"Have you read any?"

"Nope. I don't need to." He gives me what I'm sure he thinks is a charming smile, but there's a chunk of basil caught in his teeth. "But I'm sure you know this already."

I don't at all. I want to point out all the ways he's wrong and that self-publishing has *benefited* authors and readers more than anything, but the confrontation gets caught in my throat. I've actually been looking at the mismatched snippets I've been writing and wondering whether to "throw" those up online. My publisher would never accept them. Even as part of a coherent story, they're too niche.

"What do you write?" he asks.

"I thought I already said." I did. I mentioned it at least once this week when he messaged to ask what I was doing. "Fantasy."

"Ah, nice. Like *Game of Thrones*?"

I'm so sick of that comparison. So I decide to fuck with him. "More like *Harry Potter*. Or *Twilight*."

"Ah." Now he doesn't look so impressed.

And I hope he never plans to read my books because I say, "Oh, yeah, it's the full-on chosen one trope. Barry Trotter is obsessed with Eddy Carlisle, and they go to magic school together, and—oh, there's *dragons*. And a *giant centipede*. And at one point, Eddy's decapitated, and Barry

190

has to do a spell to stick his head back on, but it always chooses the most random moments to pop back off and roll across the ground."

The people at the table beside us are looking at me in horror, and Lee's clearly confused, but I'm past caring.

"That sounds ... interesting."

"Sells like hotcakes."

He clears his throat. "There's a market for everything, isn't there?"

"Including dinoporn."

"Dino ..." He scrambles for his drink. "Umm ... that's fascinating. Hey, did I tell you about that time at work Marty and I had that battle with the office across the street? Where we'd send the other—"

"The most disgusting lunch dishes you could find, and the ones who bowed out of eating it first had to pay for the others to go on a golf retreat?"

"A couple of times, huh?" He tilts a bashful expression my way.

Like, six, but who's counting?

"So what's the deal with Payne?" he asks. "I know you said you've never dated, but he was ... I don't want to say rude, but ..."

But he *was* rude. Payne wasn't happy to see Lee, and that should piss me off a lot more than it does. Payne doesn't know Lee, so the only reason I can think of for him to not like Lee is me. It makes me hopeful that there's something there even when it really shouldn't. Because if he's jealous, even the smallest, slightest bit jealous, that means I might actually have a chance. One day in the future when he's moved on from his divorce, could something actually happen?

I'd wait my whole life to find out.

"He's protective of me," I lie. Though ... it's not *really* a lie, is it? Protective might be a strong word, but Payne has my back a lot.

"I think he has feelings for you."

I almost laugh because Lee doesn't need to worry about that. And not only because I don't have feelings for Lee, but if Payne wanted anything with me, he already knows it's on the table. "Payne's my roommate. That's it."

"Well, I won't pretend that's not a relief." He tries for a smile again, but I'm not feeling it. I'm not feeling any of this. I *should* be. I should be focused on him and not picking at the things I don't like, but looking for the things I *do* like instead.

So, Lee has some outdated thoughts when it comes to publishing—that's not a *big* thing. All it would take is a quick Google search to show him where he's mistaken. And the food thing? Next time I'll tell him I don't like hot things.

I remind myself I need to make an effort, but I can't stop thinking of Payne. Is he actually waiting up? What's he doing right now? If I was at home, would I be cuddled up next to him, his heavy arm resting in my lap as I draw over his skin? Before I can stop myself, I find myself asking Lee the same question I asked Payne the other day.

"So, hypothetical. If a twenty-five-hundred-pound dragon jumped from the top of my apartment building, would it have enough time to unfurl its wings and take flight, or would it crash to the ground, creating a massive crater?"

Lee opens his mouth, then snaps it closed again. "Umm, Beau? Weren't we talking about Payne?"

"Oh, I thought we were done with that."

He gives me a pitying look. "I'd like to continue with it, if you don't mind."

"Sure, but dragon question first."

"Why? Is it important?" And then he gives me the look. The look that clearly says he worries about my sanity. The look I get at least once over the course of a date and is usually the sign I take that it's time for us to take off, hook up, and call it a night. But I don't want to hook up with Lee.

"I, umm, need to piss." I drop my fork onto my almost full plate and head for the bathrooms. I need any excuse to get out of here, so when I reach the hall for the bathrooms, I pass them and turn another corner, where I pause to pull out my phone.

My first instinct is to call Marty, but Lee is his friend, and he'll only encourage me to give him more of a chance. So instead, I hit Call on Payne's number.

"'Lo?"

"Payne?"

"Ohh ... it's Bo-Bo ..."

Jesus fuck. "Are you drunk?"

"Bit tipsy, yeah. Don't worry, I'll buy you another bottle of scotch."

That's not the part I'm worried about. "Do you have someone over? Or are you drinking alone?"

"Alone. But why are *you* alone? Where's Liam?"

My lips twitch. "Lee?"

"Is that his name?"

"You really expect me to believe you forgot it?"

"I didn't forget. I just don't care enough to remember."

"Of course." I tilt my smile toward the floor.

"Wait. Why are you calling? Where is he? Did he do something?"

"Do something? Like what?"

"I dunno. Upset you or something? Because you don't need to change for him. You shouldn't be changing or improving for anyone, especially a douche like him." Payne hiccups a laugh. "Did you *see* the gold clip on his blazer? Who does he think he is, a fucking sea caption?"

Caption? Payne is way more than tipsy. It's sort of adorable. "Can I tell you why I called now?"

"If the sea captain hurt you—"

"He didn't," I assure him before he can go off on another rant. "But the date blows. Can you call in like five minutes with an emergency?"

Payne snorts. "Why can't you tell him you're not interested and leave?"

"You must underestimate the number of awkward situations I've sat through."

"You need to learn to be more assertive."

"Sure. Of course. But tonight, can you?"

"Call?"

"Yes."

"With an emergency?"

"Exactly."

"There's no way he'll believe that." Payne burps loudly, and it's in this exact moment I have to question my taste in men.

"Yeah, but it's not like he can call me on it, can he?" And with any luck, he'll think it's Payne being overbearing again.

"Yeah, not doing it. I promised I wouldn't interfere again."

"Come on, Payne, please?" I inject a little flirtiness into my tone, feeling bolder since he's been drinking. "I'll thank you later."

His hum is gravelly and reminds me of what he sounds like when he comes. "How exactly?"

"Make the call and find out."

There's silence for a moment, and I'm so worried Payne has passed out.

"Maybe."

"Uh, what?" I laugh, because this isn't a "maybe" type scenario.

"I will *maybe* call you."

"Can't you just give me a yes or no? Preferably a yes?"

"*If* I call, you get your excuse and can blame someone else instead of telling poor Lucas—"

"Lee."

"—the truth, and then, what? Continue to string him on for the rest of your lives? *Or* I give you the opportunity to be assertive and tell him you're leaving."

"You give me way too much credit."

"Nope. I give you the exact right amount of credit, which is a shit load more than you give yourself."

"I can't do it." I inhale deeply and confess, "I didn't even want to come on this date at all, but I couldn't say no when he asked."

"Wow. Can't wait to be there for your wedding day."

"Payne ... I can't. I really can't."

"Fine. Then I guess you just have to hope I'm a nice guy."

I smile. "I know you are."

"Someone's about to be sorely disappointed, then." He hangs up before I can respond, and I'm left staring at my phone. Does that mean ... is he not going to call?

Fuck, I've been gone too long to call him back, so I fire off a text on my way back to the table.

Me: *Please don't let me down.*

DMC Group Chat

Payne: *He's not home yet.*

Art: *Beau?*

Payne: *Yes. Beau. Beau's not home. Why isn't he home?*

Orson: *Ohhhh boy.*

Payne: *What? What's oh boy?*

Griffin: *To be fair, we warned you.*

Orson: *I don't think he needs "I told you so" right now.*

Payne: *WHY ISNT HE BACK?!*

Art: *Do we really need to explain to you what's happening when a date goes late?*

Payne: *Duck off Beau's not like that.*

Payne: *Suck.*

Payne: *FUXK.*

Payne: *I give up.*

Orson: *Have you been drinking?*

Payne: *Just a little.*

Orson: *A little what?*

Payne: *Bottle.*

Griffin: *Now are you going to admit you like the guy?*

Payne: *I ... WHY ISNT HE HIME?*

Art: *For someone who owns a brewery, I have a very low tolerance for drunk people.*

Payne: *Shit I think that's him, what do I do?*

Orson: *I suggest you don't demand to know where he's been.*

Griffin: *Especially because you probably won't like the answer.*

Chapter Nineteen

PAYNE

It's close to midnight when there's *finally* noise in the hall outside. I've been turning my decision not to call Beau over and over in my head, questioning whether I actually made the right choice.

I wanted to be his knight in shining armor, but I also know that Beau is going to keep getting himself into these situations unless he can learn to say no.

I've been expecting him for hours. Hoping he'll balls up and tell Lee to go fuck himself, then come back here and get drunk with me.

But nothing.

Until now.

I jump up and have to hold back from running to the door. Beau's probably going to be pissed at me, which is fine, because the alternative would be that their date turned around, and I don't want that either.

I give them a second or two outside, not at all being creepy and listening to the muffled voices, and when there's a pause, I cross from the kitchen to the front door and yank it open. Beau topples backward, and I barely manage to catch him in time.

"What the hell?" I might be tipsy, but apparently my reflexes are still spot-on.

I look from Beau in my arms to where Lee is standing, arms extended, and take in their wet lips.

Were they ... *kissing*?

I almost crack a molar.

"Good night, was it?" I help Beau back to his feet and whirl on Lee. "I've got him from here. Thanks, buddy." Then I close the door in his face.

When I turn back to Beau, for the first time since I've known him, his eyes flash with anger.

"Excuse me?" He shoves me aside and pulls open the door. "Sorry about that."

Lee's stare flicks to me over Beau's shoulder. "It isn't your fault your roommate has issues."

Beau starts to say something when it cuts off as Lee leans in for a kiss.

My gut churns as I anticipate it happening, but Beau turns his head at the last moment, and Lee connects with his cheek.

And takes entirely too long to pull away.

"Done yet?" I growl.

Beau pulls away from Lee and smiles. "I'll text you."

And as Beau turns back to me, Lee shoots me a victorious look over his head. Fucker.

"K, bye." I swing the door closed again, and this time, Beau doesn't reopen it.

"What the hell was that?"

"Welcome home, sweetheart."

"Payne."

"Bo-Bo."

He plants his hands on his hips. "Don't Bo-Bo me! You slammed the door in his face. That's just rude."

"And here I was waiting for gratitude."

"Gratitude?" His voice pitches high. "What the hell for?"

"Well, *clearly* the date turned around. If I'd called with an emergency, you never would have had the opportunity to find out how Lee's dinner tasted."

Beau scowls, goes to reply, and then ... stops. "You're right. Thank you."

That's unexpected. "Ah ... sure."

"I'm glad you didn't call." Beau leads the way into the kitchen. "He was a perfect gentleman."

"Good for him."

"And he's a great kisser."

I huff. "What, like it's hard?"

"Well ..." He pins me with his gaze. "Some people are too sloppy."

"That better not have been directed at me."

"I didn't mention you." Beau blinks at me innocently. "Guilty conscience?"

"We both know I can kiss."

"Right." He pats my arm as he steps around me. "Keep telling yourself that."

"The fuck ..." I follow him down the hall to his room, where Beau strips off, unconcerned about me standing there watching him.

"I'm about to be naked any minute now ..."

I narrow my eyes. "Why are you like this?"

"Like what?"

"All ..." *Relaxed. Playful.* Oh, fuck. "You guys hooked up, didn't you?"

"Wow. Judgy much?"

"Did you?"

He whirls on me, shirt open, belt hanging loose, and stalks closer. "What's it to you?"

"I ... well ..."

He cocks his head. "Careful, Payne. Someone sounds jealous."

"And someone is avoiding answering the question." Two can play at his game. I step forward, leaning into his space. "Afraid to tell me you sucked his cock?"

"Is it any of your business?" Beau presses forward, his chest against mine, and walks me backward until I'm in the hall. "Great talking with you, but if you don't mind, I'm beat."

He doesn't make a move to step back though.

And neither do I.

We stand there, gazes locked, his body warmth seeping into my shirt and his bodywash filling my nose. He isn't fidgeting. The calmness throws me. Hollows out my stomach as I think of the reason he might be so calm, the reason he's meeting my eyes head-on. Lee. Lee's hands on him. Lee's mouth. His tongue.

My gaze drops. Beau's lips are wet. Can he still *taste* him?

I want to find out.

If I lean down and kiss him, will he let me? Or has the crush run its course?

I inch closer. Lips tingling. Nose almost touching his.

Beau sucks in a breath that brushes my skin, and I want to ask him to do it again. To catch it with my mouth this time.

But I can't.

No matter how foggy with alcohol I am, no matter how confused I might be, no matter how much I might hate Lee, I'm not a selfish person.

And kissing Beau right now, as hot as it would be, would be beyond selfish.

I can't hurt him.

So instead of closing the few inches between our lips, I say, "I thought you were going to bed."

His nose brushes mine. "Join me."

"Beau ..."

The tip of his tongue darts out and swipes my lip. "It's okay. No feelings."

And him saying that at all proves it's bullshit.

"No."

Beau jerks back, and the hurt that flashes across his face gets me right in the chest. He eyes me for a moment, then turns around, stalks into his room, and slams the door behind him.

If I'm hoping the next morning that everything will be forgotten about like it was last weekend, I'm very, very wrong. The moment I walk into the kitchen, Beau walks out of it without even a good-morning.

Well, fuck me. I knew I was going to screw this up at some point.

My head is too dusty to deal with this shit.

I make a coffee, then go and join him in the living room. "Can I sit?" I ask, nodding to the place next to him on the couch.

His feet bounce, so he definitely heard me, but his lack of answer doesn't seem good.

I sit anyway, keeping more distance between us than I normally would. "I'm sorry."

"For?" he asks like he can't stop himself.

"For being a dick to your date."

"Whose name is ..."

I huff. "Lee. His name is Lee."

Beau's lips twitch, and fucking hell the relief that flows through me is intense. "Is that all you're sorry for?"

"Okay, full disclosure ..." I scoot closer. "I'm not actually sorry for that. I don't like him, he's not good enough for you, and if we relived last night, I'd probably do it again."

"Then—"

"I'm sorry for the stuff that came after. Outside your room. Almost kissing you."

His inhale is sharp and loud. "You ... that was ..."

I wait him out.

"I wasn't sure what that was."

I give him a sad smile. "That was me not being fair to you."

"What do you mean?"

"You made how you feel clear, and I'll admit when I look at you, I ..." Fuck, I don't even know how to say it. "I think you're gorgeous, and I think you're amazing, but I don't know where *I'm* at. It's not fair of me to lead you on."

"When did you lead me on?"

Is he not listening? "Last night."

"No, you already told me where you were at. You don't want a relationship—that's fair after what you've been through. But you said you still want to hook up. Why can't we do that?"

"Because it might hurt you."

"And I can't decide that?" He turns to me fully, drawing one leg up underneath him. "You're the one who said last night that I need to be more assertive, so how's this for assertiveness? I wanted you to kiss me. And then I would have dragged you inside my room, stripped you naked, swallowed your cock, and had you fuck me into the mattress.

And this morning when I woke up, I would have felt incredible and had no regrets. You want to know how I woke up instead?"

I'm gaping at him, unable to answer after what just came out of his damn mouth.

"Instead, I woke up feeling like shit for pretending I liked when Lee kissed me and worried that I scared you off instead."

There's so much there to break down, but all I can focus on is "You ... didn't like it?"

"He backed me into the door and kissed me before I knew what was happening. Thank fuck you opened it."

"Asshole," I snarl. "So, why did you pretend you liked it, then?"

"To try and make you jealous, but after everything you've been through, I never should have done it. I feel terrible."

I get what he's saying, but even while trying to make me jealous, he was so ... uncommitted to it. He just admitted that he was one hundred percent ready to take me to bed, and when I look at Beau, all I can see is a man so steadfast in his ... whatever he thinks of me. And even with his terrible attempt at making me jealous, he feels bad.

Beau is a *good* guy. A seriously good, pure guy.

And it's just occurring to me now exactly how far out of my league he is.

I laugh into my hands. "So you're not going to see him again?"

"Nope. I already sent him a text thanking him for the date but making it clear I wasn't after another one."

"Well done."

"No need to sound so smug."

"Sorry, but ..." I rub my chin. "I don't know why everyone thought it would work."

"To be fair, he didn't sound douchey at all with his texts. And the things that annoyed me probably never would have come up with anyone else."

"I knew he wasn't good enough for you."

"Yeah, I'm sure."

"Seriously. *A gold pin*. On his *blazer*."

"He only tipped ten percent too. After whining all night about poor service ..." Beau trails off. "The date was horrible. He tried to give me a handie in the theatre."

"Is he a teenager?" I ask, trying to hold back the jealousy that rears up at hearing that. "Did you let him?"

"Believe it or not, that one I *could* say no to." Beau taps his fingers on his thigh. "Still, trying to convince him *not here* wasn't code for let's go to your car and make out wasn't easy." He meets my stare. "You're right. I need to get better at telling people no."

"You do."

"Starting now."

I groan. "You're not supposed to use this new super-power on *me*." But even though I joke, it feels sort of good to know that I'm one of the few people Beau is comfortable enough around to do it.

"I'm not going to let you tell me what's good for me. I

don't care if it's a rebound thing for you, but sex is on the table. You want it, you take it. We're both single. We both like each other. I promise it won't get messy, because I've had these feelings for a long time, and I've kept them in check."

"But—"

"Nope. You're not in charge of the way I feel. That's up to me. And the way I feel is that I'd like to see your cock again. Many times. Maybe we even send a video to your ex of us going at it. And I wish I could say that was a joke, but I know how much it'd piss him off that I got to sleep with you when he knew about my crush the whole time."

My eyebrows shoot up. "He did?"

"He did." Beau grins cheekily. "And he hated it."

"Like he had ground to stand on."

"Right?"

We fall silent as I think about what Beau is offering. Hot sex, no expectations. But I can't trust his assurance that he won't get hurt. That's not something he can control.

"I just don't—"

Beau holds up his hand. "Don't answer right now. You don't actually need to give me an answer at all. Just know that if one day you decide you want to fuck me, I'm here."

"Fucking hell ..."

He shuffles closer, blue eyes bright. "Now that's out of the way, can you teach me how to make those paper cranes?"

The question is so unexpected that I immediately agree. And that's how we spend our Saturday. Last night forgotten, both of us ignoring our phones, and going through almost a whole pad of Post-it notes until the living room is covered with bright yellow paper birds.

It's peaceful, and maybe this is what Art meant about taking my time. Instead of fighting the nerves that hit every time our eyes meet, I embrace them. I let myself have fun and get close to him. I could listen to him talk for days.

Beau finishes the crane he's folding and sends it sailing my way. I snatch it carefully from the air and inspect his work, finding there, on the wing, a sneaky little love heart.

My gut gives a tiny flip, and a smile shoots across my face.

We both pretend not to notice.

Chapter Twenty

BEAU

My body has tripped back to kinda nocturnal but mostly fucked-up mode, so after the weekend, I barely see Payne. I'm up and down through the night and day and end up crashing hard over the afternoon when he's home.

It sets me on edge because after our talk, things feel fragile between us.

When I wake up after midnight on Wednesday ... well, Thursday, I guess, I find Payne passed out on the couch. His mouth is hanging open, and his light brown hair is splayed across his face and the cushion he's lying on. He looks adorable.

And also, ridiculously uncomfortable.

I creep over and kneel in front of him before brushing the hair back off his forehead. He makes me feel so soft and happy, but I meant what I told him. If we keep hooking up, I'd never expect it to lead to more. I can be his rebound and die happy with that.

"Payne?"

He grunts, snuffles a little, and turns his face into my palm.

"*Payne?*"

"Wha's happening ... huh?" He jolts awake, eyes unfocused as he blinks my face into view. "Bo-Bo. I missed you." His voice is heavy with sleep, and I'm not convinced he's fully awake, but I want to bottle his words. They're like sunshine.

"I missed you too, man. But it's late, and you have to be up early."

He yawns widely and checks the time on his phone with one eye squeezed closed. "Fuck, I must have drifted off. I tried waiting up."

I peck him on the nose, just because I want to, then grab his hands and help haul him to his feet. "Bedtime for you."

"K." But before I can let him go, he closes his arms around me and pulls me close. "Night, Bo-Bo."

I can still feel him even after he releases me and staggers down the hall.

My heart swells.

But I'm sure he's going to kill me with wanting.

How, *how* did Kyle give that man up?

If I ever see him again, I'm going to make sure he remembers exactly what he's missing.

I try to stay awake until six so I can see Payne before he

leaves for work, but by four, I'm exhausted. I crash, and when I'm up again, he's long gone. At least it'll be the weekend soon and I will finally get to see him again, because him saying he misses me makes me miss him more.

I'm still foggy with sleep when I stumble into the kitchen and grab my morning mug from the cupboard, so it takes me a second to register what I'm seeing.

A yellow crane. In my cup.

I pluck it out and read the words *good morning, sunshine* written along the wing. It comes with me to my desk, and every time I glimpse it through the day, my smile is out of control. Words are flowing on a stupid piece about unrequited love, and I'm having so much fun with it, the usual guilt about not focusing on my book is absent.

I sit on my balcony for lunch, looking up at Kill Pen that looms over the hilly streets dotted with magnolia trees.

I take an extra-long shower where I don't even jerk off.

I cook dinner, then wrap half and put it in the fridge, along with another crane that says, *I hope you had a good day*, followed by a heart.

The next day, when I find cranes hidden in random places all over the house, I'm not sure what this is, but know it's *something*.

Maybe it's fragile, and maybe it amounts to nothing, and maybe it means more to me than it does to Payne, but every crane I find through the day and night gets pressed flat and put in my drawer, where I can easily retrieve them and read the notes.

I dreamed we went to the beach together last night.

Ford showed me how to change brake pads yesterday.

Your smile is amazing.

I hope your muse hits soon.

I'll pick up milk on the way home.

Everything from cute to funny to FYIs makes me grin like an idiot, and I'm so happy he's not home to see me find these things.

Half an hour before I'm due to meet Marty, I shower, change, then head out. And when I get to the Killer Brew, I find Payne leaning against the wall by the door. His strong legs are planted wide, hands tucked into the pockets of his shorts.

"Hey," I say.

"Hi."

"What are you ..." I glance around, but he's still watching me. "Shouldn't you be at work?"

"I asked to take a late lunch since I knew you'd be catching up with Marty."

"Damn, I'm predictable."

"There's *nothing* predictable about you. I like it."

I shiver, and it makes his face light up. "Is that your nice way of calling me weird?"

"Damn, Beau," he says, following me inside. "Enough with the weirdness shit."

I order three coffees, and Payne doesn't say anything about me paying. I've never realized before how much I love that. We step aside to wait, and I give him a shy look. "I guess we both failed."

He scoffs. "I don't fail at anything."

"The deal was if you move in, you help me be normal."

"Normal is boring." He gives me a look that dares me to argue. "But what did *you* fail at?"

"The deal I made with myself is that I'd use this chance to get to know you better, then pick at your faults like I do with every other guy, and it would make me get over you."

"You talk about your feelings so easily."

It's a lot harder than he thinks. I shift. "Well, uh, it's not a secret anymore. We both know. I'm not embarrassed."

"Well, if it helps, you were always going to fail."

"I was?"

"Of course." He snorts. "I don't have faults."

I know he's joking, but he's absolutely correct about that. Our order is up, and we grab the coffees, then head over to meet Marty.

"You should join us every week," I say.

He shakes his head. "Nah, this is yours and Marty's thing. I'll only impose this once."

"Why? Because you missed me?" I tease.

His gaze finds mine. "I did."

"Me too." Then I press my coffee to my lips so he can't see the way he's made me smile.

Marty's waiting in the usual spot, and he lights up when he sees Payne with me. "Where did you find this guy?"

"Lurking around a coffee shop."

I watch them hug, and it makes me happy that their affection hasn't changed from when we were kids. Payne's never been that older brother who acted embarrassed by Marty.

"We're not going to have to put up with you every week now, are we?" Marty asks.

Payne clutches his chest like he's wounded. "The love ... It hurts ..."

"Beau sees you enough at home. I doubt he wants your ugly mug cutting into this time too."

Actually, Beau does want his ugly mug cutting into any and all time. But I know what they both mean. This is the only time Marty and I actually get solo.

"Please." Payne slings an arm around my shoulders. "Beau loves me."

"Like a hole in the head, maybe." Marty nods in the direction we usually walk. "Come on, I want to get my steps in before I need to get back. We can't all have fast metabolisms."

Payne lifts the bottom of his Ford's Garage polo, revealing his lightly sculpted abs. "Don't know what you mean."

I whack him, and he releases me.

Payne clears his throat. "Actually, I have news."

"Yeah?" The wide smile he's wearing should set me at ease but instead makes me nervous.

"We got an offer on the apartment, and as of an hour ago, it's sold."

"Shit, that's great," Marty says.

I go to agree, but my stomach gets tight and distracts me.

"Yeah." Payne runs a hand through his hair. "I feel great, you know? Like, things are starting to happen for me." He catches my eye. "Good things."

Good things? The dread loosens. "I'm really happy for you."

Even if I have no idea what that means for our living arrangements, it doesn't matter. If Payne's happy, that's all I need.

We walk along, with Payne filling us in on how his week has been at the garage, and the whole time, I can tell that Marty wants to ask me something. I already know it will be about Lee, and I'm dreading it. Maybe Payne feels the questions coming too, though, because he doesn't let Marty get a word in.

"And the number of times I pick up something covered in oil when—"

"Fascinating," Marty says over the top of him. "But that's enough work talk for one day. Beau, how was your date last weekend? And that's mostly rhetorical because Lee has been walking around the office like a kicked puppy."

Ouch. I should never have agreed to go out with him. That wasn't fair. But I also called him immediately after to let him know there wasn't anything there between us. It was one date, where he shouldn't have wanted to see me again either, so the moping is a bit overboard.

"How does that look exactly?" Payne asks. "Like is he limping? Whimpering? Staggering sideways?"

"Sad, Payne. He's *sad*."

"And why is that Beau's problem?"

"And why is this *your* business?" Marty turns back to me. "Come on, out with it. What was wrong with this one?"

I don't want to answer because anything I say will sound

like I'm making excuses, but Marty won't let this drop. "He ordered for me. Stuff I didn't like."

"Uh-huh."

"And he wouldn't stop touching me."

Marty jerks back. "Like, inappropriately?"

"No, just ... my hand and my back and my face."

"It was a date. What was he supposed to do? Build a twenty-foot wall between you?"

"If Beau doesn't want to be touched, he shouldn't be touched, end of story."

Marty levels Payne with a look. "He told me about *you*. An asshole? Since when are *you* an asshole? What was up with that?"

Payne shrugs and turns away, leaving Marty to eye him for a second before refocusing back on me.

"Did you ask him not to touch you?"

"Well, no, but I kept moving away."

"Beau ..."

"And he was grumpy when the restaurant was taking too long."

"*I* get grumpy when the restaurant takes too long." He pauses to take a sip of his coffee, but I can hear him thinking. "I don't understand. You say you want to find someone, but I set you up with these great guys, and you don't give any of them a chance."

Payne snorts.

We both ignore him.

"I guess I was wrong. I like being single. *Available*," I throw in for Payne's benefit, but I drop my gaze to where

I'm spinning my cup in my hands so I don't have to see either of their expressions. "Not everyone is built for a relationship, and I'm learning that I'm okay with that. I'm not the dating kind. And that's *fine*. I love my life, with or without someone to share it with."

Let's see if I'm still saying that once Payne moves out and finds his own place.

"Okay, no more setting you up."

"Thank you." When I'm brave enough to look back up, Marty's giving me a soft smile.

"As long as you're happy, I'm happy."

"Good. Because I'm actually really, really happy."

Marty turns to look at the water, and I take the chance to glance at Payne. He's already watching me, lips bunched in confusion, so I nudge my shoulder against his.

His expression doesn't change, and at first I worry what it means, but then ...

Payne's hand closes over my nape. He squeezes gently, skin warm, and his fingers skim my hairline as he pulls away.

Butterflies explode in my gut.

They stick around for the whole walk.

I try to wait up for Payne to get home from work, but I end up crashing, and when I wake again, it's 1:00 a.m. Sighing, I haul ass out to my desk, surprisingly well rested and ready to write.

But before I can sit down, my gaze catches on my shelf.

The first book is back, and the second is missing, and there in its place is a yellow crane.

Grinning, I pull it down, but when I read the words, my heart stops.

You're the most perfectly un-normal person I've ever met.

I didn't fail.

There was nothing to improve.

When my heart starts again, it explodes.

I drop the crane.

And head for Payne's room.

Chapter Twenty-One

PAYNE

My door slamming open jolts me awake, and I blink into the darkness to find Beau standing there.

"What time is it?" I ask.

He ignores my question. "Perfectly un-normal?"

It takes me a second to remember I wrote that. All I know is that this week, I'd needed that connection with him, even if we didn't see each other, and getting those cranes back made my heart feel full. "Ah, yeah ..."

"Even when I'm nervous and don't know what to say?"

"Of course." It's adorable.

"And when I ask strange questions?" His voice cracks as he steps closer.

The intensity in his stare has me answering. "They're entertaining."

"And when you find I've taken over the living area with

every piece of furniture in the house?" Beau's final step brings his thighs into contact with my bed.

My heartbeat kicks up a notch, and I find myself answering honestly. "I think moments like that are my favorite."

Beau doesn't respond. He isn't nervously fidgeting. He's ... calm. Certain.

He leans forward and crawls on my bed. The air is humming between us. "I want to kiss you."

Fuck, I want that too.

"Beau ..." I want it so much more than I can ever tell him.

He lowers himself so his chest rests on mine. He's warm. Solid. His breath puffs against my lips. "I'm *going* to kiss you. Unless you tell me to stop."

"I ..."

"Yeah?"

"I *should* tell you that." But my lips are already tingling with anticipation.

He brushes his nose against mine. "So say it."

"Beau ..." My skin feels too tight. Too tense. His scent is filling my nose and sending rational thought from my brain until all I can concentrate on is the thrumming need racing through me, begging me to get closer to him. Goddamn him. "I *can't*."

His mouth slams against mine.

My grunt is immediately swallowed by the heated kiss. I need this. Every part of me has been begging for it. Just another taste, another touch, another night with his skin against mine. Only this time I want to make it a whole night. This time I want to be pressed against him *everywhere.*

I tighten my arms around him and flip us so Beau is on his back. The sheet falls off my waist, and this time when I cover him, our bodies line up exactly.

Our kissing turns deep, hungry. I can't get enough of his mouth. I have enough self-control to pull back long enough to shove his T-shirt over his head, and then I'm on him again. I bite his plump, pink lips, making them look swollen and wrecked. Marking them as mine. My tongue surges into the back of his mouth, and Beau's fingers tighten in my hair, the arm around my back holding me closer as he wraps his legs around my waist and pins me to him.

"I need these off," I growl into his mouth, and I yank at the waistband of his sweats. There are too many clothes between us.

"I'll lose these if you lose your boxers."

"Deal."

I push onto my knees and shove my underwear down as Beau wriggles out of his remaining clothes. He flops back onto the bed, and I hungrily drink in his long, manly body, hairy thighs, and hard cock. He's fucking beautiful.

I want to devour him.

But even as lust drunk as I am, there's still that niggling voice in the back of my mind, warning me to be careful with him. "You sure this is okay?" I ask as I slide off his glasses and set them on my nightstand.

"Ask me that again and I'll sac-whack you."

I laugh despite myself, then lie over him again. We both

let out a soft moan as skin meets skin. Beau's eyes are sleepy, looking at me with that same hazy focus as last time. It drives me wild to see him like this. I shift so our cocks line up and give a roll of my hips.

"Holy shit that feels good."

I lower my mouth to his neck and trail openmouthed kisses down to his shoulder, where I suck a mark into his skin.

"More," Beau says.

"Yeah?"

"Cover me in them."

I don't question him, because his answer goes deeper than wanting to remember a hookup. And if I'm honest with myself, it does for me as well. With every mark I suck into his skin, each bruised circle I leave behind, I'm hit with a surge of satisfaction at making him mine ... and also a twinge of regret that he's not really.

Beau is ... *perfectly un-normal*, which makes him fucking perfect to me. He deserves someone who can give him the world, and while my feelings are building to a point I can't deny them anymore, I'm so worried I'm getting them confused with a rebound. Then we'll hook up a few times, and that will be it for me.

I don't have a lot of regrets in my life, but hurting Beau would be the biggest one.

Things are still too messy.

My emotions too fragile.

I want to be able to tell Beau I'm all in, but I'm not there yet, and I'm scared I never will be, no matter how bad I want it.

"Tell me what you want," I murmur, licking his nipple.

"I want you to fuck me."

"Oh, shit yes." I crawl back up the bed to give him another long, filthy kiss. "Can I taste you first?"

He whimpers and nods fast, looking as desperate for it as I am.

I kneel up and grab his hip, rolling him onto his front. I haven't had the chance to notice Beau's ass, but I'm sure as hell noticing it now. It's firm and round, a perfect bubble I want to sink my teeth into, so I lean down and do exactly that.

Beau hisses.

I bite him again.

Then suck a bruise there too, and then another. I leave a trail of them over his ass cheek until I reach his crease, then bury my face in his ass. Beau twitches, then immediately parts his legs and arches up toward me. It's the sexiest fucking sight to see him offering himself like that, and I can't hold back. I pull his cheeks apart, exposing his hole, and then close my mouth over it.

"Holy shit, Payne ..." His words come out on a long whine, and it only spurs me on.

I give his hole all the attention I can manage, getting high off the feeling. My cock is begging me to get on with it, to sink inside him, but while I can't wait to fuck him into the mattress, I'm also pretty goddamn eager to get him to make more of those needy sounds for me.

I lick and suck and nip at his flesh until he softens enough for me to work my tongue inside. I moan, fucking loving this. It's been way too long since I've been so consumed by another person.

I should have known my marriage had issues well before I did. *He* never responded to me like this.

Beau reaches around to grasp my hair as he rocks his hips back. "I think ... I think ... I think ..." His rough voice is high-pitched and needy. Desperate. I love that he can't get his words out.

I withdraw my tongue and replace it with my finger instead. "Tell me."

"I think you need to stop," he begs.

"Why?" For a hot second, I'm worried I've gone too far when he replies.

"Because I'm so goddamn close, and I want you inside me when I come." He scrambles away from me, yanks open my dresser, and tosses my lube back to me.

I snap it open and pour some over my fingers, filling his ass with two this time, and he continues to search. "Where are they?"

"What?"

"Your condoms."

I freeze. "Fuck. I forgot about those. I don't have any. Where are yours?"

Beau face-plants into the bed. "I think you're underestimating how long it's been since I had sex."

Oh, fuck no. "Should ... should one of us duck out, or ..."

I go to remove my fingers when Beau makes a noise of protest and grabs my wrist.

"I ... I used to be on PrEP. Back when I was hooking up a lot. I've had tests since, and they were all clear."

Is he ... does he mean ... "Me too. Since I found out about ... you know. I got tested. Twice. All negative." Plus we hadn't had sex for a while before it ended.

He peers back at me over his shoulder, tongue swiping over his bottom lip. "I'm fine with it if you are."

I press another finger in, and he gasps at the intrusion before pushing back to meet me.

"I'm ready."

I grab the lube again and cover my cock as Beau repositions in the middle of the bed. I blanket his body, chest to his back, and press my nose into the hair behind his ear to greedily inhale his scent. "Any man you've ever dated would be lucky to be where I am."

"I never wanted any of them. Not like this."

I almost agree. Almost tell him that I've never had someone respond to my touch the way he does. I've never had another man driven completely crazy over being with me. There's lust, and there are hookups with hot sex. Some of it is exaggerated, some of it isn't. But as soon as it's over, that neediness disappears.

It's not like that with Beau.

Because the need isn't all physical.

But I can't lie and say it wasn't like that with my ex, at least in the beginning. Though it's been so long now, it's hard to remember.

And right now, all I want to focus on is Beau.

I guide my cock toward his hole and slowly sink inside. He's so tight my toes curl, and my teeth latch onto his ear. When I bottom out, I need to pause for a minute, otherwise things are going to be over before they get started. If I'm lucky, I'll have a round two in me tonight, but since it's not a guarantee, I'm going to make the most of this.

I start out slow, each rock of my hips gentle and deliberate, feeling the way Beau's body grips me and sucks me back in. My lips find his neck as I take my time, drawing out every second from this moment and trying to make it last. I love this feeling. Filling another man. And knowing it's Beau makes this moment deeper than it should be.

Then he reaches around and slaps my ass.

"*Argh.*"

"Fuck me like you mean it." His sexy rasp pools in my balls.

"Gladly." I grab his hips and pull him up onto his hands and knees, then let loose.

Beau takes my pounding by meeting every thrust, and I fuck the most delicious sounds out of him. His hands have tightened in my bedsheets, sweat is prickling along my spine, and the pornographic noises that fill the room are making it hard to concentrate on anything other than the need to blow my load.

The sight of him bent over and taking my cock, head thrown back and tilted so I get a glimpse of those puffy, parted lips, is sending me crazy. I never want this to end. I've never been so thankful I learned origami in my life.

I have no idea if we'll do this again after tonight, but if Beau offers it, I'm there. Because how the hell do I say no to this man? For anything? Ever?

And somehow, this feels a thousand times more intimate than anything I've ever done before.

I slide my hand over Beau's ribs, then pull him up against me. My arms wrap securely around his torso, and I plant one foot on the bed. Then I grind deep inside him.

"You love this, don't you?" I ask.

"Mmm ..."

"Tell me how much you love taking my cock. How much you love me fucking you."

"It's ... I never ... never ... umm, shit. Wow." He's panting, babbling words that don't make sense.

I hold up my hand to his mouth. "Spit."

He does without question. Then I hold him tight with one arm across his chest and wrap my other hand around his cock.

Beau's head drops back on my shoulder with a moan. I stroke him in time with my thrusts, this time aiming for his prostate and pegging it over and over. His string of nonsensical words is fucking music, and I beg my body to hold out. Just a bit longer. A bit longer.

"I'm ... I'm so close ..." he pants.

"Me too." With a last rush of energy, I give him everything I have. My balls slap against his ass, and I'm getting sweaty, overheated, and so damn close.

Beau picks up speed, fucking himself desperately on my cock, and I jerk him as fast as I can until his cock pulses in my hand, and he unleashes. His ass clamps tight, sending me off rhythm as pleasure races from my spine to my balls, and my orgasm crashes into me. I grip Beau close and bury myself as deep as I can while I spill my load inside him.

It feels in-fucking-credible.

Slowly, my breathing returns to normal, and we collapse onto the bed, me gripping him tight so I don't slip out.

"What are you doing?" he asks, wrapping a hand back to play with my hair.

"Waiting to see if I can go again."

Chapter Twenty-Two

BEAU

Waking up with Payne's arm wrapped around me, his dried cum over my ass and between my legs, I expect things to be awkward. But when he notices I'm awake, he gives me a quick kiss, slaps my ass, and throws his legs off the side of the bed.

"Up you get, sleepyhead."

I turn and bury my face into his pillow. If I get up, it's over. And I stayed awake for as long as I could to get the most out of our night. The second time he fucked me was slower, longer, more kissing and touching, less desperate pounding.

I'm torn over which was best.

I also don't care.

Because the ache in my ass is amazing.

There's only so long I can put it off, and when the smell

of bacon cooking reaches me, I know it's time to give up. I drag my ass out of bed, shower the smell of sex off my skin, then join him in the kitchen.

I watch him move around with confidence, cracking eggs and flipping pancakes. He's got a feast set up for us. When he slides my plate over to me, I take it in with wide eyes.

"This is a lot of food."

He shrugs where he's standing across the island from me and takes a bite out of a sausage. "Sex makes me hungry."

"I bet. I don't think I've taken that kind of pounding in my life."

Payne's laugh sounds completely normal, which is a relief. "Maybe next time you can do me?"

"Really?" I'm not sure what look I'm wearing, but dear fucking fuck, he cannot drop that on me over breakfast while I'm still tired as hell.

"Sure. I love bottoming, but ..." He cringes.

"Yeah?"

"My ex would never."

"Kyle didn't top? But ..." I think back to that disgusting video. Is there some kind of etiquette when it comes to pointing out his husband didn't mind topping *them*?

"*Yeeep.* Apparently it was only off the table when it came to me. That's definitely not going to make a guy self-conscious or anything."

"He was an idiot."

"Thanks. I know." Payne puffs out a breath. "Just ... that was maybe what pissed me off the most."

"Good for me though," I say, wanting to distract him.

"It is?"

"Yeah. Just think about how tight you're going to be."

He cracks up laughing.

"Can we go again now?" I ask.

"Holy shit, there is no way that's happening." He rubs his dick through his pants. "This thing is down and out for a bit longer. You're only four years younger than me—there's no way you can tell me you're good to go again already."

I shift back so he can see where my dick is thickening. "What can I say? He likes you."

"Eat your breakfast."

"Fine." I roll my eyes, like this whole thing is such an inconvenience, but he's feeding me and offering more sex. If that isn't the best morning ever, I'm out of ideas for what is.

"And stop looking at me like that."

"Like what?" I blink up at him and he lets out a shaky breath.

"Damn, Bo-Bo."

Neither of us say anything for a moment, then he clears his throat and looks away.

"I have to duck over to Marty's today and pick up my mail. You want to come?"

"Come ..."

"For a *drive*, horndog."

I should work. I really should. This week I've been even more distracted than usual. But I also don't want to be separated from him yet. "Sure."

We finish breakfast, then rinse our dishes and go change.

Payne might have failed at the "pointing out my flaws" part of our arrangement, but he's kept this place spotless, and having him here makes me more conscious of picking up after myself as well.

Neither of us brings up what sleeping together means, but I keep my expectations low. I told him we could have sex without me wanting more, and I'm sure as hell going to stick to that. Payne has enough to work out in his life without me adding the pressure of a relationship as well.

For right now, I'm happy to see what happens and to be there for Payne however he needs me to be.

As soon as we walk into Marty's place, Bridget and Soph jump into the hall and fire Nerf bullets at us. I duck behind Payne, holding him in front of me like a shield, and when the bullets finally stop and the noise dies down, I glance up to find him staring at me. Completely unimpressed.

"Good to know if we're ever mugged on a dark street corner, I can count on you."

"Hey, when it comes to kids, it's every man for himself."

"Or ... we could combine forces against them."

"I'm listening."

He glances over at our giggling nieces and says, "I'll take the big one, you get the little one."

"You're on."

Sensing danger, the girls take off as we lunge at them, but Payne scoops Bridget off her feet, and I nab Soph a second later.

I swing her wriggling body over my shoulder and carry

her out into the living area. "Where do you want this monster?"

Lizzy waves a hand. "Just throw it in the backyard. We don't need any monster messes in here, thanks."

"Backyard it is."

"No," Soph screeches between laughter, struggling against my hold. "I'm not a monster."

"One monster for the backyard, here we go." I drop her outside and slide the door closed behind her.

"Uncle Bo-Bo!"

I cup my ear. "Sorry, I can't hear you!"

"Let me in!"

"Not by the hair on my chinny-chin-chin."

"See? You can hear her," Bridget points out.

"Okay, smarty-pants." I relent and open the door again.

Soph glares at me. "That wasn't funny."

"It was for me."

Payne puts Bridget down again. "Go pick up your toys."

"*Fine.*" They both run off.

"Geez, two seconds with them and I'm exhausted already," Payne says.

"You need to build up your stamina." I don't realize how those words sound until they leave my mouth, but thankfully Lizzy and Marty don't pick up on it. Or at the way Payne lifts an eyebrow in my direction.

Marty picks up a stack of envelopes and drops them on the table. "All yours."

Payne pulls out a chair and sits down before flipping through the pile. "Who said being an adult is a fun time?"

Well, what we did last night was damn fun.

"Hey, Beau, come help me with this?" Lizzy asks. Her tone isn't subtle. At all. Luckily, Marty and Payne are both chatting and don't notice.

I follow Lizzy down the hall when she spins suddenly and crosses her arms. "How's Lee?"

I should have known this was coming. "Don't act like Marty didn't tell you."

"Of course he did. He also said you're suddenly totally happy being single, and neither of us believes that for a second. So spill."

"There's nothing to spill." Except that I want to be single so Payne can fuck me as much as he wants.

She pins me with her mom-stare. The one that makes me want to confess my deepest sins. "It's Payne, isn't it?"

"What's in pain?"

"Funny, but that was basically a yes."

"Does it matter what the reason is? I don't want to date. And whether Payne was here or not, I wouldn't want to date Lee."

"And I'm not saying to date someone you don't like. I'd never want that for you." She uncrosses her arms. "I just don't want to see you spending your whole life pining after him."

"Maybe I want that."

"There's no way you—"

"How do you know?" It feels weird to push back, especially about this. "At the moment, we're spending time together, we live together, and we're getting to

237

know each other more. You don't know it could never happen."

"If Payne was smart, it would. You'd never treat him like … well, you know. But from what Marty says, a relationship isn't even on his radar, and if you keep holding out for him, you're going to get hurt."

I plant my hands on her shoulders. "I love you. *Both* of you. Because I know this worry comes from love, and that's great, but I also need you to trust me. If I get hurt, I'm doing it with my eyes wide open. I'm not naive. I know it'll probably never happen. And that's fine. But give me space to fuck this up on my own."

"You're not filling me with confidence."

I laugh and kiss her on the head. "I'm a big boy. I'll be fine."

"*Jesus fucking Christ!*"

We both jump at the loud voice and exchange wary looks. Payne does not sound happy. And when we return to the main living area, I find him with his hand buried in his hair, staring down at a piece of paper.

Marty looks pissed.

"What is it?"

I move closer, and Payne hands over the paperwork he's holding.

Divorce papers.

With a note clipped to the front saying, *I won't do this unless it's in person.*

"That fuck!"

"Uncle Bo-Bo said a bad word," Soph says in the doorway.

Lizzy crosses her arms. "Sometimes those bad words are needed—when you're an adult. Go and play with your sister."

Soph looks from her mom to Marty to Payne. Then she darts across the room and climbs into his lap.

His back stiffens for a second before he wraps an arm around her. "Thanks, sweetie. I'm okay now."

She doesn't leave though.

It's taking all of my self-control not to go on a rant. "When did you last see him?" I ask.

"Before ... before it all went down."

"You haven't since?"

"Nope. I stayed at a friend's place in Boston and made it clear that if he came near me at work, I'd let the school know about his extracurricular activities."

"Why the fu—why now? What's his game plan here?"

"I have no idea."

"Are you going to do it?" Marty asks.

"I ... I don't know." Payne pinches his nose.

"You could ignore it," I suggest. "There's no rush here. Give it a bit of time, and once there's some distance, it might be easier then."

"I don't want anything tying me to that ... *man*."

It's lucky he has Soph to hug because otherwise I probably would have folded him in my arms already. He looks so lost, staring at the paper and Kyle's stupid note, and I want to fix it. To make it better. I can't do that here, and it sucks that literally no one in this room knows what he means to me.

Not Marty, not Payne, not Lizzy, and fuck, sometimes not even me.

The thing about loving someone is you don't get to do it with conditions attached. I don't love him, expecting him to return it. I don't love him, hoping I'll get over it, or that I can transfer that love to someone else.

I just *love* him.

I'm starting to realize that maybe that's enough. It's not the easiest option, but it's the one that makes me happy.

Chapter Twenty-Three

PAYNE

"Turn into this driveway up here," Beau says.

I don't question him, just switch on my turn signal and follow his instructions. It's a gravel driveway, and Beau tells me to keep going all the way to the end. "Where are we?"

"Don't worry, no one lives here. This block has been for sale for months." He unclips his seat belt, then whacks my thigh for me to do the same.

I have no idea what we're doing here.

I want to go home, face-plant on my bed, and ignore the world for the rest of the day.

Beau's waiting for me in front of the car, and when I reach him, he immediately steps forward and wraps me in his arms. Like that, some of the stress loosens its hold.

My hands find his lower back, and I tilt my face down to smile into his shoulder. "What's this?"

"You looked like you could use it."

"You're not wrong."

His fingers play with the hair at the back of my neck, and neither of us moves for a long moment. Holding him close, breathing him in, it settles me like nothing else can. He's quickly becoming my rock, and I wish I could be the same for him.

When he loosens his hold, I let him go reluctantly.

Then look around.

The driveway has a dense wood pressing on one side and a large open paddock on the other. More trees cut off the view of the road we were just on, and the land goes past another tree line and toward the mountains a half mile away.

"Want to go for a walk?" Beau asks, nodding toward the field.

"Are we allowed?"

He grins and heads toward the timber fence separating the driveway from the paddock. "Who's going to stop us?"

Good point.

Apart from the occasional car passing back on the road, it feels cut off from the rest of Kilborough, like it's a secret oasis away from the always busy town center. Birds call to each other from the trees, dragonflies skip over the longish grass, and when we round the second tree line, we find a pond with ducks lazily drifting across the surface.

"I didn't even know this place was here," I say. It's nice. Calming.

"I've never been here before." Beau holds up his hand in a wave, and I turn to see what's caught his attention. A man's sitting outside a small stone cottage.

"Shit," I mutter. "I thought you said no one lives here?"

"I think that's Trent Briller. Come on."

We cross the distance to the cottage, and when the man stands, he does look vaguely familiar. He's around our age with a thick beard and a broad hat planted on his head.

"Hey, Beau." His eyes squint up kindly. "What brings you around here?"

"Sorry, I thought the place was empty. We just needed to get outside for a bit."

"It's a good place for it." Trent extends a hand to me. "I think I've seen your face, but ..."

"Payne." I shake his hand.

"Oh, yeah, Marty's brother."

"The one and only."

"What are you doing out here?" Beau asks.

Trent huffs. "Every month we have to come out and mow this son of a bitch, so I usually stay for the weekend and do it in parts." He points toward where the grass is green and clear on the other side of the paddock.

"I'm surprised it hasn't sold yet," I say. "You'd think a developer would have jumped straight on it."

Trent shakes his head. "That other half is protected land because of some of the species that breed in the pond, and the part up front we've been offered a fat sum for, but none of the family wants to let it go and see a bunch of houses or apartments go up."

"I take it you're not in a hurry to sell, then?"

"Yes and no. We want it off our hands, but Kilborough gets bigger every year, I swear, and we prefer knowing that this area is useful for more than just condos."

"But if not a developer, who would want this much land?" Beau asks.

He has a point. It's huge.

"It's good farmland. Maybe a horse-riding school? Not sure, but there has to be someone out there with better ideas than me."

Agreed, because like Trent, I'm not an ideas man. I'll leave the creativity to Beau.

We stay for a while as Beau and Trent catch up and then make our way back to the car. Being out here, getting some perspective away from it all, has settled my annoyance over Kyle's note.

The divorce is going to happen whether he wants it to or not, and it's not as though he can force me to meet with him. I have no idea why he'd even want that, unless he's hoping for a broken nose, because seeing his face again ... there's no telling what I'll do.

Just the sight of his handwriting was enough to almost ruin my day, but it didn't. Because of Beau.

When we get home and walk inside, I'm just debating the best way to grab Beau and drag him to my bedroom when he heads straight to his desk.

"What are you doing?" I ask.

"I've had a cool idea, and I need to get it written before I forget."

Aaand there goes *my* idea, then.

I watch in bemusement as Beau drops into his desk chair, wakes up his computer, and starts hammering away at the words. He loses himself in them completely, not even pausing when I move around the apartment to clean up and pull ingredients out for dinner.

It's funny that he can go from devoting his afternoon to me one minute to completely forgetting I exist the next, and honestly ... I think it's adorable.

Which is weird, because when *that* fucker used to ignore me while he was playing on his phone, I'd get mad. It was rude and disrespectful and rubbed me the wrong way. I guess the joke is on me because he never had any respect for me anyway.

Whereas with Beau ... I know he respects me. He's never told me that, but he hasn't needed to. It's there in the way he acts, the things he does, how he doesn't push me to talk about feelings when after last night, he'd definitely be in the right to.

It would be childish for me to think I'm not feeling something for him. Something bigger than wanting to sleep with him or flirt with him or even be friends. And if he pushed ... what would I tell him? That I can easily see myself falling for him? Because fuck if that isn't true.

I *want* Beau. I want to be the man he finds happiness with. But I can't offer him happiness with this divorce hanging over my head.

It's too distracting. All it took was one note today and I felt like my whole world was coming apart at the seams.

That's not a healthy reaction.

I shouldn't need Beau to fix things. To put me back together.

That sort of need is what makes me doubt my feelings for him are real and not a product of proximity and timing. I've never even thought about Beau in this way before—and as worried as I am about hurting him, I'm just as desperately hoping this is real. That I could be so lucky.

Beau works for hours without a break, and I have no idea how he manages it. My hands would be aching by now.

When dinner is ready, I grab Beau's book that I'm reading and sit on the couch, not wanting to distract him by putting on the TV.

I think I've figured out why Beau wants to live in this world. All his characters have their eccentricities, and none of them are judged for it. They're accepted for exactly who they are.

When I first started reading them, I didn't know what I was getting myself into, so I was relieved when he asked me not to tell him what I thought. If I hated the books and he asked me about them ... well, talk about awkward.

Instead, I love them. I want to tell him how much I love Jaciel and how I think Klein is a bit of a douche, but Tombra is a badass motherfucker, and he and Jaciel should bone already. The more I read, the more I'm convinced it's going to happen too.

I want to ask Beau about it, but I don't want to spoil the ending, so when I reach the last pages and Tombra has just taken Klein, instead of worrying how Jaciel will get him back, all I can think is *good*.

But still ... Beau said Jaciel had to save his love interest, which makes me think he isn't setting up Tombra at all. I swear it's there though. Those two have chemistry for days.

With Beau still tapping away behind me, I open my phone and do a little googling. If his books are as popular as he's said, there should be ...

Damn.

There are a *lot* of fan sites and fan fiction, and ... wow. I do a quick scroll to the bottom of the page, then go back and type *Jaciel and Tombra boning*.

Bingo.

I'm far from the only one who thinks that's where Beau is taking this thing.

I turn on the couch and watch him, dying to ask my question, and thankfully, ten minutes later, his fingers slow and he slumps in his chair.

"How'd you go?"

Beau jumps and swings around. "Shit, I didn't know you were there."

I hold up his book. "Just finished."

"You did?" He hesitates, then reaches over to take it from me and sets it back on the shelf. "I don't want to know."

"You sure?"

He bites his lip.

I wait patiently.

"Urg, fine. Did you hate it? You totally hated it, didn't you?"

"Nope. I mean this with total honesty, and not at all because I want to get in your pants again tonight ... that was fucking incredible."

"Yeah?"

"Yeah." I shift. "Your writing is insane. Like I was there with your characters."

He ducks his head. "Thanks."

This next part is the one I'm cautious bringing up with him. He's the only author I know, so I'm not sure how he'll take my opinions on characters *he's* created. It's not my business to tell him how to write his books.

"Looked like you got some good words in," I say instead.

He nods, eyes drifting toward his computer again. "A couple thousand. That scene came easily."

"What was it about?"

"When we were out at that land and Trent was talking about how it could be used, it reminded me of how I wanted to write a scene with a full training facility for Jaciel to prepare at, but I couldn't decide how I wanted it to look. I made it into this full outdoor obstacle course thing. It was fun."

"That's awesome. Does that mean the muse is back?"

"Nope." He scowls. "I don't know where to go from here. I'm getting further into the book, and I swear it's like Jaciel couldn't care less that Klein's waiting for him."

Interesting ... "What makes you think that?"

"Every time I try to write a scene, the focus is on Tombra

instead. I did a word search the other day, and Klein was mentioned three times. I'm worried he's *not* worried enough about the guy he's supposed to be in love with and that it feels ... empty."

"Huh."

His attention snaps back to me. "That was an odd *huh*."

"Uh, nope. Nothing odd here."

"Payne ..."

"Can I say something that you might not like?"

"Sure."

I'm not convinced I can believe him, but here goes nothing. "I think it seems that way because ... I don't think Jaciel is in love with Klein."

"What?"

"Yeah, I'm pretty sure he wants to bone Tombra."

Beau stares at me. "No ... No, they're mortal enemies."

"Are they though? You can't tell me they didn't almost kiss in that last fight they had."

"He was trying to slit his throat."

I snort. "Wasn't trying *that* hard. I mean, he might be a badass sword fighter, but Tombra has magic and could realistically obliterate him. Like, when Jaciel got hurt and Tombra sent an army just to check he was okay?"

"They were sent to finish him off."

I hold back my skepticism, because apparently, what I was reading wasn't actually what he was writing. "Interpretation, maybe, but I can't be the first person who's mentioned that to you. There are a *ton* of theories online."

Beau's whole body is twitching with nervous energy. "I

... I don't go on social media because it makes me too anxious ... *Tons?*"

"A whole fuck ton. You really weren't planning to throw that plot twist in there?"

"Shit ..." He stares across the room blankly, and I wonder what's going through his mind. He isn't angry about me pointing it out, so that's a bonus at least. "Now I'm confused."

"You know what helps to clear your head?" I ask.

"I don't feel like drinking."

"I was actually going to suggest fucking me, but if that—"

He shoots to his feet. "Deal. Now? Whose bed?"

I laugh to hide the sudden onset of nerves. It's been a long time since I've bottomed for anyone so I'm not overly confident on how this will go.

"Yours."

But when Beau takes my hand and leads me down the hall, it's easy to ignore the nerves because it's him.

Chapter Twenty-Four

BEAU

Seeing Payne stripped and lazing across my bed is my wildest dreams come to life. He's physically mouthwatering, but the thing that has my cock standing at full attention is his eyes. His full focus is trained on me as I undress, weighted in lust and a million other things I can't name.

I lick my lips, so desperate for this I want to rush through it, but I'll hate myself forever if I don't take my time.

"You're going to have to ease me into it," Payne says in that sexy, deep voice of his, reaching for the lube in my bedside table. "I organized things in the shower earlier, but it's been a really, really long time."

They were together, what, a decade? If his ex didn't top him, then he's not exaggerating. I need to make this good.

"You never used toys?" I ask.

Payne scowls. "I tried. *He* didn't like it because it—get this—made him feel insecure."

"Fuck ..."

"Asshole."

I hate Kyle with every cell in my body. Fuck him for making Payne feel that way. "Just saying, if you want to buy yourself a dildo and put on a show for me, I'm one hundred percent here for that."

He grins. "I'll keep that in mind."

"Good." I drop my boxer briefs and step out of them, giving my cock a slow, loose stroke before I climb up onto the bed.

Payne greedily watches every movement as I crawl over him. I'll never be able to tell him how amazing I think he is, so when I lean down to kiss him, I try to make him feel it. I want him to know, without a doubt, that no matter what that asshole might have done, Payne deserves the world.

His big hands palm my ass, dragging me over until our cocks line up.

I chuckle into his mouth. "Someone's impatient."

"You just feel so good against me."

"Wait until I'm inside you."

His groan rumbles in his chest. "I don't think I can. Fuck, I need this."

I press another kiss to his lips, linger, kiss him again. Being with him like this makes me indescribably happy. I chuckle and kiss him deep, and when I finally drag myself away from his mouth, he's smiling too.

I take the lube from him and cover my fingers, then

kneel between his legs. His hard cock is resting against his stomach, begging me to taste him again, so I lean forward and run my tongue from base to tip.

He's so goddamn perfect. And okay, that's me wearing Payne-goggles, but there isn't a single thing about him I'd change. Including his cock. It's long and thick, has a prominent vein running along it, and the head is swollen and red and ... I lean forward to seal my mouth around him as I reach between his legs. I hum at the taste. That's perfect too.

My fingers find his hole, and I rub at the skin, softening the resistance as I bob up and down on his cock. I listen to the way Payne's breathing deepens, the way it cuts short when I wrap my tongue around him, and stops altogether the second my finger breaches his ass.

"Damn, that feels weird."

I pop off his dick. "Good weird, or ..."

"Just *weird* weird."

I slowly move my finger, watching his face for signs of discomfort as I stroke in and out. "This okay?"

"Yeah, keep going. It'll take me a minute." Payne spreads his legs more, and I watch the way his balls flex, mesmerized by the sight. "Get another finger in there."

"Ohh, bossy. I like this side of you," I say but do as I'm told. He moans, and not in an entirely good way, so I dive back on his cock again. I'm determined to make him feel good, to want to do this with me all the time, and because I'm not about holding back, I spill exactly what's on my mind.

"Anytime you want me to suck your cock, or touch you,

or fuck you, or if you want to fuck me, I'm always on board. Just so you know."

His stare gets heavier as he reaches down to stroke my cheek. "What if I want to suck your cock? I haven't had a turn of that yet."

I whimper and tug on my balls. "Oh yeah. That too."

"And if I want to touch you? Or kiss you?"

"Whenever you want it."

Payne's sexy grin sets off butterflies in my gut. "I wish we'd done this sooner."

"It would never have worked," I point out. I don't mention Kyle's name because I don't want Payne thinking of anyone but me right now. Even before his ex though, we were teenagers, and that shit rarely turns out to be forever. "Besides ... if we'd done it before, we wouldn't be going through exactly this now, and I've gotta say ... this is in the top three hottest moments of my life."

He laughs. "What were the other two?"

"You should know."

He frowns like he's thinking.

"You were in both of those too." Blinking up at him, I suck his cock back into my mouth, never breaking eye contact. He watches me greedily until I rub over that spot inside him that makes his toes curl into the sheets and his head drop back.

"*Nrgh*, yes, that's it."

I focus my attention on his cock as I work another digit in and stretch him open. Prepping has always been one of the hottest moments for me, and I never like to rush it, but with Payne, I'm in a constant battle with myself between getting him as ready as possible and finally being inside him.

I peg his prostate between stretching, and his cock is leaking, leaving salty spurts on my tongue with every swipe over the tip.

Then his hands close under my arms, and he hauls me up the bed. His lips crash against mine, tongue surging into my mouth in a way that leaves me breathless and wanting more.

"Fuck me," he begs.

My cock throbs at the sound. Husky and needy. Payne is ticking every one of my boxes and setting my imagination alight.

I coat my cock in more lube than I'll probably need, but I'm not risking hurting him when he's wanted this for so long. I hesitate a second. "Still okay with no condom? I didn't even think to buy—"

"Why? Have you slept with someone between last night and now?"

"Of course not."

"Then quit stalling and get inside me."

A shiver races through me, and I squeeze his thigh. "I want you on your side."

He rolls over, and I close in behind him. It puts my nose at his neck, and his hair brushes my cheek. My heart feels so fucking full of him as I reach down and grab my cock, pressing it to his hole. He shifts his top leg forward, and I push in, immediately engulfed by the tight heat of him clenching around me.

"You okay?"

"Mm. Doesn't hurt."

Perfect. I hold his hip and slide in slowly, barely keeping myself from slamming home. Because, as I work myself inside him, I can't help feeling this is ... perfect. Right. Exactly the way we're supposed to be. The feeling sort of settles over my mind, and I don't try to argue or push it away. It's so intense, I'd be surprised if he can't feel it too.

I bottom out and still for a moment before kissing his shoulder. "All good?"

He presses back into me. "Just give me ... one more second. Shit ... I want you to fuck me so bad. Don't hold back, okay?"

"Jesus, you want me to come already?"

"Depends. Do you have a round two in you? Because if so, have at it." He squeezes his ass around me, and it feels so good, I sink my teeth into his shoulder to distract myself.

"Payne ..."

"Beau ..." He wriggles. "I need you to move now."

"And if I don't?"

He pulls almost the whole way off and slams back against me. "I'll use your cock as a dildo and fuck myself with it."

"*Nrgh.*" I start to move. "We'll add that to the list to try later."

"Perfect."

I hook my arm under Payne's top leg and lift it, pressing deeper. I keep my thrusts slow and shallow until I can tell he's getting impatient, and then I pick up speed.

Each roll of my hips sparks tingles in my balls until I'm vibrating out of my skin. Getting to hold Payne like this, to be inside him and taste his sweat, and be here for him in a way that no one else gets to is intoxicating. I'm addicted to him. The sounds coming from him are delicious, and I vary my thrusts between short and sharp and long and deep to draw out all the different noises I can get him to make.

I try to clear my mind and let the pleasure drive me. To take what I need without thinking about what it means.

Payne's cock is leaking steadily onto his abs, and I watch over his shoulder as it bounces with every thrust, needing attention neither of us is in a hurry to give it. I want to draw this out and make him come so hard he can't live without those types of orgasms in his life. So I alternate my thrusts, take him to the edge, and back off again. Change angles. Aim for his prostate and then keep clear.

Payne's pushing back to meet every thrust, sending me crazy with his grunts and muttered curses. He reaches back to tangle his fingers in my hair. "Mark me," he pants. "Like I did to you last night."

I moan as I lower my mouth to his neck and suck a bruise into his skin. Then another. And another. All the way along his shoulder before I lean forward and nudge him to turn his head so I can drag him into a filthy kiss.

"I'm so close," I warn him.

"Me too."

"On your front." I wrap my arms around him and ease us forward, careful not to slip out.

Then I plant my knees on either side of his thighs and do what I've wanted from the start: I unleash.

My thrusts are hard, fast, uncontrolled, stabbing his prostate until he's squirming beneath me. We're both panting heavily, our sweat building between us. My brain is reaching that staticky place it goes right before I come, where I'm running on feeling and instinct, and driven only by the need to reach the finishing line.

"Holy *fucking* shit," Payne says, as he grabs my pillow and then shoves it underneath him. "I'm about to ruin this."

"Do it. I want you to mark every goddamn thing in my room."

He groans, thrusting into the pillow as I pound into him from behind. I'm taking him the way I've always dreamed, and I'm not going to be apologetic about it. My gaze rakes over his broad back, following his tattoos down his arm to where his bicep is bulging. I'm so close, desperately chasing that high that will tip me over the edge.

"Come, Beau. Please. Fuck. Come. I want to feel you inside me."

"Want me to mark this hole as mine?"

His hips are thrown off rhythm, and then I hear the most beautiful sentence that's ever been uttered during sex. "Yes. I've never needed anything more."

Shit. I let go, hips taking on a mind of their own as I fuck him so hard the bed knocks against the wall with heavy thuds. Over and over and—

"*Shit.*"

I come. My vision blinks in and out, but somehow I manage to keep moving through it.

"So ... close ..." Payne says, and then he stiffens underneath me, letting out the longest, sexiest noise I've ever heard.

His thighs twitch, and when my cock stops throbbing with my release, I collapse against his back.

I'm speechless.

Overwhelmed.

If it was up to me, that's the sort of thing we'd be doing every day. Forever.

I have to remind myself that pushing something so fragile isn't a good idea.

But when Payne wraps his arm around my back and tilts his head back to give me soft, sweet kisses, the worst thing imaginable happens.

I hope.

DMC Group Chat

Payne: *Is it too soon to be in love?*

    Art: *You and Beau fuck again?*

    Griffin: *It must have been good if you caught feelings. Feel free to give us a full rundown.*

    Payne: *That won't be happening.*

    Griffin: *You ruin all my fun.*

    Art: *Back to your question, short answer, no.*

    Payne: *Long answer?*

    Art: *Emotions are complicated and multifaceted. They're not linear, they're a spectrum. You can love someone and hate what they did. You can love someone and have it not be enough. You can love many someones with varying intensity.*

    Payne: *Worrying about not being enough is the problem.*

    Griffin: *I don't think you need to worry about that with Beau.*

    Payne: *That's the problem. I know he'd settle for whatever I could give him, but I don't want Beau to settle. Ever.*

Orson: *HOLY SHIT PAYNE'S IN LOVE <3*

Chapter Twenty-Five

PAYNE

I want to feel you inside me.
I've never needed anything more.

Well, fuck you very much, past Payne. So much for not confusing this thing and leading Beau on.

My ass feels pleasantly raw, ruined pillow on the ground beside the bed, and the smell of Beau's shampoo fills the room from the shower we took to clean up.

He's sleeping peacefully beside me, and every time I catch a glimpse of his face in the low light from his window, my heart twists.

He deserves so much better than this.

He deserves someone who can be one hundred percent committed to him and only him.

I want to be that man.

I want to be the one to treat him how he deserves to be treated.

And the only way to do that is to work toward it.

I have no house, a shitty job, and a divorce that's barely even pending.

I'm a real catch.

I sigh into the darkness, wishing I could snap my fingers and fix shit.

The more time I spend with Beau, the less hold that doubt has though because when I picture settling down with someone, it's not as overwhelming when he's the one I picture doing it with.

We could have this. Exactly this. The spending time together and living together and fucking each other's brains out, because how is what we're doing any different from being in an actual relationship?

And considering what I've been through, I should be wary or holding back. I should be protecting myself better than this. But I trust Beau, and I don't know what he's done to earn that, but fuck if I can picture him hurting me.

But if I want to even think about asking him for more and being who he needs me to be, I need to sort my life out. The sale on my Boston apartment has a short close and goes through officially this week, which means I'll have financial independence again.

First step, finding a place to live.

Second step, a job.

Third step, get this goddamn divorce finalized.

Fourth step, telling Beau I want more.

Careful not to wake him, I pull out my phone and search apartment listings. There are a few around, but the more I look at them, the more it feels like taking a step back to what I had in Boston. Prices are cheaper here, being two hours away from the city, so I could technically go for something a bit bigger.

But bigger to me screams family. It's something I've never thought about beyond a husband because Kyle didn't want kids, and I didn't have much preference either way. I have my nieces, who are the world to me, but if I had the option, *would* I want one of my own?

I delete apartments from my search and check all the places available. Big homes, rooms for rent, condos, and ... I pause over the listing for the land we were at yesterday. It doesn't have a price, but I'd bet it's a lot. Too much.

Which is a shame because I felt an immediate boost being out there. I'm grateful to Ford for taking a chance on me and giving me a job to get through, but being inside all day isn't me. Even as a teacher, I took the class outside as much as I could, and I had a big window in my office that overlooked a leafy quad.

I've left my resume at the high schools, but they close for the summer soon, and kept on top of job advertisements, but there hasn't been anything close to what I'm after except a part-time summer camp counselor, and I'm about twenty years too old for that, plus it was an hour and a half away.

I look at the land again. It actually would be a good location for a summer camp. It's a huge parcel, and the cottage there looked weather-beaten but sturdy. It was also the perfect size between an apartment and a house.

I groan because it doesn't matter how perfect it *could* be; I don't even have to ask to know the price is too far out of my budget, especially when I'm making shit all at work.

"What's wrong?" Beau asks sleepily.

"Nothing. Go back to sleep."

His eyes snap open. "You're not having regrets, are you?"

I laugh softly. "None." It's the opposite, but I can't tell him that. I nod to my phone. "Been thinking and trying to work out what my next steps are."

"And is there a reason you're suddenly doing that right after sex with me?"

I lean forward and kiss him. "I promise there are no regrets. Stop stressing. I couldn't sleep, and it's no secret I'm not happy with where my life is at the moment."

"Because of your job?"

"Yep." And before he can doubt again, I add, "It's like I'm twenty-two again and trying to build a life for myself. I'm a forty-year-old man starting from scratch, and that's a huge deal to me."

Beau shuffles up onto his elbows and looks down at me. "Why are you starting from scratch?"

"I have to find a job, a place to live—and yes I love living here with you, but it was only ever supposed to be short term. I need a place that's mine. A place where I can settle and know that's it for at least the next twenty years."

"You could live here for twenty years." He pouts, and it's adorable.

I slap his bare ass. "And as much as I love living here and having regular sex with you, I need my own place. For me."

He perks up. "Regular?"

"Of course you'd focus on that." But it proves we're on the same page. "But I'm not in a hurry to stop if you aren't."

"No rush on my end."

"Good." I know I shouldn't say this next part, but I can't stop myself. I want Beau to know that me wanting a place has nothing to do with not wanting *him*. "And even when I move out, I don't think I'll want to stop then either."

"Payne, that, umm ... that almost sounds close to a relation—"

I cover his mouth with my palm. "I really care about you, but there are things I want to figure out before jumping into whatever comes next."

Still, when I remove my hand, his smile is enormous.

"Don't look at me like that," I warn.

"Like what?"

I roll on top of him, pressing him to the bed. Nose to nose, I kiss him. "Like I'm better than I am."

"You do know that *things* aren't what make you, right? I liked you before your job and fancy apartment. I liked you before getting married or divorced. I *still* like you because you're working hard, no matter what it's at, and you never make me feel ..." His nose wrinkles. "Umm ... different. You're there for me in a way I've never had before. I've had you on this ridiculous pedestal our entire lives, and you've still managed to surpass the image I built."

I sigh, pressing my forehead to his collarbone, not feeling worthy. "I don't know what I did to deserve all that, but I'm going to earn it."

"You already have."

I cup his face and kiss him slowly, taking my time and enjoying the moment. He shifts, and his hard cock brushes my leg, and it almost makes me laugh. I'm nowhere near ready to go again, but that doesn't mean I can't help him out.

I break from his lips and push back, settling between his thighs. "My turn." I swallow him to the root, then do everything I can to drive him mad. He tastes like soap and precum. It's so fucking hot to watch the way my mouth drives him crazy, and when Beau squirms on the bed, one hand gripping my head, I tighten the suction and work him over as fast as I can.

His thighs flex as he comes, and seeing Beau lose his damn mind is something I don't think I'll ever be sick of. It's glorious.

When he slumps back into the bed, I pull off and prop my head on his stomach. He's still breathing deep, and his red lips are begging me to kiss him again, but somehow I manage to resist.

"Goddamn you're good at that," he says.

I pump my eyebrows. "I love it too."

He lets out a long, happy exhale and strokes my hair for a

minute before he shifts, and my phone lights up where I dropped it.

Beau gestures to it. "What were you looking at?"

I reach over and open the page again, showing it to him. "Trent's land?"

"I was trying to think of ideas on what it could be used for, but it'll be too expensive."

"What ideas did you have?"

"A summer camp was one of them."

He nods, and I can tell he's thinking. I give him time. "A summer camp limits the market though, doesn't it?"

"Yeah, I guess. This town *is* seasonal though."

"It is, but you need to make a living the rest of the year."

He's right. "Like I said, just daydreaming."

"Well, hold on. I think you're on the right track."

"You do?"

"Yeah." He tugs his bottom lip between his teeth, and then it pops out again as his face lights up. "You *could* do the summer camp and then through the rest of the year offer something that would cater to schools."

"What do you mean?"

"Well, something like what I wrote today. A training ... *something* or—"

The idea pops into my head, fully formed and addictive. "Like an adventure land type of thing. Obstacle courses and team-building exercises. Get some local schools on board. And if I do a summer camp, I'll have accommodation I can offer for school groups who come from further away ..."

"*Yes*. You could do some sport-type things, have animals

... *oh*! A paintball range you could hire out for parties. Maybe spooky themed twilight mazes—"

"Match everything else in this damn town?"

"Exactly."

My heart is beating fast in excitement. I can see it all. Everything he's describing. Cabins lining the far woods at the back of the block, animals in the front paddock, and all the equipment in the back one. Behind the cottage is a big enough space to set up a paintball range—maybe even lasers for the younger kids and ...

I sigh and close my phone. "It's a nice idea."

"Then make it happen."

"Beau ..." I laugh. "Imagine how much that land costs."

"It's not specified."

"Yes, but it's huge. I made a good profit off my last place, but not that good. Not to mention the set-up costs."

He shakes his head. "Is this something you want to do?"

"Well, yes, but—"

"Then we'll make it happen."

"Make it happen," I repeat. "It's not that—"

"Stop. One thing I know about you is you don't give up when you want something. If you want this, we'll *make it happen*."

And when he says it like that, I can imagine it. It doesn't sound impossible. "We?"

"You've done nothing but help me when it comes to my work. Let me return the favor."

"You're not going to offer me money, are you?"

"Would it matter if I did?"

Hmm. On one hand, I've never been one of those people who worries too much about money so long as I have enough coming in to live a decent life. That said, I also don't like handouts, and the money we're talking about here would be a lot. I don't want to have to rely on Beau for every little thing. "If I keep leaning on you when I need something, I'll never learn to do shit myself."

"Do you need to learn that?"

"Of course I do."

"Says who?"

I tickle his ribs and make him squirm. "Literally every self-help person goes on about being self-sufficient."

"I think that's the worst thing you can be. I offered you a room I wasn't using, and in return you showed me I could be myself around someone and they'd accept me. Whether anything happens between us or not, I'm not going to settle for less. What I gave you was material and worthless to me but meant a lot to you. And what you gave me can't be replaced. When did sharing what we have with people become this huge deal? Pooling resources used to be necessary for survival, and now all people do is hoard what others need."

"Yes, but me showing you basic decency isn't the same thing as you giving me a place to live."

"Says who? You're the first person to offer that to me. I needed it. I was the first person to offer you a room because you needed it. Seems the same to me."

I tip my head forward to press a kiss to the trail of light

hair running down to his groin. I'm still not sure I agree with him, but he does have a point.

His fingers run through my hair, and he gives it a tug, coaxing me to look up at him. "We can at least look into it, can't we?"

Every stubborn bone in my body is telling me to say no, to do this myself. But ... I *want* Beau's help on this. "We can try."

Chapter Twenty-Six

BEAU

Since Payne pointed out that Jaciel is supposed to be with Tombra, this book has been flying out of me. It's like the whole plot exploded in front of my eyes, and suddenly those snippets I was writing make sense. Klein is the ultimate betrayer, and somehow, I set the entire thing up without even realizing I was doing it.

High fives to my erratic brain.

I've been pulling all-nighters, and Payne's been working all day, but somehow we've found our way into each other's beds a few times this week, and every time it happens, I have no idea what I've done to get so lucky, but I swear the second I figure it out, it'll become part of my daily ritual.

We might not have planned anything more than what we are, but whenever we're together, he holds me like I'm precious, like he's in awe of me, and seeing Payne look at me that way, makes me fall deeper and deeper in love.

Emotionally, we're still in limbo, but hooking up is better than nothing, and Payne made it clear he wants to at least continue that side of things once he finds his own place, so I'm being Helpy McHelperson and trying to make that happen for him.

Even while I desperately pray that him moving out won't be the end of … whatever this is. I need to trust him, and I'm trying so hard to focus on the fact that if this is meant to be, it'll be.

I set three different alarms today, but I'm still ten minutes late getting to the Killer Brew, and I cross my fingers Trent hasn't left already.

Thankfully when I walk in, I find him sitting in one of the booths, basket of wings in front of him and half-finished mug of beer beside it.

"Sorry I'm late," I quickly say.

Trent waves me off. "Ten minutes is nothing to worry about. I was enjoying the music."

I nod, though I can barely hear it over the sounds of the market on the other side of the old warehouse.

"So, you wanted to talk about the land?" he asks.

"Yeah, it's for Payne actually, but he got held up at work. We're both proving our reliability already."

Trent lists his head. "Reliability for what?"

I know Payne wanted to be here for the conversation, but Ford couldn't let him out early today, so he told me to go ahead. It sucks he couldn't do it himself like he wanted, but I'm excited that he trusts me with this, and I'm determined to prove he was smart to.

"We've had an idea for the land you're selling."

"Really?" Trent leans forward, small smile almost hidden behind his beard. "What's that, then?"

I fill him in on the plan Payne came up with, along with some of the logistical things we've worked through. Payne's drawn up numbers and a list of the planning permissions needed to create his vision, and I'm excited to be able to help him with it all.

"That's interesting," Trent says. "We want the land to be used, and that sounds as good a use as any."

"Yeah, Payne's been working really hard on it."

"So why are you bringing this to me?"

I cringe. "That's the tricky part. Without knowing the exact price you're selling the land for, Payne's confident he doesn't have enough, and no bank is going to lend him the kind of money he needs to put into the place without some collateral."

"Okay ..."

It suddenly hits me what his wary tone is about. "Oh, no. No, no. We don't want it cheap. We—"

"Sorry!"

I glance up at Payne's voice and find him crossing the brewery toward us. His Ford's Garage polo clings to his chest, giving a peek of his tattoos under where the buttons are undone.

"I got caught at work." He holds out his hand and shakes Trent's. "Did Beau fill you in?"

"He's given me a rundown of your plans so far."

"Awesome." Payne shoots a smile my way as he slides into the seat beside me, and I'm caught, totally off guard, when he presses a kiss to my cheek. "In that case, I'll cut to the chase. Money is my number one barrier. How much are you selling the land for?"

"One point two."

Yikes. Slightly more than we were expecting.

Payne looks as relaxed as always. "I have a third of that."

Trent looks between us. "So what's your request? Because four hundred isn't going to cut it."

"No, I know. So obviously my biggest barrier is funding. What I'm hoping we can talk about is me leasing the place for twelve months while we get everything set up. In the meanwhile, Beau is going to be applying for small-business grants and funding for the type of place I want, and I'll be organizing the build. We'll start small with the accommodation, permissions, and licensing and begin some of the setup for the smaller activities. Once that's in place, I'm confident I'll be loaned the remaining amount."

Trent rubs his beard. "What rental amount are we talking?"

"I was hoping to negotiate that and the sale price. Whatever we pay you, a percentage comes off the final price."

"And if you don't get the funding?"

"Then you keep whatever I've paid and built, and the place goes back on the market."

"Interesting …"

There's no way I'm letting Payne throw away all that money though. "If the bank doesn't front the money for it, I will. I have it. I'm not using it—"

"Beau."

"No, like I said the other night my money is literally sitting there doing nothing. I could buy the place outright and save you the stress and headaches, but I've agreed to letting you try it your way first. If that doesn't work, we try it my way."

Payne's expression softens. "Since when did you become so stubborn?"

"Since I'm determined to see you succeed."

He looks like he still wants to argue—or thinks he should, at least. And then, he relents. "Fine. If I fail, we do it your way."

I turn to Trent. "How does that sound?"

"I'm interested. Very. It means keeping the land together and seeing it used for a good purpose. I'll have to run it by my parents and our Realtor, but I think they'll be on board."

My excitement skyrockets.

Trent finishes up his wings and leaves us to it with a promise to call later in the week. I wait until he's out of sight before I throw my arms around Payne's neck.

"Holy shit, I think it's happening."

His warm laugh is loud in my ear as his hands settle on my lower back. "Here's hoping."

"I'm buying you a drink. Multiple drinks. Let's have lots and lots of drinks to celebrate."

His eyes are soft as he pulls back, and it makes my heart feel funny. "It might not happen yet."

"Of course it will."

"And if Trent's parents say no? Or the agent points out it's not a smart move?"

"Then your plan fails and we move to mine."

"After twelve months."

I tilt my head and squint my eyes like I'm trying to remember. "I don't think that was stipulated."

"Ah, so you're stubborn *and* sneaky?"

I smile innocently, and Payne shakes his head.

"In that case, I guess celebration drinks are in order. I'll buy."

"A rusty shank, thanks."

He leaves and buys the round, then returns with two glasses each. "Couldn't be bothered getting up again."

"Fair enough."

We toast, and I'm fighting fluttery feelings the whole time.

Payne takes a long drink, watching me over the top of his glass. He swallows, sets it down, then clears his throat. "You know, the reason I wanted to do this solo was, well, I've never had anything that was mine. And look at how that turned out. My apartment, my husband, my job, my life ... all gone. Because I shared them with the wrong person."

I give his hand a squeeze. "I get it. And I respect the hell out of you for wanting to do this by yourself. But ... I don't want a claim to any of it. Sure, if I end up putting money in, we'll have to get something drawn up to show my investment, but that's all it is. An investment in your business, and one day when you're absolutely killing it there, you can pay me back."

"And if I don't end up killing it?"

"Then you sell the place and give me back what I've put in, even if it's worth a crap ton more."

He chuckles. "What if it's worth less?"

"Then I'll take the same percentage loss as you."

He looks conflicted, so I reach over and take his hand. His fingers immediately lace through mine.

"I know you can do this. And it will be yours. Even when we stop hooking up, I don't want to take this from you. I don't want to own you or for you to feel indebted to me. We'll have a contract drawn up that we're both happy with and then never mention it again until we need to."

He stares at me for a long moment. "This being a possibility makes it feel like I can breathe again. I'm excited, which isn't something I expected after everything that went down."

"I'm happy for you."

"The weird thing is, I don't doubt that for a second." He squeezes my hand. "Even though I hope I don't need to rely on you again, you have no idea what this means, Bo-Bo."

"Well, if you don't want to rely on me, I guess we only have one option here."

"Oh yeah?"

"Yeah." I lean forward. "We make sure your plan fucking works."

"Deal." We toast again and down the rest of our drinks

before Payne pulls me from my chair. "Come on, celebratory drinks are done. It's time for some celebratory sex."

"Sounds like the perfect ending to the day."

Chapter Twenty-Seven

PAYNE

Is it possible for the worst moment of your life to lead to the best?

A few months ago, I would have told those *everything happens for a reason* people to go and suck a fat one, but now I'm on a trajectory that feels so undeniably right, I'm finding it hard to be negative about anything.

Well, except the message I got from an unknown number last night.

All it said was we need to talk, but I know without asking that it was Kyle. Normally that kind of thing would have prompted me to reach out or to turn to his OnlyFans to remind myself of why I left, but all it did was make me feel sad for the life we were building together.

And then I went and climbed into bed with Beau, and the sadness miraculously went away. He's shown me that there are people deserving of my time and others who aren't, and I've wasted enough of it on my ex to be able to confidently walk away without doubts now.

Which is why I stopped by the store on the way home and bought every coloring book I could find. I figure a guy like Beau isn't going to be impressed by flowers or chocolates or whatever, so this can be my offering.

A way of asking him to stick it out for a little longer, because I'm almost there. I have a goal and drive to get there. Only a few things to bump off my list, and then I'll be able to be the man he needs me to be.

Sure, I've been wrong in the past when it comes to who I've put my trust in, but as much as I'd like to say Kyle's behavior was totally out of character, there's a small part of me that wasn't surprised. It's not that I didn't love him, but I also didn't turn a blind eye to his faults.

He liked attention and being the best-looking man in the room. He suggested filler for the wrinkles I was getting and tried to convince me to have injections in my lips. None of that shit is me. And while none of it was malicious, it does make me question if, in the end, I wasn't enough for him.

He didn't like my tattoos or messy hair. He didn't like when I went weeks without shaving. I'm sure there was a part of him that did love me, but to him, my faults were clearly more than he was prepared to deal with.

Beau's seen me at my lowest. He knows I have sweet fuck all outside of an idea and motivation to make it happen, and yet somehow, we *work*. He's a neurotic workaholic, and I'm a struggling divorcé, but when we're together, we're just ... us.

Which is why I want to tell him how I feel.

I'm sure he knows. It's not like I've been subtle about it. But to move forward with him, I need to put my past behind me.

I pick up dinner from a steak place on the way home, and I walk in to find Beau at his desk like he so often has been lately, hammering away at his computer. He must be finishing up because as soon as I enter the kitchen, he stops what he's doing and swings around in the seat to face me. His glasses have slipped down so only half of his eyes are magnified, and his white T-shirt has the telltale markings of spilled coffee.

But when I look at him, I see a future I never could have thought was possible, especially not so soon.

I leave dinner on the counter and approach him.

"I bought you a little something."

"What?" Beau eagerly reaches for the white paper bag I'm holding and pulls out the coloring books and new markers. I've wrapped a ribbon around them so they look almost fancy. But instead of the smile I'm expecting, he squints up at me. "Is this your way of saying you don't want to be my art project anymore?"

"Dammit, no. They're a gift. A gift that I clearly messed up. I just know that you ran out, and when I'm at work, or once I move out, you'll need something for the times I'm not around."

"And ... will there be a lot of those times?" he asks.

"I really hope not."

His inhale is shaky. "Tell me more."

"More ... Okay, I think you're cute and funny. I never know what I'm going to be walking into when I get home. And you make me laugh."

"At me?"

"Of course." I cut off his protest with a quick kiss. "You're nonstop entertainment."

"Ah, good, my life goals are complete."

"Was one of your other goals being incredible at sucking dick? Because you've mastered that one too."

"Well, now I can die happy."

"So glad I could help make that happen." I rest my forehead against his. "But seriously, Beau, you make it so easy to trust you, and I thought that would be the hardest thing to do moving forward."

"Really?"

"Yep."

"Well then, in the spirit of trust ..." He leans over for one of his desk drawers and reaches in to pull out ... coloring books?

"Where did those come from?"

"Right after the first time you let me use your tats, these showed up. I hid them so I could keep up the excuse of not having any."

My expression feels smug. "Couldn't get enough, huh?"

"I don't think I ever will."

"Beau ..."

"No pressure." His expression is teasing. "You're just an extremely irresistible hunk of flesh."

"Kinda sounds like you're objectifying me."

"You say that like I don't do it often."

"And here I was thinking you were a nice guy."

"I'll show you how nice I am." Beau immediately closes his hands behind my neck, and the kiss goes from sweet and innocent to scorching hot in a second flat. I wheel his chair closer and wind an arm behind his back, holding him against me. I love the feel of him in my arms and the way his glasses brush my face and his stubble scrapes my skin. The groan that rumbles in his chest is low and echoes the want I'm feeling.

I reach for his cock and find it hard, straining against his sweats. "So nice," I breathe into his mouth. "I'm going to need a closer look."

I sink onto my heels and yank his sweats down his thighs, revealing the cock I'm becoming addicted to.

"Oh ... I could get used to this," Beau says.

"Feel free to keep working if you need to." I lean forward to tongue his slit. "I'll just be here having fun."

He makes a noise in the back of his throat, and his hand lands on my head. "You think I can concentrate on anything when you're on your knees? Fuck, I've only dreamed about this since high school."

I don't bother saying that I wish he'd mentioned it or let me know because he was right. Who knows what would have happened then? Right now is where we're supposed to be, and I'll go through the pain it took to get here if it means ending up with Beau.

I want to think long term and get ahead of what this is, but going from one long-term relationship to promising someone else another is too overwhelming to consider. I want to take it slow this time, to learn everything there is to know about Beau, to start small, and if we're lucky, one day we'll have the kind of life I always imagined with someone. No coming home to sit in front of the TV all night. No making plans with other people all weekend. No sitting on our phones before bed until we trade obligatory blow jobs once a week.

My marriage had gotten stale, and I'd never realized it.

Beau's injected passion back into my life again.

I sink farther onto his cock, lapping at the tip and tightening the suction. His breathing is getting heavier, and it's music to my ears—until the phone's piercing ringtone cuts through the apartment.

"Fuck," Beau says, scrambling to shut it off when he pauses. "It's Trent."

I pop off but replace my mouth with my hand. "Answer it."

Beau's teeth sink into his lip for a second before he takes the call. "Hey, how are you?"

I watch, straining my ears to try and hear the other side of the conversation, but Trent's voice is too low to make out clearly. Beau's making a lot of affirming sounds, but I can't get a read on his face.

He reaches down to grab my hand that I didn't realize had been absently stroking over his cock.

"Yeah, that sounds amazing. Of course we can." His face explodes in a smile, and my gut flips as he gives me the thumbs-up.

"He said yes?" I whisper.

Beau hurries to nod.

I'm so happy, I lean forward and swallow his cock down my throat. The whole time Beau is talking to Trent, I give him the blow job of his life. I suck and slurp and drive him wild, all the while his "uh-huh"s and "yeah"s are getting more and more breathless. He's trying so hard to hide it, death grip on my hair trying to hold me in place, but the pain only spurs me on. I tongue his sac, sucking each of his balls into my mouth before taking his cock again.

Beau's awkward laugh fills the apartment as his grip twists my hair painfully. His legs lift on either side of my head, and I watch as he hurries to mute the sound right before he cries out and the first salty spurt hits my tongue.

I take every drop, loving the way he falls apart for me, and when he catches his breath, he clears his throat and takes the sound off mute.

"Yeah, that's reasonable. We can meet you tomorrow afternoon?"

I rest my cheek on his thigh as his cock softens in my mouth, and his fingers ease up their grip. He strokes my hair, finishing the call, and when he hangs up, I release him from my mouth.

"I'm going to kill you," he says, but the relaxed way he's slumped in his chair takes the bite out of his words.

"What did he say?" Because even though the thumbs-up was good, I need to know for sure.

"They want to accept your offer." Beau leans down to kiss me. "Congratulations. It's all happening."

Chapter Twenty-Eight

BEAU

Not getting excited. That's definitely not a thing that I am doing.

Even if we're acting like a couple.

And things are great.

And I feel more for him now than I ever thought it was possible to feel about anyone.

All the sex is great, but when we're talking or eating together, when he drags me out of the house for walks, or helps me with problems on my book, or lets me relax by coloring his tattoos, I can feel the connection. And I fall in love with him even more.

It's a windy summer day when I get to the Killer Brew and grab coffees to go and meet Marty. I'm early, so once I have our order, I take the long way, walking past Ford's Garage, hoping to run into Payne. It's a big lot with a shiny office building up front and a huge open garage where they work on the cars out back. I scan the lot, looking from one person to the next, but he mustn't be out there.

A car pulls up in the parking lot just as I'm about to keep walking, and Ford jumps out.

"Hey, Beau. What's up?"

"I was on my way to meet Marty and thought I'd see if Payne was on lunch, but he must be busy."

"Lunch?" Ford chuckles. "He took the day off today, didn't he tell you?"

"No." It's surprising, but then, I was in bed this morning until right before I had to leave, so it's not like he had the chance to. "Is he sick?"

"Don't think so. He said yesterday he had to drive down to Boston to meet someone."

Meet someone?

I force a smile and thank him, then numbly head to where I'm meeting Marty. If Payne knew he was going to meet someone yesterday, I don't understand why he wouldn't have mentioned it last night. If it was a friend, that's the sort of thing that would have come up when we were cooking dinner together. Well, together is a teeny exaggeration since I didn't do much but stir a pot, but still. We were there. We were talking. Payne tells me everything.

Right?

Right?

The panic that grips me is a good indication of my suspicion on who Payne has gone to meet.

Kyle has been trying to get in touch. Did he manage it? What does he want, to get back together?

Fuck no.

No, no.

He doesn't deserve Payne. He fucked up, and it's my turn now.

I want to say with complete confidence that there's no way Payne would go back to that asshole, but then ... why wouldn't he have said something?

He's told me everything about them, even things he hasn't told Marty. He's shared how the whole thing made him feel, the porn, the real story that he's glossed over with everyone else.

I knew Kyle wanted to see him.

So why didn't he tell me he was going?

The only reason I can come up with is that he's not sure *how* he feels about seeing Kyle again.

And if he's not sure, then how can I be sure he'll come back to me?

We're not official. We haven't discussed dating for real.

I thought we were waiting to see what evolved, but what if what evolves is that he and his husband work things out, how am I supposed to deal with that?

I'm well on my way to panic-town when I reach Marty and hold out his coffee.

His eyes immediately narrow in concern. "What's wrong?"

"Nothing." I shake my head because it's not like I can tell him I'm in love with his brother and we've been sleeping together. I almost wish Lizzy was here so that I could tell her the full story, have her yell at me for being a dumbass, and then get squashed in reassuring hugs.

"You're seriously pale, man. Here, sit down."

I shake off his concern and step away from the bench he's trying to steer me toward. "It's fine. I'm fine. Just … things on my mind."

It's clear he doesn't believe me, but I'm not doing a convincing job either.

"You know what I want?" he asks. "A beer. Maybe I can call in for the afternoon and we'll go to the Killer Brew? It's been ages since we've hung out properly."

"You're not subtle at all."

He laughs, and my heart pangs at how much it reminds me of Payne. "Come on, man. Drinks? Please?"

"It's not like I have anything else to do with my day." Because there's no way I'll be able to focus on work, knowing where Payne is.

We ditch our coffees, then walk the two blocks to the brewery. As usual for the day, the market is full and the bar side is quiet, apart from people grabbing lunch in the booths.

We take a seat at the bar and order our drinks, before I say, as casually as I can, "Talk to your brother today?"

"Nah, why?"

"No reason." *Because I want to know if he's seeing his stinking ex.*

Marty turns on his stool to face me. "Well, that was a lie.

What's going on? Did you guys have a fight? Please say no—I can't handle him back on my couch."

I stifle my dislike at the thought of us fighting. "Nothing like that."

"Then what is it?"

There's a spot on the mirrored wall above the bar, and I stare at it, mentally running through what I can actually tell him. The annoying part is I can't come up with any tidbit to throw him off because ... I want to tell him. "I don't think I can say."

"Why?"

"Because it's not just about me."

"For fuck's sake, Beau. I'm your best friend. You can tell me anything."

Damn, I wish that was true. "I don't know how you'll take it."

"Take what?" I can feel him watching me.

"The thing I need to say and want to tell you but can't."

"And now you're speaking in riddles." He runs his hand back over his short hair. "You're upset, and if I didn't know better, I'd say you've had your heart broken, or—"

My head snaps toward him.

Marty's eyes get wide. "You ... wait, *what*? Who have you been—" His mouth drops. "Oh, fuck no."

"Umm ... 'fuck no' what?" My gut hollows at the way he's looking at me because I'm on the fence about whether he's about to throw fists or start yelling.

Surely he doesn't actually give a shit? He wouldn't be mad, right? I mean, Payne *is* his brother so—

Marty cracks up laughing. "Payne? There is no way. Please tell me I'm wrong."

I cringe. "And if I can't?"

The amusement slips from his face. "*Payne?*"

I hum.

"And *you?*"

"You *could* sound a little less disgusted."

"Sorry, I'm ..." He looks away. "Processing."

"Can you process a bit faster? Because I'm scared you're mad, and I really need to talk about this."

"I'm not mad, I ... I don't get it. He's just left his husband, like ... are you guys fucking around or, wow. I have no idea what's going on."

"That would make two of us." I take a long gulp of beer.

Marty cringes. "I *knew* I spotted a hickey on Payne's neck when you two came over the other week."

"Guilty."

"Let's move to a booth. This isn't a bar top conversation."

I think that's actually the perfect setting for regurgitating your every thought and fear onto a person, but I follow Marty anyway.

He's quiet for a minute after sliding in, and then he sighs. "All right, I think I need you to explain, because I don't understand. How did it happen, and why are you looking so upset?"

"Well ... I guess the first thing you should probably know is that I have feelings for Payne."

"Okay ..."

"And have since high school."

"Fucking what?" He tips his beer up and drains the glass. "You mean, like, you had a crush? And it's back?"

"No, I mean I've had real feelings for him for maybe twenty years, and every time I see him is hard."

"But ... you were at his wedding, and ..."

"Yeah, that was torture."

"You've dated people."

"And it's never worked out." I take a steadying breath. "I've been able to ignore it and resign myself to the reality that I'd never have that chance with him, and then he showed up, newly separated and looking for a place to live."

"Which I begged you to give him." Marty cringes. "Is this my fault?"

"No. It was my choice, and I'm glad I did it. We've gotten to know each other and started hooking up, and until maybe an hour ago, I'd thought there was a chance it could be going somewhere."

"Then what's the problem?"

"I stopped by the garage to see him, and Ford said he was off today to go and meet with someone in Boston."

"Okay?"

"In *Boston*." My voice breaks. "And he didn't tell me. That can only be one person."

"You think he's seeing Kyle?"

I slump in my booth. "Yes. Wait, no, I don't think, I'm sure. He didn't tell me, and Payne tells me everything."

"Then maybe there's a good reason for it."

"Yeah. That he's worried they might sort things out."

All the tension melts from Marty, and he watches me with sympathetic eyes. "You actually think that, or are you being insecure?"

"How am I supposed to know? We haven't talked about us further than seeing what happens, and even though he knows how I feel about him, he's never mentioned how *he* feels. Isn't that a massive red flag?"

"No, it sounds like Payne."

I play with my nail as I say, "He's always said that if he was weaker, he'd go back to Kyle and try to make things work. How do I know that isn't what's happening here?"

"You're right, you don't."

Ouch. That isn't the response I'd been hoping for.

"What do you like about him?" Marty asks. "Why is it feelings for you and not just superficial attraction?"

I frown and think. "He's ... genuine. And nice. He's always made time for me, and even before he knew me well, he'd make conversation and not be pushy or feel like he wanted to be anywhere else. He's ... relaxing. And he has a big heart. And he leaves me paper cranes when he thinks I need them, and lets me draw on his tattoos, and keeps my dinner warm if I'm working and he doesn't want to interrupt me ..." Yikes. Just thinking about those things is bringing a lump to my throat. I can't lose that. I really, really can't.

"Exactly."

I glance up at Marty, and he leans closer.

"Payne is a *good* guy. And while he's my brother and I totally think you could do a thousand times better, I also know he's not going to fuck with you. Do you trust him?"

"Of course."

"So trust that he knows what he's doing. If he knew you had feelings for him, he wouldn't have started anything with you unless he thought there might be something there. Kyle is a dickweed. Maybe he said he'd go back if he was weak, but that's one thing Payne isn't. He takes the hard road if it's for the best, and you need to believe that whatever he's doing, he's doing it for the right reasons."

And I ... can't argue with any of that. I scowl. "I know you're right, but ... even the smallest hint of losing him ... I don't think I can do it. I'm so in love with him even the thought of it makes me feel sick."

"Why did you do this to yourself?"

I give him a self-deprecating smile. "Because I finally had a chance with him. It's worth it, even if I ended up heartbroken."

"Oh yeah? And how does it feel now?"

"Horrible." And it occurs to me that even feeling like this, even if Payne came home tonight and told me it was over, I'd still do it all again. "But so worth it."

Chapter Twenty-Nine

PAYNE

Seeing the land and making plans with Beau went a long way toward opening my eyes to the way I was living. I've spent so much time resenting what happened, and somehow, I've run right to the best thing that's ever happened to me.

I've never been more excited for the future.

And that's saying something because after college, I thought I had it made.

Here I am, starting over at forty, and it's easy to worry that it's too little too late, but even if it takes me another year or two to get my plans off the ground, I still have an entire lifetime to enjoy it.

With Beau, if I'm lucky.

So, I made the decision last night that it really is time to move forward.

And to do that, I need to leave my regrets behind.

Which is why I'm on my way to Boston.

I'd love more than anything to show up, present the divorce papers, and make Kyle sign them all without breaking a sweat, but I can't see that happening.

I've done well not to think about him lately, and now he's front and center in my mind.

I still can't understand why he threw away the life we had together. The more distance I'm getting from us, the more I'm able to acknowledge that it wasn't perfect, but our problems are things you fix together in a marriage. You don't spend two years sleeping around with other men.

The rage and betrayal come back hot and thick, and my hands tighten on the steering wheel. The nerve of him to think he can reach out and make me talk simply because he wants to.

I'm happier than I've ever been, and I want it to stay that way.

So even though Kyle would have forced this at one point or another, I'm going there on my own terms. I've already been married to him for far too long and I don't want it to last a minute longer than it needs to.

I follow the directions I've plugged into the GPS from the address he sent me this morning and find myself out the front of a pastel-colored town house. The street is lined with trees and has low wrought iron fences along the front of each of the houses.

Our apartment block was nice but impersonal. This is ... well, it's exactly what I wanted when I first moved here.

And now, looking at it, I'm relieved that it's not what I want anymore.

My phone lights up, and I check the DMC chat to find they've written back to where I told them what I was doing today.

Orson: *This is for the best, you can do it.*
Art: *Kick the fucker's ass.*
Griffin: *If you feel stressed, just remember Beau and how good he is in bed. Feel free to pass on the details if you'll need me to remind you ...*

Well, they're being supportive in their own way, I guess.

I unclip my seat belt, grab the papers from the passenger seat, and steel myself to see him again. The last time I saw my husband in person, I'd kissed him goodbye as he left for work, and he told me he'd be home after his workout that afternoon. By the time he walked back in the door, I was probably getting shitfaced in Kilborough.

Nerves hit my gut as I cross the street, pass through the small gate, and take the stairs to the front stoop in one step.

In and then out.

I can do this.

And when I get back, I'll have Beau there waiting for me.

The thought of Beau launches the nerves into butterflies, and the lightness helps me to lift my hand and knock.

There are quick footsteps on the other side, and just as I hear them reach the door, I brace myself, prepared for that familiar hit of nostalgia when I see his face. Or a surge of rage. Or the bottomless pit of betrayal.

But when the door opens and there's Kyle looking exactly the same as he ever has, I feel ... nothing.

Huh.

"Hello." My voice comes out strong and impersonal. It takes me by surprise, but damn do I like it. I lift the papers I'm holding. "You wanted to see me?"

He steps aside. "Yeah, come in."

"I'd rather not."

"Payne ..." Kyle widens his eyes. "Please. I want to talk."

"Why? Are you planning to give me a step-by-step on how you cheated on me for years?"

He recoils like I hit him. "You're angry, I get it—"

"I'm not. Being angry at you gives you a right to my feelings, and ... I've decided you don't have that right anymore."

He reaches up to tuck his longish hair back and then tugs on the ends like he does when he's nervous. It used to be enough to get me to back down from whatever fight we had. Now I can see it for the manipulation move it is. "Please come in. Just give me five minutes. Surely after twelve years together you can spare me that."

"Actually, I don't owe you a second of my time," I say but step into the house. "You do owe me answers though, so let's do it."

I don't wait for his reply as I make my way down the

short hall into a living area. I'd say I have no idea how he afforded this place, but I'm not that naive.

I stand in the middle of the room as he perches in an armchair.

"You can sit."

"I won't be here long enough to get comfortable." I drop the papers on the table and cross my arms. "You're also signing those while I'm here."

Kyle sighs and pulls the papers toward himself. "I guess you want to know why I did it."

For the last few months, hell, even for the whole drive here, I've wanted the answer to that question. I wanted to know why. I couldn't wrap my head around how he could betray me like that.

Now ... holy shit. I don't actually care. "Explain if you want to, but nothing you say will be a reasonable excuse."

"I'm not trying to excuse my actions—"

"Of course you are. You want me here to hear you out so you can fool yourself into thinking you tried. But it's too late for that. It's too late for you to try and feel better about yourself. What you did was fucked-up, and there's no way you didn't know that the whole time it was going on."

"Can you blame me?" He throws himself back in his chair, and while his tone sounds wrecked, the expression on his face doesn't change. His skin is flawless and eerily still.

"I can."

"You weren't an easy man to be married to."

I almost ask what the hell he means by that, but I'm not

falling into that trap. "I'm sorry you thought so. It's a good thing I brought papers that will make all of that go away."

"Do you even care what I have to say? Don't you care why our relationship was so terribly off track that I had to turn to other men?"

"Surely I made it clear since I arrived that I really, really don't."

"Right." His eyes go shiny like he's about to cry, and it kills me I can still know him so well, even when he deceived me for so long. "I made a mistake."

"Mistake? You think doing the same thing for two whole years is a *mistake*?" The burning rage I've felt since the separation is bubbling up inside me again. He's trying to draw it out. Trying to force an argument that might escalate to makeup blow jobs like it often has in the past.

But that will never happen again.

And maybe I wouldn't be so strong if I didn't have Beau, who knows? But I also think he's onto something with letting people help where they can, and the thought of him has never been more welcome.

"All I'm asking is that you give me a second chance. That we work on things. Don't throw away twelve years together and make me out to be the bad guy when you're not exactly innocent in all this."

"Work on things?"

"Yes." Kyle pushes to his feet and takes a tentative step forward. "I'll delete my account, and we'll go to counseling. I want to try. Maybe this had to happen so we'd take this time to miss each other and remember what we had."

Is he ... holy shit, he's serious. I'm suddenly very, very grateful that I haven't seen him before this moment because I know there's a small part of me that would have agreed. That would have done what I needed to make this mess go away.

"Let's say we did take each other for granted. Let's say the romance was dead and we didn't show each other the attention we once did. What then? We go to counseling and I spend that time learning how to trust you again, while you ... what?" And suddenly, the calm I was feeling snaps. "*Fuck our counselor?*"

"Baby—"

"Don't *baby* me. Maybe we were shitty to each other, but I'm not the one who slept around with other people. I'm not the one who went back on our vows. And I'm not the one standing here and trying to blame you for the shitty thing I did. There isn't enough money in the entire fucking world that would entice me near you or your cheating ass ever again."

His bottom lip trembles.

"Save it." I pull out my pen and shove it into his hand. "Sign the goddamn papers. There's no point in us talking anymore because you're clearly set on trying to save something that no longer exists."

Kyle sniffs but thankfully doesn't fight me. He pulls the papers toward himself and signs the marked spaces. "All I wanted was an adult conversation."

"Here's an adult conversation for you. If you'd asked me before you started all that shit, we could have done it together. Who knows? Maybe it would have brought us closer, maybe we would have ended up right back here anyway. But if you ever date someone again, I hope you've learned your lesson, otherwise you're going to end up very alone."

Kyle rolls his eyes. "Like you can talk. Might want to remove that stick from your ass if you ever want to be boyfriend material."

I take the paperwork and tuck it under my arm before he can think to change his mind. "I dunno, I think Beau likes the stick I have shoved up there." I wink. "It's easier to fuck me with."

I turn on my heel and leave, and as I reach the front door, I hear him say, "If you mean Beau Rickshaw—"

The front door slams behind me, cutting off his words and that chapter of my life.

It might have been petty, I might not have handled that the way I wanted to, but damn it felt good.

And now I can finally move on.

Chapter Thirty

BEAU

When I get home, a little tipsy, and Payne still isn't there, the worry kicks in again.

I remind myself of what Marty said, of why I like Payne and the fact he's a good person. The best person. And those kinds of people don't mess with others' feelings.

Especially not after what happened to him.

But when you're boning with a mystical creature, i.e. The Perfect Man, you find it hard to believe. And damn am I finding it hard. When I look in the mirror all I can see is a neurotic mess who's in his midthirties and hasn't even begun to get his life together.

Sure, I have money, but the rest of my life is a mess. Whereas Payne has his shit together, *emotionally and mentally*, which is the kind of headspace you can't buy.

And I know that because I would have by now if I could.

Money means nothing; character means everything. And when it comes to character, Payne has me beaten by a mile.

I flick the lights on inside, rather than open the curtains. It's late afternoon, so it's still light out, but I want to block out time until Payne is back and I get some answers.

Then I spot something that clears the worry like nothing else has.

A little yellow crane.

It's perched nonchalantly on my desk, exactly where Payne would have left it if he wanted me to see it first thing, and if I hadn't woken up so late, I would have.

I pluck it from my desk and immediately check the wing, finding five words in his handwriting.

You deserve everything and more.

That's positive, right?

The door clicks open, and when Payne walks in, I have to resist the urge to fling myself at him. I'm feeling needy and hopeful, and I have no idea where I stand. My hands are turning the crane over and over, and I can't stop. The last thing I want to do is immediately launch into quizzing him about how it went, because I'm not sure if I'm supposed to know.

Payne is smiling, and I'm finding it hard to know if that's good smiling, or ... The idea of Payne ever getting back together with Kyle is slim, but that insecurity is still there. He loved him at one point.

"Not working?" Payne asks.

I shake my head, and he does a double take.

"You okay?"

"Yeah, fine. Totally."

His eyes are trained on me as he crosses the living room to stand in front of where I'm standing.

I swallow around the obstruction in my throat and force myself to meet his gaze. "Umm, hi."

"Hello."

"Did you have a nice day?"

"I did."

Because ... why? "Oh."

He chuckles and takes my hand to lead me to the couch. When he drops down on it, he pulls me into his lap. "Isn't me having a nice day a good thing?"

"Umm. Yes. Maybe. Well, it is, but it depends what was nice about it ..."

"Well, you're definitely *not* okay. What's going on?"

"Nothing."

"Don't start lying to me now, Bo-Bo." Then he leans in and brushes his lips over mine. "Tell me."

Relief flows through my body, and I grab a fistful of his shirt. "Ford said you went to Boston, and I was worried you were seeing Kyle and going to get back with him."

"Huh."

I bite my lip. "Did you?"

"See him or get back with him? Because if I did one of those things, I wouldn't be holding you right now."

"You went though?"

"I did."

"And you didn't, umm, tell me."

"No. It was something I had to do for myself. I didn't

tell you because I wasn't sure I'd get the outcome I wanted, and then you'd know I failed. I didn't want to disappoint you. I thought I'd duck down there and back before you'd even know I was gone, then I could have surprised you with the good news."

"Good news?" I ask hopefully. "You got him to sign the divorce papers?"

Payne's grin is immediate and butterfly inducing. "I did."

"Wow. It's over. You ... you never have to see him again. Shit. How do you feel?"

"Fucking incredible. He still had so much hold over my life, and now it's over. Which means ... now I can move on properly." Payne's low voice dips. "You've done something I never would have thought possible. When I left my old life behind, I'd been convinced that was it for me. All I wanted was to become a bitter, grumpy asshole who only ever wanted to rely on cheap hookups. And yet ... here we are."

"Cheaply hooking up?"

He presses a kiss to my forehead. "I trust you. More than anyone I've met. And my self-preservation is trying to warn me against it, but I can't stop myself. You're fun and quirky. You're gorgeous and have a big heart. And I know I'm not in a position to offer you much more than, well, me, I guess, but if you still want me, baggage and all, then I'd like to see where this goes."

"You are one stupid guy if you think that isn't all I've ever wanted," I say, cupping his face. My heart is in my throat. "But if this is too soon for you ... if you think you need time to see what else is out there ..." I wish I could force myself to shut up and take those words back, but even though it would kill me if he walks away now, it'd kill me more if he does it in a year or two because we happened too fast.

Payne kisses me again. "No. I don't need to see what's out there, when everything I want is right here. I was worried that maybe you were a rebound, and I didn't want that for you, but after seeing Kyle, I've figured it out."

"What's that?"

"You're the one who was always meant for me. And I'm sorry it took me so long to figure that out."

I can't hold back. Our mouths collide, and I moan at the contact and the way I'm able to actually do this. For real. Maybe forever.

"You're mine?" I murmur against his lips.

Payne nods. "Just ... promise you won't hurt me."

"I couldn't. Ever. Not even if I tried." I bury my fingers in his hair. "You're perfect. I'll remind you of that every day."

Payne's mouth finds mine again, and we sit there kissing until my cock hardens and needs to be touched. I squirm and start to whine.

"I need you."

Payne wraps his arms around me and stands. "*Oompf.* You are not a light guy."

"Maybe you're just getting weak in your old age?"

"We'll see how weak I am when I'm fucking you into the mattress."

"I'll believe it when I see it."

He chuckles because we both know I'm full of bullshit.

As he strips me down, kissing every bit of exposed skin he can, I lean into the touch. Knowing Payne is the one touching me wakens every nerve in my body. It doesn't only feel incredible physically, but emotionally, I'm in heaven.

He lays me back, grabs some lube, then draws my cock into his mouth as he works me open. My fingers find their way into his hair, loving the things he's doing with his tongue. The tightness, the heat, it's where I want to be forever.

He pulls off too soon, but then he's positioning his cock at my hole and gently pushing forward. My body is drawn tight with lust, but I relax and let him in, and when he bottoms out, I change my mind. *This* is where I want to be forever.

"There's nothing like being inside you." His lips brush my temple.

He fucks me with steady, measured thrusts that gradually get harder and faster. I press back into him, heels digging into his ass, and with the angle he's nailing me at, the pressure he's putting on my prostate is insane. I'm oversensitive, right on the edge.

I cling to his shoulders, bringing his sweaty forehead flush with mine, before I reach down and wrap my hand around my leaking cock.

"Come, Payne," I beg. "I want you to fill me up. Own me. Make me yours."

"Oh, *fuck* yes." He slams home, and feeling his cock twitch, knowing he's unloading deep in my ass, is what sets me off too. My orgasm slams into me, and I stroke myself through it, cum landing on my chest and stomach as I tug him down to kiss me.

We stay like that for as long as possible—happy, trading lazy kisses—until Payne's cock softens and slips out of my ass.

I wriggle under him. "Okay, let me up. I need to shower."

"Urg, fine." He presses another kiss to my mouth, then rolls off me.

I jump up and head for my door when Payne's voice stops me midstep.

"Stay right there."

I glance back over my shoulder. "What is it?"

"Just ... one moment."

I wait, trying not to squirm as cum slides out of my ass and runs down my legs.

"There it is ..." Payne's gaze is trained on my ass, and seeing the twisted smile that crosses his face makes my dick desperately want to regroup.

"There ... what is?" I sound breathless as hell.

"I fucking love seeing my cum running out of your hole."

I shiver. "Yeah?"

"It's the hottest thing I've ever seen."

I reach down and run my fingers through the mess, then slide them up into my ass crack.

Payne growls and climbs out of bed. "*That* was the hottest thing I've ever seen."

He pulls me back against his chest and ducks his head. "I forgot to give you this." Then he sucks a mark into my neck.

I tremble. "Join me in the shower?"

"Try and stop me."

He follows me, and even though I'm well and truly fucked out, we're all roaming hands and soft kisses while we wash.

It's not until we're back in bed, falling asleep, that I remember one very important thing.

"Ah, so, also. There's something you should probably know."

He hums sleepily to show he's listening.

"I was sad today and went to Marty, and now he knows about us. Good night."

"*Beau.*"

I pretend to be asleep, and Payne lets out a long sigh. "Well, better you than me, I suppose. Just tell me, how much does he want to kick my ass?"

"Oh, yeah. You should probably steer clear for a while."

"Motherfucker."

I muffle a chuckle with my pillow, happy to let him think that until morning.

Chapter Thirty-One

PAYNE

The Killer Brew is rowdy as we approach. The market side has been packed up for the night, but the bar is full and loud, live music is playing against the backdrop of conversation. The heavy thud of axes hitting targets comes from the back rooms, and the huge bar is thrumming with activity.

I squeeze Beau's hand as we pass the bar and climb the stairs to the mezzanine area above.

Art invited me for drinks for Orson's birthday, and I took the invitation as a request to show off Beau as mine.

We walk into the room, holding hands, and I try not to act too smug at having Beau with me. Especially when Griffin eyes us.

Orson points as we approach. "Oh, hey. This is a fun development. Griffin, Art, pay up."

"Pay up what?" Beau asks, but I spin on Art.

"Dude, you were part of it too?"

He shrugs. "It seemed like an easy bet at the time."

"You bet on us?" Beau asks, and *now* the asshole thinks to look guilty.

"I have a very boring life where I'm desperate for entertainment," Art says.

Beau eyes him. "Who bet we'd end up together?"

Orson lifts his hand.

"I like you. The other two of you are dead to me."

I laugh and pull him against me to kiss his head.

He stays with Griffin and Orson as Art and I break away to get drinks. There are a fair few people here, most guys from the DMC, some who I've met and some who I haven't. Art keeps inviting me to catch-ups, but before now, I haven't felt ready to embrace my divorced status. That's all changed since I saw Kyle. Being divorced isn't something to be pitied for. It was the best move for me, and without it, I wouldn't be back in Kilborough, planning a kick-ass business idea and sharing it with a man who makes me smile all fucking day.

Art taps the bar top and signals for drinks, but before the woman behind the bar can reach us, the male server side-steps her and slides in first.

"Hey, Arty."

My friend sighs. "The good bourbon, thank you."

"Anything for you, cutie."

I hold back my amusement as the guy bats his eyelashes at Art in a very over-the-top way. He looks younger than us, maybe early thirties, with a stubbled jaw and shaggy brown hair, tied into a knot. His name tag reads *Joey*.

"Friend of yours?" I ask Art.

"Pain-in-the-ass employee."

"What do you want to do to my ass?" Joey asks.

"I'm going to fire you one of these days," Art warns.

Joey just smirks. "And lose this eye candy? I don't think so."

I smother my laugh, but Joey's not wrong. He's tall and built, with a face that's somewhere between pretty and handsome.

And by the way Art's eyeing him, he knows how good-looking his employee is. "One day I'll get to work and find your resignation letter, and it will be the greatest day of my life."

"So you're saying threatening to quit is your idea of foreplay?"

"If it shuts you up, I'll be in heaven."

Joey's stare turns challenging. "There are *lots* of ways you could shut me up."

"Starting with reminding you who you work for and who you're currently making wait."

Joey grabs the bottle of bourbon and holds it out.

Art reaches for the bottle, and Joey tugs it out of reach before leaning in. "You'll take me up on my offer one day."

"Maybe when hell freezes over." He takes the bottle, and Joey moves off down the bar to serve someone else.

"He's a handful," I say.

"You're not wrong."

"I'm surprised you haven't taken him up on his offer."

"He's not serious." Art reaches over the bar and hands me a stack of glasses. "He takes a different woman home every night, despite my no hooking up with customers rule."

"Then why don't you fire him?"

Art's mouth forms a line. "*So*, Beau?"

I know what he's doing, but I let him change the subject. "Yep. I didn't expect it for a second when I moved in with him, but I'm so glad we happened."

"See what I mean? Divorce isn't the dead end people make it out to be. It's a fork in the road to your true destination."

"I might be more on board with your theories if you weren't so dramatic about them."

"We've been friends since high school." He cuffs my shoulder. "It's too late to pretend to be embarrassed now."

"I clearly can't be trusted to make good choices."

"Speaking of good choices though, what's this I hear from Trent about you buying his land?"

I'm hit with excitement at the thought of all those future plans and fill him in.

He nods. "Well, let me know if you need any help. With that many people about, you're going to need to feed them somehow."

"And let me guess, you're happy to supply me?"

He cuffs my shoulder. "I thought you'd never ask. Don't worry, we'll work out a friends-and-family discount."

"I don't for a minute believe you give your family any kind of discount."

Art laughs. "Yeah, okay, you're right. But you'll be buying in bulk, so we'll sort something out."

"Thanks, man."

"Don't thank me. This is pure selfishness. I'm hoping you'll hire some gorgeous drill sergeant that I can flirt with every time I make a delivery."

"You realize this place is a good year or so away, right?"

He shrugs. "That just means I have a year of sleeping around to get through first."

"Well, I don't know about you, but this settling down business is for me."

Art smirks, big lips pulling up at the sides. "It's a pity. I know a few guys who would have loved to get you naked."

And somehow, that isn't at all appealing to me. It actually sounds like too much energy, for little reward. "Well, they're never going to get that chance now. With any luck, Beau is it for me."

"Really?" Art glances around and tilts his head. "In the nicest way possible, how can you be sure? You've been wrong once, right? Aren't you scared it will happen again?"

It's a fair question. "I thought I would be at first. I didn't think trust was possible again. But ... there's something I can't even explain when I'm around Beau. This complete confidence that we're made for each other, and I don't doubt for a minute that he's always been committed to me."

"You didn't think that with your ex?"

"Nope. Obviously I loved him, but it's hard to explain. There was always that feeling of not being enough for him, no matter how hard I tried or how much I had. With Beau, I literally have nothing, and he wants me anyway."

"Better you than me, brother." He gestures toward the table. "Let's get back to your man."

We join the others, where Griffin is trying to explain his situation to Beau.

"So, your son leaves at the end of summer?" Beau asks.

"A little sooner. Felix is heading to Franklin U in California, so we're taking a road trip across the country with his things, and then Poppy and I will come home and sort out the divorce."

"Wow."

Griffin nods. "One last family trip. It feels good to know things are finally happening."

"You don't think the trip will make you rethink things?" I ask.

"No way." Griffin looks like he's trying not to laugh. "Heath has been counting down the days until he can get me laid."

"Heath is ..." Beau prompts.

"My ride or die. He's been there for me through everything."

I smile at Beau and tug him closer. "Having someone like that is invaluable."

Griffin eyes us and then says, as though he can't stop himself, "I know I talk a big talk, but I've only ever been with Poppy. I have no idea how I'm going to handle whatever comes next."

Art plants a large hand on Griffin's shoulder. "With our

support. And Heath's. We're going to get you through this ... and we're sure as hell going to make sure you have all the sex you can handle."

As the night goes on, Beau becomes more and more comfortable. Given his issues with meeting new people, it makes me so happy to see Beau joking around, even if he looks set to vibrate out of his skin.

That constant energy is always there, and it comforts me. Because it's him.

Distinctly Beau.

And I'm fucking crazy about him.

Chapter Thirty-Two

BEAU

A week later, and the paperwork is signed for Payne to take on the lease for the land.

"We'll need a good name for when we launch," he says, driving down the long driveway to get to the cottage on the grounds. He hasn't stopped smiling, and while I wish I was paying for the place outright so he didn't have to lease it, I'm not going to say anything when he looks as happy as he does right now.

On the way along, he's been pointing out where he wants to put things and brainstorming what everything might look like once it's finished. We clear the tree line and take the dirt road between the two main fields and pull up at the front of the house.

"Maybe I need to get some horses and a cowboy hat," Payne says, jumping out of the car as soon as it's off.

"Calm down there, Boston. The country air is going to your head."

He grins and rattles the keys. "Should we see how bad it is inside? Trent said he stays here on the weekends he tends to the place, so it can't be too bad, right?"

"We're about to find out." Secretly, I hope it's a total shithole so Payne has no choice but to continue staying with me. Logically, I know he needs his own space if we want this thing between us to work. We need the chance to date properly before jumping into a full-blown relationship. That doesn't mean it will be any easier when I have to go home to an empty apartment again though.

I follow Payne inside, and it's ... well, cute is the only word for it. There's a wooden kitchen on one side, a small living area on the other, and doors leading to what I'm assuming are the bedroom and bathroom on the other side. It's painted a happy blue color, with whitewashed hardwood floors and large windows letting in pools of sunlight.

"Damn ..." I whisper.

Payne turns to me with a questioning look on his face.

I try for a smile. "I'm going to miss you. This place actually looks great."

"I know." He crosses back to me and wraps me in his arms. "It will be strange at first, and I know it's hard to take someone at their word, but this isn't going to change how I feel about you."

I quickly nod. "I get that." But I don't really. What if this whole thing between us is some kind of friendly version of Stockholm syndrome? Or falling for his hero complex?

What if all it takes is Payne finding his own place to realize everything he thinks he feels for me is a misconstrued rebound.

I don't mention any of that though because I don't want to put ideas in his head.

It's just so hard to believe that after so long I could be getting exactly what I've always wanted.

"Come here." Payne takes my hand and drags me over to the two doors. The first one opens to reveal a generous bedroom, and the second one that I assumed was a bathroom is ... another bedroom? It's much smaller than the first, but Payne strides inside and throws his arms out.

"What do you think?"

My eyebrows creep up. "Umm, it's a nice, ah, space."

He laughs, then walks to the wall closest to me. "I'm picturing a huge bookcase here—maybe I can try my hand at building one, and then there, by the window—" He walks to the place he's pointing at. "—we can put your desk."

"My desk?"

"But the best part?" Payne shoves aside the curtains to reveal an enormous window overlooking a pond, a part of the forest, and a huge clearing behind it. "No more feeling claustrophobic while you work."

I stare at him with my mouth hanging open. "You want me to set up in here?"

"Well, I mean ..." He rubs the back of his neck. "You don't have to. I saw it on the plans and thought it would make the perfect office, but I know you didn't like using your spare room, and if you'd prefer to only work at home

..." He shakes his head. "Wow, I'm killing this. I only mean that I'd like you to be able to stay over whenever you like and then not have to rush home to work the next day. I know how anxious being away from your work for too long makes you."

"You want me to stay over?"

"Well, yeah."

"And set up my own space here?"

He shifts his weight to the other foot. "It would be nice to have. If I'm doing this whole business thing, I'll probably need to throw a desk in here for me too."

I'm hit with the most vivid image of me and Payne working in silence side by side, and I ache for that. For us to have that future. "Holy shit, yes, that would be so freaking perfect."

Payne crosses the room and hauls me into a kiss. I have no idea how long it lasts for; all I know is the shivers rattling through my body are making me light-headed.

After writing a list of repairs needed for the cabin, we go for a walk around the grounds. We'll spend time out here drawing up plans and spray-painting to-scale sizing in the grass another time, but for right now, we just want to enjoy it.

The smell of the trees, the bugs darting over the grass in the field, the hot sun beating down on us. I can see Payne here.

I can see him walking kids through obstacle courses and strapping others into a harness on the zipline he wants to install. He's talking about a boot camp in the afternoons and a large meeting space for companies to come up from Boston and hire the place for the week. His ideas are big and exciting.

And dammit, he's going to make them work. I'll do whatever I have to in order to support him, but I'm trying to stay hands-off for now. This is Payne's thing, and I'll be involved as much or as little as he likes.

We approach the larger pond at the front of the house, and the heat is making my glasses slide down my nose. I'm about to suggest we head back inside when Payne turns me to face him.

"Is this okay? I don't want to push or move too fast, but I can see a future here. With you."

Lucky my man is pretty. "I've edged myself for twenty years. We could get married tomorrow and it wouldn't be fast enough."

His face falls. "Ah, about that. I'm not, umm ... I don't want that again. After everything that happened, the word 'husband' means nothing to me but heartbreak and broken promises. I don't want to think of that when I look at you."

"Fair." I struggle to talk around my enormous smile. "And I don't need that. I told you I only need you. That wasn't me exaggerating."

Payne lets out a long exhale. "Thank fuck. You deserve the world, but I think that's the one thing I can't promise."

"My love doesn't come with stipulations."

His lips part, and for a whole second, I can't understand the wide-eyed look he's giving me. Then, "Love, huh?"

I could deny it and pretend like it's nothing and this is all so totally casual, but ... my heart won't let me. "Are you surprised? I haven't exactly been relaxed with how I feel about you. I've loved you for a really, really long time."

"And here I was stressing it was too soon to say anything. Fuck, Beau, I love you too. I've never been more sure of anything in my life."

I don't know why, but that's what helps me stop doubting things. Marty was right—Payne doesn't mess around with people's feelings, and once he sets his mind to something, he commits completely.

It might have taken twenty years for me to get to this point, but nothing has ever been more worth it.

Epilogue

PAYNE

One Year Later

"Beau?"

I let myself into his apartment with the key I never returned, and even though he said he'd be ready to go ... I have no idea where he is.

I check his bedroom and the bathroom, then get back to the living room and pause, looking around, wondering if he somehow forgot I was picking him up in the hour since we spoke.

A light breeze tickles my side, and I turn toward it, finding the sliding door to the balcony cracked open.

I approach, no idea what I'm going to find, but when I slide open the door ... it isn't this.

Beau's got earbuds in, leaning over the rail where he's got ... I'm not even sure what that is.

I approach without him noticing and lean over to look too.

Ah.

Bedsheets.

I nudge him, and Beau almost jumps out of his skin.

"Shit, I didn't hear you," he says, removing one of his earbuds.

"Clearly." I nod toward the sheet. "What are we working out today?"

"If it's actually possible for someone to tie bedsheets together and climb down the side of a building."

I blink at him. "And how are you planning on testing that?"

Confusion crosses his face, and he waves toward the railing. "By putting it into practice."

Of course he is. I plant my hands on his shoulders before steering him back inside. "Yeah, we're not doing that."

"But—"

"*Here.*" I give him a stern look. "After the party, we'll head back to my place and test it out. The zip-line platform should be high enough, and I've got crash mats we can use and—"

He cuts me off with a kiss. "That sounds perfect."

"Good. Now go get ready." I smack his ass on the way past

and hunt down the gift he bought for Soph to make sure we don't forget it. Even though we're a couple now and technically only have to get the one gift, neither of us wanted to deprive our nieces of being spoiled, so we both went shopping.

I find the gift bag in the laundry sink and hold back the urge to laugh.

He's still as scatterbrained as ever, but since learning to write with music playing, he's been able to get a cleaner in without it interrupting his work.

We hit the road and ten minutes later pull up out the front of Marty's place. There's a huge bouncing castle set up in the backyard and balloons dotted on the fence out the front.

To think, Lizzy was worried people would get lost.

Inside is the mayhem I'm expecting. My parents and Lizzy's are here, but other than the occasional friend or school parent, we're completely outnumbered by kids. They're tearing through the house and the yard, shrieks matching the heavy pounding of footsteps on the hardwood floors.

Beau gives me his big *help* eyes, so I take both gifts and catch Soph on her way past us.

"Uncle Payne, put me down."

I throw her over my shoulder. "I guess I could, but then I'll have to keep these gifts we brought."

"Presents? Gimme."

"*Hey*." Lizzy plants her hands on her hips and gives Soph the stink eye. "What do we say?"

I place a squirming Sophie on her feet, and she morphs

from energetic monster to sweet princess. She clasps her hands and bats her eyelashes at me. "Thank you so much. I'm sure I'll love whatever you got me. It's the thought that counts."

Beau sniggers, and I shoot Lizzy a look.

"My children are such angels," she says, rejoining one of her friends.

As soon as her mom is gone, Soph drops the act. "Can I have it now?"

Beau scoops up the gift bags and holds them out to her. "Happy birthday, sweetheart."

"You're supposed to wrap these. It's more fun." But wrapped or not, her face lights up in excitement when she pulls out the ninja costume, complete with weaponry that she *had to have*, and then my soccer goals and ball.

"Yes," she squeals. "Will you play with me?"

"Of course."

Then she drops the presents unceremoniously onto the floor and disappears outside with her friends.

"Did that go well?" Beau asks. "It's always so hard to tell."

"I think it's the sugar."

He packs the gifts back into the bags for us to leave in her room for later. I haven't told her, but we bought the same soccer goals for my backyard for when the girls stay over on my fold-out couch.

My main concern has been setting up the equipment and accommodation for our business, but months of prebookings on the place was enough to get the bank's attention, and as of last week, my loan to buy the place was officially approved.

The next step is extending the cottage so the girls have rooms of their own.

And maybe so kids of our own will too.

I'm nervous as I glance at Beau and then back to the groups of children who don't. Stop. Moving.

"You know ..."

He hums to show he's listening.

"I've been thinking lately. I'm forty-one soon."

His eyes light up when he turns to me. "Did that take a lot of thought to realize?"

"Hush, you. What I'm trying to say is that the business opens in a few months, and I have all that land, and we both have a lot of flexibility in our schedules ..." Fuck, the nerves ramping up in my gut are making this hard. "I, uh, I've maybe been thinking I could see a kid or two ahead."

He blinks at me, slowly looking from me to the backyard and back again. "You want that?" He hooks his thumb back toward the mayhem.

"At first, I wasn't sure, but, *yes*. My own kid, *shit*." My chest warms. "I can see it. And you. I think you'd be an amazing father."

He sucks in a sharp breath. "You want a kid *with me*?"

Ah, fuck. I can't read that tone. Is it ... is that a yes or a hell fucking no? "Well, I don't see you going anywhere in a hurry. And if it's too much for you—"

"Are you kidding? Too much? Of course it will be too much. I'm an anxious mess the majority of the time, and you want to add a kid to that? I'll ruin them. I'll mess it up and cause the child issues, and holy shit why do I want to say yes?"

"You do?"

"More than I've ever wanted anything while being simultaneously terrified."

I bark a laugh of pure relief. "That's a yes?"

"Yes. Hell yes."

I scoop him into my arms, overwhelmed at how happy I am, and kiss him just because I'll never get enough of it. "I want you to move in. And to have kids with you, and to run the business with you, and to help you with your quirky book experiments. I want everything."

"You want me to move in?" Beau's smile is blinding. "Wouldn't having a roommate at forty-one be more pathetic than forty?"

"Nah, I figure once you cross that milestone of forty, all bets are off."

"Ice cream for dinner?"

"And breakfast."

"Jumping in the fountain at the mall?"

"Only if I don't push you in first." I pump my eyebrows at him.

"Can I have a turn on your zip line?"

"Of course." I pause for a second. "Once you're forty-one. Please, Bo-Bo, you need to earn the awesome."

"Why do I get the feeling I'll turn forty-one and you'll turn around and be like, 'oh, did I say forty-one? I meant forty-five,' and then I still won't be at your level?"

I shrug. "Guess you'll just have to stick around and find out."

"I think I can do that."

"Good." I kiss him. "And you're fooling yourself if you think I'm not the one punching above my weight."

"Agree to disagree?"

"Never." I screw up my face. "I read once that compromise was a terrible thing in relationships."

He tilts his head. "Somehow that doesn't sound right."

I kiss him again. And again. Because fuck, I can't stop. "So who gets to tell Marty and Lizzy we could have niblings coming their way?"

"Hey, I think I'm still regaining my ability to breathe after telling Lizzy we were together. You're up this time."

"I'll allow it." Because I'm realizing when it comes to Beau, I'll give him anything.

Thanks For Reading Roommate Arrangement!

To keep up to date with future releases, come join Saxon's Sweethearts.
www.facebook.com/groups/saxonssweethearts/

Making Him Mine

My best friend is the love of my life ... he just doesn't know it yet.

Ever since Barney finalized his divorce, I've been his biggest support.

He needs a shoulder to cry on? I've got him covered.

He needs someone to answer his late phone calls? I'm here all night.

He needs to be fucked to within an inch of his life? Climb on up, big guy.

But when he mentions he's finally ready to start dating again, watching him meet up with guy after guy is not on my checklist.

It's time for the best friend gloves to come off.

Find out how the DMC got started with this sweet romance between two best friends. Grab it here:

https://www.subscribepage.com/saxonjames

My Freebies

Do you love friends to lovers?
Second chances or fake relationships?
I have two bonus freebies available!

Friends with Benefits
Total Fabrication

These short stories are only available to my reader list so join
the gang!
https://www.subscribepage.com/saxonjames

Other Books By Saxon James

FRAT WARS SERIES:

Frat Wars: King of Thieves

Frat Wars: Master of Mayhem

Frat Wars: Presidential Chaos

NEVER JUST FRIENDS SERIES:

Just Friends

Fake Friends

Getting Friendly

Friendly Fire

Bonus Short: Friends with Benefits

LOVE'S A GAMBLE SERIES:

Good Times & Tan Lines

Bet on Me

Calling Your Bluff

CU HOCKEY SERIES WITH EDEN FINLEY:

Power Plays & Straight A's

Face Offs & Cheap Shots

Goal Lines & First Times

Line Mates & Study Dates

Puck Drills & Quick Thrills

PUCKBOYS SERIES WITH EDEN FINLEY:

Egotistical Puckboy

Irresponsible Puckboy

And if you're after something a little sweeter, don't forget my YA pen name

S. M. James.

These books are chock full of adorable, flawed characters with big hearts.

https://geni.us/smjames

Want More From Me?

Follow Saxon James on any of the platforms below.
www.saxonjamesauthor.com
www.facebook.com/thesaxonjames/
www.amazon.com/Saxon-James/e/B082TP7BR7
www.bookbub.com/profile/saxon-james
www.instagram.com/saxonjameswrites/

Acknowledgments

As with any book, this one took a hell of a lot of people to make happen.

First, my cover designer Story Styling Cover Designs did a fantastic job on making this smoking hot cover.

Thanks to Karen Meeus for the thorough beta read.

To Sandra at One Love Editing for my amazing edits.

Lori Parks, you were a gem as always with my proof read and I always appreciate how timely you are with your work.

Thanks to my wonderful PA, Charity VanHuss for wrangling my scattered self on a daily basis.

Eden Finley, your notes and ongoing commentary were fucking incredible, and thank you for letting me pick your brain while talking absolute smack at each other. You're the bestest bestie I could ever ask for.

Louisa Masters, AM Johnson, Riley Hart, CE Ricci thank you so much for taking the time to read. Your support is incredible and I really appreciate it!

And of course, thanks to my fam bam. To my husband who constantly frees up time for me to write, and to my kids whose neediness reminds me the real word exists.

Printed in the USA
CPSIA information can be obtained
at www.ICGtesting.com
LVHW040439070923
757498LV00013B/19/J

9 781922 741071